The Gypsy's Lie

By CJ Heath

Copyright 2015 CJ Heath
Published by Chris Heath

All characters and events described in this book are fictitious and products of the author's imagination. All locations are correct as believed to be in the time of the story (1953).

License Notes

This book is licensed for your personal enjoyment only. It may not be re-sold or given away to other people. If you would like to share this book with another person, please purchase an additional copy for each recipient. Thank you for respecting the hard work of this author.

"Love is composed of a single soul inhabiting two bodies"

Aristotle

Chapter One

Wednesday 8th July 1953

Naked to the waist, Mickey Ray stepped into the light between the four open fires in the wooded clearing. The rough terrain should be to his advantage but on this night, the dark haired youth wished he had concrete under his feet. The unease he felt had nothing to do with the man opposite, if anything, the older man would struggle to keep his feet on the uneven ground.

Mickey could feel the compacted, fire-scorched earth beneath his bare feet; the cinders had been swept clean a dozen times with besom brooms and there was no stone or twig to distract him. It was as close to home ground as the gypsy could ever expect but still he was nervous.

The Irishman stepped forward between the two fires at his end of the square and grinned at Mickey; the awkwardly angled nose and the missing two front teeth an indication of the man's experience. Raising his hand, the bare chested Irishman took hold of the crucifix hanging around his neck and raised it to his lips to kiss it. His mind may have been on heaven but his eyes were locked hard on the teenager facing him.

While the young gypsy had a tousled mop of black hair slicked back from his forehead and tucked behind his ears, the older man's hair was cropped short. A sheen of moisture prickled at the short spikes of hair and in the flickering firelight, Mickey imagined it to be silver. It would fit with what he'd heard of the man. Flynn Burn was said to be in his fifties but still not one to underestimate. You didn't play this game long if you weren't up to it.

Shuffling from foot to foot, Flynn began the hypnotic swaying Mickey's father had told him about. Keeping his expression neutral was a challenge; he wanted to grin at the predictable nature of the man. It may have been intended to unsettle him but the fact was the young gypsy found the routine comical. It was what he needed. The last traces of uncertainty left him as he furrowed his brow and stared intently at the rocking figure.

A sparkle caught on the brow of the Irishman and Mickey squinted to try to tell if the man was sweating or if he'd put oil on his face. He drew a breath and shook his arms out to help limber up. What did it matter? He was old.

A pewter tankard appeared before him and the gypsy gripped it as he turned to see who was handing it to him. The dark haired girl beside him leant in hard against him, pressing into his side as she offered the ale her puri-daj brewed. Her face was flushed and her eyes were alight with a passion that was only partly a response to his bare skin.

"Kill him my darling, put him down" she whispered. "Show them what my man can do!"

Placing one arm across the girl's shoulder, Mickey leant over and placed a delicate kiss on the top of her head and remained impassive. Still holding her beside him, he lifted the tankard and drank the contents in one long, smooth action. He thrust the empty tankard back into the hands of the girl by his side and avoided grinning as she was pulled away by his own family.

A voice in his ear whispered last words of advice as his father repeated his observations of the older man. Mickey locked eyes with the Irishman again as he barely listened to warnings of the left roundhouse he could expect. He muttered just loud enough for his father to hear his concerns that the man opposite had oiled his brow and was rewarded by silence as the olive skinned parent peered to try and see the reflective, tell-tale sign of an advantage. After a moment he grunted and said "Don't be toying with him, he's a tough bastard; be quicker, be tougher."

With his words said, Mickey's father retreated from the glow of the fires and joined the substantial crowd standing at the gypsy's back. With a grin, the young fighter crossed himself and raised his hands before him, alternately flexing and clenching his fingers. Behind the Irish champion he could see faces shinning as the flickering flames lit up their eagerness for the bout. This wasn't just about putting the Irish in their place, this was about money; enough money to maybe get his own caravan.

Jacky Ray had promised his son a horse and a caravan but they weren't going to appear until a year after his wedding and though tradition may say he and his bride had to live with his family for a year first, it was a tradition the young gypsy was eager to break. Marriage may be a foregone conclusion but it wasn't going to be the restriction everybody planned it to be. If he had to marry, he was going to make damn sure his every move wasn't watched by the family.

Mickey took his anger at his arranged marriage and let a proportion of his bitterness rise up inside him. Staring back at his opponent he summoned the pent-up rage he'd had to keep contained for the past two years. The face before him changed, the gap toothed grin and broken nose were replaced with an image of his father, frowning his disapproval. A voice called out clearly but Mickey didn't hear the words, he was aware of the staging area clearing of bodies and of the hubbub of voices dying away as somebody from the Irish camp took charge of the situation.

A short, rotund man stepped between Flynn and Mickey and beckoned the two of them closer. Stepping forward, the men closed on each other. A few words were spoken but unheard; both fighters knew the rules. Flynn was a good eight inches taller than his opponent and his reach was going to be an issue for the younger boy to deal with but he was ready.

When prompted, the Romany nodded his understanding, still with his gaze locked on the green eyes of the man opposite. The Irishman nodded when his turn came and the little man withdrew from the improvised square. Flynn raised his hands, interlocked his fingers and pushing his elbows out, he cracked the joints of his knuckles and rolled his head from side to side, eliciting the same bone breaking cracks from his neck. He backed away a half pace and took the fighters' stance, his left foot a half step behind his right. Raising his hands, he clenched his fingers into his palms to make fists and cocked an eyebrow at the youth facing him.

Standing with the bare-knuckle fighter in front of him, Mickey ignored posture and simply raised his fists in front of him as though ignorant of the skill required at this level of fighting. He noted the momentary flicker of Flynn's eyebrow as the more experienced boxer suddenly doubted the ability of the Romany champion. Mickey deliberately made his cheek twitch. It was a ruse that his cousins no longer fell for but the Irishman was fighting an unknown quantity in the young man the gypsies had put up.

The hush that had fallen over the gathered crowd was broken by a strident voice calling out "Fight on!" The Irishman threw the first punch; a left handed jab shot forward with full force directly at the youngsters jaw. Mickey dodged left just far enough for the blow to pass by his ear and then he powered a hard left into the ribs beneath the Irishman's right elbow. Flynn flinched as he made to withdraw his left for a new shot but his age showed; before he could adjust his position, he took a harsh blow to his clavicle and felt the collarbone break with the impact of the youngster's right fist. Though used to the pain of a fight, the youth's speed had been a surprise and as he grunted at the discomfort, the Irishman felt a third punch crack into his jaw as the boy whipped his left arm wide and round.

Staggering back, Flynn turned his body so as to lead with his right. He knew he was disadvantaged with his left arm all but out of action but he was right handed, he knew his own strength and though the boy was fast, he could never match the older man blow for blow.

Keeping his guard up, the older man held his left fist close to his body and lunged forward, swinging his right fist in a roundhouse blow; it didn't connect as Mickey ducked under the blow and struck an uppercut with his right fist directly under the chin of the champion.

Flynn's feet left the ground as the punch connected and he landed hard on his back. Coughing and wheezing, the older man rolled quickly on to his knees and keeping his left arm close to his body, he rose tentatively back to his feet.

Mickey waited for him to gain his feet again. If this was a brawl he'd have been in fast with a boot in the man's face but he was well schooled by his father. Never hit a man when he's down; at least, not in the ring.

Back on his feet and with a wariness in his eyes, the Irishman circled the youth, careful not to close on the boy with his left side exposed. The man was angry at himself for assuming the boy was less than he'd thought. Years of training his own children and grandchildren not to get over confident and he'd made the mistake himself. Eyeing the Romany boy carefully, Flynn noted that the naivety and innocence had gone from the youth. He was positioned perfectly to block a right handed roundhouse and an uppercut was out of the question. The stance Flynn had taken at the outset that the boy had appeared ignorant of was present now. The little bastard had played him for a fool and played him well.

Mickey held his posture and waited. He could move in with either a left or right led jab and follow it with a hay-maker but he was content to wait the older man out. It wouldn't be enough for the Irishman to win the fight now; Mickey had embarrassed him and the man was going to look to win decisively. The outcome should be a foregone conclusion but the words of his father were always with him; it's not over 'til it's over.

Patiently the gypsy waited for the old man to make his move. As soon as that right arm moved forward he would either duck or lean away from the blow and then he could get a second shot into that ribcage and follow it up with a right to the stomach. As Flynn began to fold with the blow, a left under the chin would snap his head back up and he could finish the fight with a right to the face. The two men continued to circle as the Irishman looked for his opening.

Mickey watched Flynn intently and as he saw the man's pectoral muscle change shape, he knew the punch was coming, he swayed right and was jolted hard as, impossibly, a left handed jab slammed into his cheek. There was no time to puzzle through how the man had managed to land a blow from an arm with a broken clavicle as it was immediately followed up with a downward impact that jarred teeth and blurred vision as the man's right came in straight after on the other side of his face.

A roar from the crowd snapped the young gypsy back to reality and he realised he was sitting in the dirt and still falling backward. Raising his legs, the boy tumbled head over heels to come to rest on his knees and without pause, he clambered to his feet again. He spat blood and looked in a daze at the big man as he moved in for a third punch. As much through luck as judgement, Mickey managed to dodge the knockout shot and he stepped in close and pounded three rapid jabs to the kidneys. He didn't fool himself, the punches did nothing more than buy time to recover.

Flynn was an opponent to reckon against. He must have been in agony when he landed his left against the youngster but it had shocked the boy long enough to launch a stronger punch. The gypsy knew he couldn't take many hits like that last one. The man may be old but his strength was incredible. If they'd fought toe to toe as the Irish had wanted, he'd be finished long ago. Mickey needed to end the fight fast before the grey haired man managed to breach his defence again. Sense told him to back away and wait for a decent opportunity to get a series of head shots in but stalling like that wouldn't go well with the crowd. The old man had to go down and he had to go down solid or there'd be arguing over the pay-out. That was the trouble with the Irish, you could put your man on the floor but if he was able to rise again, the fight wasn't over.

Still reeling and with his vision still blurred, Mickey let one eye close and touched his cheek with the back of his hand. It came away bloody as he knew it would but he didn't look at it, he just let Flynn think he was going to and the man obliged as the boy hoped. With a roar, the Irishman swung a wide armed roundhouse in from the right and the gypsy stepped in and ducked under the arm, he punched in hard at the ribs on Flynn's side with three rapid, right hand jabs that though on target, lacked any serious force.

Circling behind his opponent, he came round on the left quickly as the Irishman turned to keep his weak arm from the youth. Quick as he was, Mickey was quicker; with his left fist raised and protecting the broken collarbone, the boy punched the shoulder-blade as he came around and the impact made the man flinch and his elbow wavered. Just below the shoulder, the gypsy hit again, this time he caught the shoulder side on and the scream from the Irishman as the broken bone pushed against the skin was loud and clear.

Sagging slightly with the pain, his arm hanging all but useless, the older fighter raised his one good arm again ready to swing but as he made to straighten his posture, he took a side on impact against the fist of the boy's left hand; once, twice, three times the jaw was hit. Flynn's head was level with Mickey's chest, one more left would put him on the floor but the gypsy boy knew it may not be enough to keep the warrior down. Flynn saw the right hand rising to meet him and unable to dodge, he closed his eyes and let the punch snap him upright, over and into the dirt on his back.

There was cheering and applause around the makeshift ring but Mickey Ray still stood over the downed boxer with his fists clenched in front of him. The man was conscious and the boy knew enough of the man's reputation to know he wasn't one to give in easy. The crowd stopped their roaring and muttered uncomfortably as Flynn Burn rolled himself to a sitting position. He glared up at the youth who had put him in the dirt and he clutched his left arm across his body, holding it tight to his chest with his right hand. The boxer shuffled in the dirt until he managed to get his legs crossed in front of himself and then called out to the gypsy.

"Hey!" Flynn yelled, loud enough for the gathered crowd to fall silent. "Well boy? Least ya can feckin' do is help an old man up!"

The glare of the Irishman slowly faded and was replaced with a gap toothed grin as he held his uninjured arm up, hand open and offered to Mickey. The boy hesitated a moment before he unclenched his hands and lowered his fists. He reached down to the man and found himself smiling back. It wasn't the easiest task to help the boxer to his feet and when he did, the bloodied, injured old man leant himself across the boy's shoulder and wrapped an arm around his neck.

Flynn leant in to whisper in the boy's ear as the crowd erupted in cheering and swearing as both sides began to argue over the winnings and the bets that had been placed. Mickey felt the Irishman's hand on his shoulder move across his chest and the hairy forearm slid under his chin, squeezing the youngster's throat tightly. "Laddie, you're gonna be one hell of a feckin' fighter when you're growed, just watch that left side."

Having said his piece, the man released his grip on the boy's throat and his grin returned. Letting go of the youngster completely, he turned away from the swept area and walked out of the light. Mickey watched him go, a little more nervous now than he had been before the fight. Just as the Irish champion left the circle of firelight, he saw a woman in a red headscarf rush over and initially she fussed over him, then as they entered the darkness, he watched her slap at his bare skin. It didn't take a lot to realise she had to be his wife.

Chapter Two

Thomas Quatrell was already awake when the front door slammed shut. Lying cosy under the single blanket on his bed, he knew he should rise quickly or the temptation to stay there was going to win and he'd fall asleep again within minutes but it was hard to force himself out of the relative warmth the bedding provided. The gap in the curtains let in enough light for him to see and on the far side of the room, he could make out his shirt and trousers draped over the back of the chair waiting for him to prepare himself for work.

Despite his drowsiness, he'd been awake for an hour listening to his mother moving around downstairs. He'd heard the shrill whistle of the kettle and through the open window, the hooves of the milkman's horse had come clearly to him as bottles had clinked onto the stone doorstep. Hunkering down under his bedding, he pulled the blanket up a little higher and hugged his bear a little tighter.

It wasn't a cold morning; the summer was already proving to be a gentle season with long evenings and bright days but the contrast between the heat of the single bed and the chill of the unheated room was a harsh reminder of just how early it really was. With a resigned sigh, Tom reached an arm out of his sheet to his sideboard and snatched up the alarm clock. He pulled the clockwork timepiece into his bed and fidgeted as he manoeuvred it up his pyjamas to bring it out of the bedding close to his face. Angling the face of the clock so the white hands caught the light of the day, he squinted one-eyed at the dial. The largest hand rested on the eleven and the shorter pointed distinctly at the five. Another five minutes would be manageable but the eighteen year old knew the alarm itself was unpredictable. It kept good time but the third hand that pointed so clearly at the five could be out as much as twenty minutes and as much as he would delight in an extra twenty minutes, he knew he couldn't trust himself to wash, dress and grab a quick breakfast if he allowed the clock to dictate when he was to rise.

Bracing himself and drawing in a few quick breaths in preparation, Tom threw the blanket and sheet that covered him back and hurriedly clambered from the bed. Pushing the pin on the back of the clock into the mechanism, he silenced the alarm before its tin clatter racketed out. Placing it back on the bedside cabinet and rubbing his hands together, he darted for the door to his bedroom and drew down his twill dressing gown from the hook. Tom wrapped it hurriedly around himself, not even bothering to slide his arms into the sleeves.

Wrapped to the knees in the blue fabric, the boy returned briefly to the bed to slide his feet into the too large pair of slippers and shuffled back to the door, careful not to raise his feet from the threadbare rug lest his slippers slide off his feet.

Stepping out onto the hallway, Tom fumbled in the dark for the bannister that ran down the wall to the kitchen and he carefully descended. Opening the door at the bottom of the stairwell he deliberately placed his foot to one side of the last step to avoid treading in whatever the cat had decided to leave him as a present at the foot of the stairs. Nothing was visible and in all likelihood, had Blackie left a portion of mouse or rabbit behind, his mother had probably already removed it. It wasn't a gamble the teenager was willing to take; he'd been caught out too many times in the past.

The kitchen wasn't as cold as the rest of the house and at least through the summer months there was no ice on the inside of the window frames, nor would he need to break the ice in the toilet. Still shuffling forward he made his way from the stairs into the room and a little warmth found him. Skirting the table and the two lonely chairs, Tom reached the rayburn and placed his hands on the steel rail that protruded a few inches from the black top of the range. He had to slide a damp towel to one side and the metal was still cold to his touch but the heat coming from the rayburn was a blessing.

The wood burning range was the centre of the house in many respects. It heated the room, cooked their food and boiled the water for their drinks. In the colder months there were nights his mother would drag the table close to the yellow and black, over-sized stove and the two of them would play cards as they took in the generous amount of heat it spat out. On more than one occasion they had made toast with the door open; last February, just after Tom had turned eighteen, his mother had even let him hold the toasting fork.

With his front warm, Tom turned to toast the back of his legs and he half leant, half sat on the rail. Resting his gaze on the kitchen table Tom saw the brown paper bag that he knew without looking would contain an apple and sandwiches wrapped in greaseproof paper for his lunch. They would be beef, made from the left overs of the Sunday roast almost a week earlier. Meat was still hard to come by in any quantity; when his mother's ration account permitted it, she would always try to buy beef as it was versatile enough to use every cut and make it last. Tom knew without having to lift the lift the lid that the pot on the table would be a beef stew for the two of them that evening. It would be for him to put it on the rayburn when he got in and depending on how much work his mother had to do, he would likely be eating alone again.

With a little warmth coursing through his body, the youth crossed to the sink and hesitated. He'd gone to bed early the night before and hadn't felt up to dragging the tin bath out to have a good clean and he knew he should really have a thorough wash this morning but the water was only going to chill him all over again now he had got warm.

Grabbing a thin, worn flannel, Tom quickly jammed the plughole of the sink with the square of fabric, grabbed the kettle from the range and poured a small amount of boiling water onto the flannel. Barely half an inch of water covered the flannel before he returned the large steel kettle to the rayburn. He turned back to the sink and turned the tap on, waiting for the clank and thud of the ancient pipework to deliver a small trickle of water into the steaming water already present. As the flow stuttered and spat, the sink began to fill but Tom stopped the trickle by turning the tap back half a dozen times until the flow ceased.

He waited a moment for the flannel to absorb as much water as it was capable of, then pulled it from the plughole. As he watched the water swirl away, he squeezed the excess water from the fabric and rapidly washed his face and hands, making sure he washed behind his ears. He promised himself a bath when he got in. There seemed little point in leaving the house spotless when he was only going to get filthy at work, Besides, only his mother would care and he'd be home long before she was.

The quick wash may not have satisfied the cleanliness his mother lectured on but it had brought the youth back to life. He dried himself on the towel hanging in front of the rayburn, then cautiously, he lifted the lid of the saucepan that sat and rattled on the black top. The porridge looked creamy rather than watery and from the sight and smell, Tom realised his mother had made it with milk today and he smiled to himself. Eggs would have been more welcome but he'd have to wait a few more days for that treat and he knew it. Milky porridge was a reasonable compromise.

Taking a large dish from the draining board, Tom then wrapped a tea-towel around the handle of the cast iron saucepan and holding it precariously in one hand, he scooped two large spoonfuls of the oat and milk mixture into the bowl. Peering into the pan, he shrugged and tipped it toward the bowl and with the spoon, he scraped the remainder out for his breakfast. It was going to be a long time until lunch and there was nobody else in the house to finish anything he left behind.

Depositing the saucepan in the sink, the youngster sat himself at the table and idly stirred the porridge in order to hasten its cooling. There were a few black burnt bits but less than usual; he could easily leave them. He stared across the table and through the kitchen window as he ate, slowly watching the sky brighten from misty white to shinning yellow as over the course of twenty minutes, the sun burnt away the last traces of the night time mist. There was a good chance it was going to be a hot day.

Finishing the last of his breakfast, Tom wondered briefly if he could get away with leaving the washing up until he came home but he eventually admitted to himself, if he left it that long, he'd likely not touch it all. It wasn't that Thomas was lazy but that he was used to his mother doing all the mundane things for him. It was true that of everyone he knew, their mothers cooked cleaned and cleared up after them all; not just the lads his own age either, the older men all considered such acts to be 'women's work'.

It wasn't as easy or as clear cut for Tom. His mother didn't have all day to keep house and to run around after him. He hadn't always appreciated just how much his mother did for him. For a long time, until just a few years before, Tom had been unaware of just how much his mother did.

Putting the last of the washing up in the sink, Tom headed back to the stairs and up to his bedroom to dress for work. He'd made his mind up, he'd wash up the dish and the odd bits and pieces but he'd leave the pan to soak and finish it off when he got back from work. With his hand on the banister, Tom climbed wearily back to his room.

Chapter Three

Mickey woke on his back with the stars shining brightly above him. The edge of the tree-line was quiet and he could smell the smoke of the all but extinguished fires drifting across him in the gentle breeze. Even without moving he knew his head was going to hurt. He remembered switching from the Romany ale to the Irish whiskey and he had a recollection of Flynn insisting he drank a toast with their poteen but he couldn't remember much beyond that.

A hint of the dawn was just visible on the distant horizon with a thin sliver of lightening sky. With no cloud cover, the full moon lit the ground around him in a sterile, frozen glare. He peered down his body at the weight pressing on his chest and saw the familiar straight, black hair of Rosa as she slept with her head against his breast and her arm draped possessively across his body. Mickey took a long breath in and let it slowly escape again as he sighed and frowned sadly at the girl.

It wasn't that he disliked the girl, they'd been friendly for their entire lives and it hadn't surprised anyone when their parents had discussed joining the families together with their wedding.

Rosa was pretty; her large, dark eyes were the same shade of brown as his and she had a very classical look to her face. If not for the Romany colouring to her skin, her high cheek bones and straight, aquiline nose would suggest Greek or Italian parentage. She was five inches shorter than Mickey's five foot ten frame and she curved in all the right places. At seventeen years old, it was late for her to not be married already but she was such a will-full, stubborn daughter her parents had been content to wait until she decided it was time before the families had been made aware an approach wouldn't be refused outright.

Mickey's father had haggled with Rosa's Da through the night almost two years previous before the darro had been agreed. The two men were accomplished at pushing negotiations close to offence but never quite crossing the line; at the conclusion, both families were happy with the deal. Neither Rosa nor her family were happy with the delay that Mickey insisted on; a long engagement wasn't unusual for the promised children but most times, the promise was made when the offspring were just entering their teen years. To keep Rosa from being a wife until she was beyond eighteen years had caused a little friction between the two fathers.

For her part, Rosa was taking to being the betrothed with an enthusiasm none had expected; she wanted nothing more than to be Mickey's romni and bear his children. Though she'd often try to find time to sneak away to be by his side, most of her day was spent with her Nana or Mickey's mother learning all she was expected to know.

With a pained expression on his face, Mickey gently freed himself from the gypsy girls' sleeping embrace and sat up, leaving her still slumbering beside him on the damp grass. Glancing around from the wood beside their sleeping area, he looked toward the camp a hundred yards distant and spotted Rosa's cousin almost immediately.

The sixteen year old was lit periodically as he drew on the pipe he held clutched in one hand; the glow of tobacco in the bowl cast an eerie orange glow to his face and it was easy to ascertain the youth was staring at Mickey. The youngster was leant against a solitary rowan tree between the fighter and the camp and Mickey was impressed the boy had managed to stay awake through the night. He knew it was just as well as if Rosa's Da had learned his watchman had fallen asleep the boy would have suffered a savage beating.

Mickey had always had a soft spot for Stefan, or Stevo as he'd always been known. Until he'd become promised to Rosa, Stevo had been the older boy's shadow and despite the age difference, the two of them had been almost inseparable. It had been Mickey who had taught the youth how to fight and had they not fallen out over Rosa,

Stevo would likely have developed into a strong fighter. The falling out had less to do with Rosa and more to do with the boy's uncle. No sooner had the bottles been opened to toast the pair than Rosa's Da had tasked Stefan with watching after her honour.

The irony was, if Mickey could be honest with himself, it would be Stefan that had more to worry about than Rosa.

Over the elapsed two years, the friendship between the two boys had crumbled into dust. Stefan had begun to both resent the lost time learning to punch and duck and also, he had grown angry that he had to spend his day watching the girl he was sweet on himself flirt and tease his former friend. He was bitter and jealous despite how much he tried not to be.

Raising a hand, Mickey acknowledged the youth and the only response back was a brighter glow from the pipe as Stefan drew harder on the stem. At least he knew Rosa hadn't had her way with him while he was deep in his cups. There were fewer reasons for him to stall the wedding as the days and months passed but if she got her way, there'd be a rapid wedding with a shotgun behind him and her swelling with every moon.

Frowning and shaking his head, he knew eventually he'd run out of excuses and he'd become the rom to her romni. There was no belief he would ever avoid becoming her husband but he was terrified of the night that would follow the day. There were some

27

duties he didn't know what he could do about. How could he become a da himself when her curves and smile failed to rouse him? The fear ate at him daily.

Glancing back down at the girl he found himself smiling at the way she lay curled close to him. He did love her but he could never love her in the way she wanted, not in the way she deserved. Rosa was his best friend, more than a sister and dearer to him than any other girl. Somewhen she was going to know his lie and he hated that he was going to hurt her.

A blanket lay pooled across his knees and he carefully shifted to the side, keeping the blanket from the damp grass and raising it above Rosa's shoulders to keep her warm. The girl must have brought the blanket to him and wrapped them both in it but it had been a warm night and he'd slid it down their bodies as he slept. Now the morning carried a cool chill to it and he covered her to keep her cosy.

Quietly Mickey rose to his feet and headed to a nearby tree to relieve himself. His head pounded and he had to rest a hand against the coarse bark to ensure his balance. Turning back and buttoning his fly he strolled back to the gypsy girl while keeping a watchful eye on Stevo as he silently watched back.

"Hey, Rosi-posie!" Mickey dropped back to his knees and gently shook the girl's shoulder. "Rise and shine" he said, a gentle urging in his voice.

With her long hair tangled around her, the girl rolled over and arched her back, deliberately pushing her breasts upward while exaggerating her need to stretch. "So? Dosta! I's awake." Mickey grinned at Rosa's irritability and she grinned back. She reached up and wrapped a hand behind his head, pulling him down to meet her part way for a kiss. The boy managed to shift slightly so as to place a delicate kiss on her cheek and then he straightened up, forcing her to rise to a sitting position or to fight against him to pull him down. There was no doubt who'd win.

Subtly breaking free from her grip, Mickey offered his hand to help her rise but the young girl simply laid back on the ground and put her hand down to her skirts and as her fingers made walking motions on her thighs, she gathered the material in her hands and inch by inch, she slowly raised her hemline. Rosa's bare feet were already exposed but as she tried to tease the fighter, she exposed her ankles, then her calves. As her knees came into view she asked if Mickey wanted to lie somewhere more comfortable.

Deliberately glancing in the direction of the camp, the boy mentioned Stevo's presence and the girl's face fell and she swore loudly, turning her head to glare in the direction of the young teenager.

"Khul!" Rosa hissed, letting her head fall back hard to the grass as she pouted petulantly. "Thee and me need being wed!"

Without responding, Mickey again offered his hand and this time, after a moment's hesitation to stare at her promised, she acceded and let the muscled boxer haul her from her grass and dirt bed to her feet.

Mickey reached to the ground and picked up the blanket, he folded it in half and wrapped it around the shoulders of the girl like a shawl and with his fingers, he gently straightened out the tangled tresses of hair that fell around her face.

With one hand, the girl reached up to cup his chin, she sidestepped him, circling him just enough that he had to shift his feet to keep his eyes on her. Once she had him positioned so the moon lit his face, Rosa began to inspect the damage the Irishman had caused to the face she loved.

An eye was closing as the swelling from the punches he had taken took effect while he slept and the cut on his brow had scabbed over. He'd be sporting a black eye for the next few days and there was a good chance by the time they reached the camp and prepared to move out he'd not be able to see out of the eye but the damage was superficial. His other eye was unmarked but the cheek below it looked red and tender; the moon reflected in his black pupils as he looked ahead while she examined him. She gently stroked the cheek while she stared into his eyes, the brown iris looking as dark as the pupil in the half-light. She reached up on tiptoe and placed a soft kiss against his split lip; he neither pulled away nor encouraged her but he turned his eyes to look down on her, a smile lighting his face. Lowering herself back to her heels, Rosa briefly leant her head against his chest.

"My man! My rom" she whispered just loud enough for his ears to catch her words.

Taking a step back, Mickey put his hand to her shoulder and turned to break the contact she had with him. He looked over the ground they had been laying on and spotting three empty beer bottles, he gathered them up in one hand, gripping the necks between his fingers. With his free hand he reached out to take her hand in his and slowly, with Rosa pulling the blanket tight around her shoulders, they began to walk toward Stefan.

"Stevo!" Mickey called, "Give these back to your puri-daj." He dropped the bottles at the feet of the young boy and walked on, not waiting to see if he picked them up. Rosa and Stevo's grandmother wouldn't be happy to find her bottles had been left behind and Stefan could be guaranteed to take them to her.

If their grandmother found out they had been left with Stevo and he'd not brought them back to her he'd suffer for it. She might not beat him herself but she was a devious woman; all she had to do was to refuse a drink to one of the men in camp and say she had no bottles because Stevo had left them behind and he'd suffer at their hands instead.

Heading toward the Irish camp, Mickey grinned to himself as he heard the glass bottles clink together behind him as the lad did as he was told.

The camp of the Irish was quiet; the tents and caravans were in darkness aside from the light from the moon and stars but Mickey could see well enough. Heading for the fires where he'd had his fight, he kept his eyes open for any Romany he could, spotting a few sleeping in the dirt. He woke those he found and continued through the camp until he found his own da.

Half under a caravan and propped against the wooden steps, Mickey's father was snoring with an almost empty whiskey bottle gripped in his hand and held across his chest. Letting go of Rosa's hand he knelt in the dirt and prodded his father until he responded by opening one eye.

The father and son exchanged no words but Jacky Ray managed to open his other eye and after a pause, he nodded once to his son who smiled back. His father was proud of him.

Standing again, Rosa's hand pushed itself into his and the two of them continued through the Irish camp toward the road a hundred yards outside of the caravans. They avoided the tarmac and walked along the grass at the side of the road in bare feet and headed back to their own camp. The news had probably gone ahead that Flynn Burn had lost the bout and Mickey was going to be lauded for a few days by those who'd won money on him. There wouldn't be much celebrating today though, today the camp would pack everything away. A few of the men would head into the local village to see what they were owed was settled and then they would all move on to a new site.

Mickey was smiling as he walked but as Rosa squeezed his fingers, his smile faltered as he realised another day had passed and he was one day closer to being joined to her. Try as he might, he found it hard to be happy for it. There were worse people to be bound to but the lie pained him as much for her as for himself.

Chapter Four

Dressed in trousers that were too big for him and wearing boots that had been bought second hand, Tom locked the door behind him. With his coat left draped over the chair in the kitchen, he looked skyward and hoped the day would stay as dry as it promised.

A slight breeze cut through the thin cotton, collarless shirt that was done up one button short of the top. It was still early and the warmth of the sun was yet to reach him but it was a long walk to the common; if he'd worn anything thicker, he'd have been perspiring heavily by the time he got there.

Checking his shirt was thoroughly tucked in all round, Tom tightened the thick leather belt on his high waisted trousers and with his lunch gripped in his hand, he started down the narrow lane to the main road.

Though it was still early and the road he was approaching was little used, he was apprehensive. They usually didn't appear to tease him until he was on his way home but Tom was wary of the local boys taking delight to go out of their way to antagonise him. With the school holidays on them, it was still barely credible that they may have chosen to wait for him this early but he worried none the less.

The bottom of the lane was quiet and when a fox slunk from the hedgerow where the lane joined the road, Tom breathed a sigh of relief. The rusty looking dog fox turned his eyes to the youth and still gripping the baby rabbit in his jaws, he scuttled across the dirt track and into the long grass opposite. With the fox so relaxed it was safe to assume there was nobody hiding in the bushes nearby. Taking a deep breath, Tom managed a smile. The day would hold more terrors but missing the first potential torment was a reassurance.

Much had conspired against the young boy to make him the object of bullying by the local children and as far as he could see, none of it was reasonable. He wasn't alone in being the only child to grow up without a father; he knew half a dozen people he had grown up with who had lost their fathers in the war. Where things differed for him was passing his eleven plus exam and going to the grammar school. It was supposed to be an achievement, it was meant to make life better; it had failed miserably.

When it came to the three R's, Thomas excelled at reading and writing but his arithmetic had never progressed as promised. Just a casual glance at a sheet of sums could make the boy dizzy as the numbers swam across the page. He'd done well in history and geography but the sciences had destroyed him, so much relied on mathematics that he hadn't stood much chance.

For five years he'd struggled on with an education as the few friends he'd had took jobs and apprenticeships. Five years later and Tom looked like the clerk life had pretended he should be. Five years wasted. That was how Tom viewed it. When he did finally leave school at sixteen he was only able to get work as a woodsman. Of the crowd he worked with, four of them were the same age as he was but whereas they were muscled after five years of hauling logs and sawing through branches, he was almost puny by comparison. Even two years of grafting with them had failed to give him the physique they bore and identified him as an outsider just at a glance.

The friends he had made at grammar school had all achieved good exam results and had moved into careers that allowed them to look down on him. Stuck firmly between both worlds, Tom didn't feel he fitted in anywhere. The biggest separation between himself and those he'd grown up with was the households in which they lived. The widowed mothers of his peers were more financially stable than his own mother as they had been in receipt of keep from their working sons. While other working mothers had been able to live on the money their children brought in to supplement the meagre widow's pension, Tom's mother still worked long hours to make ends meet.

At the bottom of the lane, Tom began to walk with a little more confidence. Not being persecuted at the start of the day should have been such a small thing but for the youth, it was a huge relief. Too many times he'd made it to the common with blood on his face, buttons torn on his shirt and his lunch either stolen or so trampled as to make it inedible.

The woodsmen he worked with may not have despised him but all too often it felt like they did. They were strong men, old school in their thinking. The foreman was the only person Tom felt any fondness for and though he hadn't given it a lot of thought, he should have realised the man only stood up for him because if he said what he thought about the boy, it would have raised questions as to why he'd hired him in the first place.

Once across the main road, the single lane tarmac road he found himself on meandered lazily with pointless twists and turns. He followed it under the over-hanging trees until he came to the bridge over the river. He stopped and leant on the stone wall, gazing down onto the flowing waters of the River Rother. Even in the summer it roiled and bubbled over the rocks and stones. There was something about how the water caught the light that mesmerised Tom and he had to pause to stare at it every time he crossed the bridge. It was the last sheltered area of his walk for a while and he liked the wooded surroundings.

The meadow just past the water was a dark green even in the height of summer. Through the wet months the grass would barely peek above the water as it flooded onto the meadow but through the summer it begged to be lain upon. He'd paused more than once on the way home to stretch out on its gentle carpet and imagine all was right with the world.

Reluctantly he pushed himself off the stone wall and walked away from the tree-line. With his hand in his trouser pocket he let his fingers toy with the matchbox in his pocket. His tobacco and papers were in his back pocket and he was tempted to roll a smoke but the small supply he had would only permit him half a dozen cigarettes before it ran out. The more he thought about it, the more he found himself wanting a smoke. Sitting down crossed legged on the side of the road, he pulled out his baccy pouch and leisurely made himself a roll-up.

A whirring sound came to his ears from under the shadows of the trees by the bridge and Tom hastily glanced around for somewhere to hide. There was no place he could keep himself from sight and bracing himself, he rose to his feet and moved off the tarmac. The bicycles came into sight with laughter and barely audible conversation. Envious of their freedom but unable to justify the expense of purchasing a bicycle, Tom endured the leers and taunts as the four teenagers rode their bikes directly at him, only veering away as they reached the edge of the tarmac. Once the teasing of those he worked with hurt but Tom was slowly becoming inured to the group. Once they started the logging, stripping and sawing of the timber, the insults and bullying petered away. Tom knew he didn't fit in just as well as those he worked with and it wasn't the graft that called a halt to him being picked on. The older men would glare at the boys if they rode the youngster, they may do so themselves but felt lording it over the newcomer was their domain.

For the most part, the woodsmen tended to leave Tom alone as long as he did his fair share of work. They pretended not to make concessions for his lack of strength and inability to handle the larger logs but in reality, they'd rather leave him to the smaller tasks than have him lend a hand where it would be hindrance.

Allowing for where the boys had cycled past him, Tom guessed it must be nearly half past seven. It'd take him another twenty minutes to reach Redford common so although the others would be there before him, he was reassured he wouldn't be late. The foreman certainly had no complaints about the youth's timekeeping; in the eighteen months he'd been working on the common he'd never arrived after the eight o'clock start and the only day he'd had away with sickness had been in the first week when he'd got knocked out by a chunk of wood that had shot away from the band-saw. He'd been teased by everyone the next day he'd gone to work, man and boy alike. After a brief and strict lecture about where not to stand when the rotary blade was running, grins had crept in and within the hour, even the foreman was calling him 'Blockhead'.

Finishing his cigarette, Tom pinched the end off, burning his fingertips in the process and unrolled the remaining half inch of paper to add the unsmoked remnant of tobacco back to his pouch. Penny-pinching it might be and he'd never be so frugal if anyone was watching him but earning barely four pound a week and giving two of that straight to his mother, Tom was loathe to waste anything. It was bad enough when the woodsmen stopped for lunch and he stayed sitting on a log unwrapping his sandwiches while everybody else headed to the Plough for a beer and a snack.

Picking up the pace, he began to stride it out as he hit the only uphill stretch of road. He passed the graveyard on his right beside the large house that hid behind a larger wall, and began to breathe heavily with the effort the incline caused. Not long to go; the road levelled out again after the hill and he was almost there. Early morning until early evening most days but being Friday, they'd all get to finish work at one o'clock. Everybody would head to the pub except Tom. Tom would be asked but even if he thought they meant it, he wouldn't go. He'd take a steady, leisurely stroll home and be in in time to put the stew on to heat up. With a few hours to himself, he'd head for his bedroom and read for a while until his mother got in.

The work on the common was harder than usual. James and Toby were partnered together with old Albert and Fred; the four of them were cutting down a stand of beech trees over the hill from the main camp. Fred and Albert's axes could be heard biting into the hard wood, their swings making a distinct double chopping sound that sounded like the pumping of a heart. The youngsters with them would wait for the first tree to fall and then they'd set about sawing through the branches to leave just the bare trunk as the men moved on to their next tree. The other two boys of Tom's age, John and Robert would hitch up the two dray horses to haul the logs back to the camp where they could be split on the saw by Percy and Mister Randall, except Percy wasn't there today.

Percy was likely the oldest man Tom had ever met and on the days he didn't turn up for work, everybody assumed the worst. Today though, he'd sent a message with his nephew that he had to get part of his roof re-thatched and he'd be back to work on Monday.

Edward Randall wasn't pleased with the news but could do nothing about it. Calling Tom to him as soon as the young lad had arrived on the common, the foreman told him he could leave the branches he usually attended to and help run the band-saw.

Nodding nervously, Tom eyed the contraption warily. Even before his accident with the lump of wood the boy had been uncomfortable around the machinery. The vast steam engine was loud and he could feel the ground vibrate with the heavy, rhythmic pounding of the pistons. Then there was the huge belt that ran from the wheel of the engine to the cog attached to the circular blade of the saw itself. The belt would slip, whine and sometimes slide free of the narrow guide rails in extremely scary moments. Tom's greatest fear though had to be the blade. The steel disc looked like a white sun while it span but before it was kicked into life, the inch long teeth on the three foot diameter blade made the boy's blood run cold.

It was Percy's job to line up the trunk on the cutting slab and once he was satisfied the angle was right, he would set a pulley loose that also ran from the steam engine and the trunk would propel itself along the slab to have a plank sliced from the massive log. Tom knew there was no way he was going to have the judgement to get the wood lined up, let alone the strength to get the pulley to activate. He knew what that meant, he'd be doing the job the foreman usually did. It wasn't skilled work but it was a heavy job and one that had to be done as quick as it took the pulley to retract the log ready for the next cut. There may only be five working hours to do on a Friday but it was still going to be a long day.

Chapter Five

The sun was high in the sky above the trees and the heat of the summer pitched down on the rabbits as they nibbled the long stems of wild grass. A black Ford Prefect crept over the stone bridge and turned off of the road onto the grass of the meadow. The rabbits scattered at the loud growl of the motor vehicle and bolted for their burrows.

The narrow tyres gained purchase on the firm ground but as the car moved into the longer grass, the three speed engine laboured in first gear to keep traction. Wisps of steam crept wraith-like from the grill under the bonnet; not enough to threaten to kill motion but enough to hint at a rising difficulty.

Wheels sank into rabbit holes and then rose over the bumps of the untended land, the black box managed to navigate it's way to the riverside about fifty yards from the tarmac. The driver hauled on the steering and rode a large circle to bring the car side-on to the running water and came lurching to a stop. The driver's door opened and

Jacky Ray made to step out, pushing the door wide as he attempted to exit the vehicle only to have the heavy door fall back onto him with the slight slope of the ground.

Sporting a dark and tender black eye, Mickey jumped out of the passenger side while his da swore and used his foot to open the door as wide as it would go. When Jacky made it on to level ground he leant one hand on the front wing of the old ford and spat in the direction of the river that flowed past just a dozen yards away.

The older gypsy scanned their surroundings as though expecting something to be wrong. There was nobody to be seen but the two of them and the rest of the families were a good two hours behind them. Jacky had driven ahead with his son to identify where each family would make camp when they arrived. Switching his gaze back to the car from his surroundings, Jacky Ray tapped a staccato rhythm on the gloss black paintwork and glared silently at the bonnet as vapour puffed erratically from under it. Despite the heat of the day, the forty year old wore a long heavy coat and ignoring the car for a moment more, he reached for his inside pocket and stared hard at his son as though daring him to speak.

Jacky unfolded a worn and yellowed piece of paper that had the scrawling his second son had drawn on it and passed it to Mickey to figure out. There were few words written as neither Mickey nor his father could read well but there were symbols to denote families and numbers beside that indicated the favours Jacky would receive for preferred pitches.

The idea of parking their caravans where they were told was a recent idea; prior to buying the Ford, families would camp where they saw fit but Jacky had decided they would set up where he wanted them so as to avoid the arguing and fights that always ensued when two families would disagree over a pitch. The only consideration was the road and the river. Nobody wanted to be beside the road and everybody wanted be close enough to the river to wash but not so close as have any spirits creep from the water into their caravan.

Mickey looked over the meadow and kept referencing the paper to work out who was going to be put where but the reality was easier than the other families realised. There were two categories that mattered, those who promised the best favours gained an area near the river, those who offered nothing got the road. Anyone else was put anywhere else but led to believe their pitch had been chosen especially for them. It was a good deal and helped keep the car fuelled while letting all the families think they had a reserved space.

Turning at the creaking sound of the bonnet being raised, the young gypsy paused his study and walked back to his da. The older man held a dipstick in his hand and whipped it at the ground to shift the excess oil from the metal rod before dipping it once more and drawing it back out to study the level.

"'s all right?" Mickey asked of his father but Jacky said nothing in return, he just frowned at the low level indicator on the dip. The boy waited, knowing better than to interrupt his father's thinking when he had a mood upon him. Stepping up to the car, he leant on the wing and peered under the bonnet at the engine block and even his inexperienced eye could see black oil spattering the steel casing.

With his head lowered as though still studying the motor, Mickey peered at the older man from under his fringe. Jacky Ray had a temper that made the Irish seem placid and Mickey knew how easy it was to become the focus of his ire. Carefully avoiding eye contact he watched as his father rummaged in the back seat and after more muttered curses, the man produced a glass milk bottle with an inch of milk remaining. Walking around to the front of the vehicle again, he swirled the white liquid against the side of the glass, raised it to his lips and gulped down the remaining milk.

Mickey reacted quickly as the now empty milk bottle was thrown his way, catching it in his left hand despite the absence of a warning. "Been quicker last night maybe you'd not be so sore."

Keeping his expression neutral, Mickey grunted as though to agree. Every aspect of the fight had been talked about by his father all morning as they'd driven north. To listen to the critique it sounded as though Mickey had been the loser but as always, he held his own temper in check. There had been no praise, no compliments, even the congratulations Jacky had given the night before had evaporated as the alcohol had slowly left his system.

As a child Mickey had complained to his daj that however well he did at something, it was never recognised. His mother had clipped him around the ear and told him he should do well for himself and then sent him outside. He'd had the same lecture and felt his father's belt that night when his mother had told his da of his complaining. It was a lesson learned.

Sitting in the car as they'd driven through East Sussex and into West Sussex Mickey let his father rail at him about his failings as they both weathered the effects of hangovers. He took comfort in the fact that despite the lecturing, he knew his da was proud of him. It wasn't the greatest comfort he had that morning, his mood was eased by the twelve notes that sat folded in his back pocket.

Mickey's hand strayed to his back pocket almost unconsciously as he took the milk bottle to the river as directed. The car would need more than a top up of water to keep it happy but if Jacky Ray said fetch water, Mickey fetched water. He just hoped he wasn't going to slip from the bank and get his winnings wet. Drying the large notes discretely wasn't going to be easy.

The car was parked on a slight slope and the young gypsy paced the small incline until his feet reached the point where the grass met sand. Mickey's knowledge was enough to see they were setting their camp at the point the river had no bank. This would be where the flooding started; when the water level rose, it would need only an extra foot in height before it left the route nature dictated and would steadily run down the grass. Once it hit the level ground, it would spread and encompass the meadow in a matter of hours. Gauging the level, the youngster could tell there would be no threat for many months.

Relieved he had no need to hang precariously from the bank, Mickey simply squatted down and held the neck of the milk bottle below the water line and watched it fill. With an inch in the bottom he raise the bottle, swilled it around to rinse the milk away and then repeated filling it. Movement in the shallow area he was situated gave the youngster a smile as he saw a fish dart away from him. It was the first time the young man had been to this camp and nobody had mentioned fishing was a possibility.

Unsure if he could credit it to instinct or peripheral vision, the gypsy boy knew there was somebody approaching. Slightly to the right of him, a figure was drawing near from along the tree-line of the river. Turning and rising to his feet in a single movement, Mickey saw a youth in brown trousers and a dusty shirt heading slowly toward him. The boy was intently watching where he placed his feet and the gypsy realised he was close enough to the edge of the water that he needed to hang to the narrow trunks of silver birch so as to not fall in the river. Despite the idiocy of the boy's actions, Mickey grinned as he watched. The boy looked to be in his early teens but his clothes looked like those of a worker. The youngster slowly drew closer to where Mickey stood but he was still concentrating intently on his feet and hands to stay as close to the river without actually being in it.

"Khul!" Jacky Ray muttered behind his son. "'e be dinilo!"

Starting at his father's presence, the young gypsy watched as the older man shook his head, took the milk bottle from his son and walked back to the car. Though his da had shocked the grin from his face, it soon came back as he watched the youngster leap from the root stock of a beech tree, catch a low branch and swing optimistically to leap and land on a grassed patch of ground beside an old oak. The boy's hands snaked out, fingers catching in the bark to steady himself and then he glanced up to check his next obstacle and froze as he caught sight of the gypsy fifty yards ahead.

Mickey was in agreement with his father, the boy was a fool. Usually when he first caught sight of local boys, Mickey braced himself and took careful stock of the gadjo. Almost every encounter became a fight but he didn't see the youth as the usual threat. The boy was slightly built; with his shirt undone it was clear he was no fighter though Mickey conceded he wasn't all skin and bone. Around his neck he wore his boots, tied together with the laces, the black, dusty footwear knocked together with his movement. The gypsy had never seen anybody so pale. Barefoot, the youth was frozen as he stared at Mickey.

Tom was puzzled who the two men were who had parked on the meadow but he was also annoyed. He considered the grassed area to be his own and after leaving work he had walked away from the road and into the wood with the intention of following the river to the meadow and just lying there in a day dream for a few hours. He didn't know who the gypsies where but they had already ruined his day.

The dark haired man standing staring at him didn't seem at all concerned he was on private land. Tom knew he had no extra privilege to be there either but he was possessive of area and in his fantasies, it was *his* land. Realising he hadn't moved since he'd spotted the strangers, Tom hastily stepped away from the tree he had been clinging to and took his boots in his hand. Acting as if he hadn't been seen swinging from branch to branch like a child, he adopted the pretence of indifference and walked forward with a nonchalance he didn't feel. He'd nod and walk on past; he'd be home a lot earlier than planned but he couldn't act as though the men weren't there.

Flicking his fringe away from his eyes and looking away to the road simply to break away from the stare of the man at the river's edge, Tom let himself slowly take in the road and the bridge. Casting a broad sweeping gaze over the meadow and back to the river, he swallowed hard. Tom was a little under forty yards away now and the man was still gazing at him.

The gypsy was curious. Mickey had encountered a handful of gadjo but never outside of a village or town. As a child he'd been able to defend himself against kids four and five years older than himself and once he'd hit his teen years, he'd begun to head into local villages in the hope of starting a fight but he'd never seen somebody look so out of place as the youngster heading toward him. He didn't doubt for a moment he could put him down with a single punch but he found himself wanting to know about the sandy haired boy. There was something about him that was unusual, Mickey didn't know what it was but something felt wrong.

Though avoiding eye contact, Tom lifted his eyes from the grass he walked across often enough to determine the man at the edge of the river hadn't taken his eyes from him as he'd approached. The nervousness that had been increasing at being stared at so blatantly was waning as Tom realised the man wasn't as old as he'd initially thought. The youth ahead was close in age to himself, maybe a year or two older but he had muscles that the woodsmen wood envy.

Calling out to ask if they had broken down, Tom was greeted with silence. The older man by the car raised his head from under the bonnet and stood straight, he glared at Tom from under his thick black eyebrows, then muttered something to Mickey that Tom couldn't hear, then he started to wipe his hands on an oily rag he'd picked up from the wing of the car.

Scratching at the half day of stubble Jacky Ray pulled his neckerchief from around his throat and mopped his brow. He leant back against the paintwork and still gripping the red polka-dot square in his hands, he looked askew at Tom who was now half a dozen feet away from his son and called out "Dilo chav shee jilling gav?"

Mickey smirked as Tom halted with one foot raised. He lowered it again where he stood and his face turned furtively to flit between both men.

Crossing his arms to match his da, Mickey translated his father's words and asked "You going to the village?"

Tom hesitated a moment and then nodded. Mickey kept his gaze on the youth in front of him and called out "Arvah."

Furrowing his brow in confusion, Tom puzzled over the man's words. He had a little knowledge of Latin from school but the men were conversing in a tongue he couldn't recognise even parts of. He asked Mickey if he was Polish and the boy began to chuckle.

The chuckle grew into a laugh and the grin that split Mickey's face caused Tom to grin along with him. The older man had something shouted to him and he too laughed. Both men uncrossed their arms and Jacky hid his face in his neckerchief as he wiped a tear from his eyes.

Initially Tom had liked the laughter but he realised the men were laughing at him rather than with him and he managed to stop laughing and he shuffled from foot to foot as they both managed to calm themselves.

"Tu never seen a gypsy afore?" Mickey asked and grinned as Tom shook his head. "Well tu can tell those gorgios of yours, tu has now. Now you seen two!"

Jacky Ray stepped up to the pair of boys and though he was still smiling, there was a harsh edge to it that Tom sensed straight away. The man held a milk bottle casually in his left hand and his neckerchief in his right. He walked past his son and placed his hand on the boy's shoulder. He pulled the boy close as though in a conspiracy. Gripping the top of the boy's shirt, he shook him lightly while still smiling and began to talk in a low, halting voice as his shoved the milk bottle at Tom's chest. Tom raised his hands to the bottle and as his fingers came in contact with the glass, Jacky released it, leaving Tom holding it.

"Tu go get oil terno rom" the man stated. "Get oil for car." The gypsy dug into a small pocket in his waistcoat and pulled out a thrupenny bit. He held it up in front of Tom's face making it plain to see. "Tu get oil, I get change." His smile broke into a grin and he leered at Tom. "Tu chor, Tu gets amria. Tu get a gypsy curse arter tu." Jacky stuffed the coin in Tom's trouser pocket and nodded again in the boy's face, he shook him by his shirt once more then he walked away grinning to himself.

Tom thought he understood but he checked with Mickey he seemed to at least understand English that the older man wanted oil for the car.

The young gypsy's attitude softened toward the boy and he found he liked the naïve youth. He'd never encountered a gorgio, a non-gypsy who was ignorant of them and to find he didn't have to intimidate the youngster was a change he found he welcomed. Telling Tom oil was what his father was wanting, he also told the boy to check his pocket for the coin.

Asking why, Tom put his hand in his pocket and found it empty. He hurriedly checked his other pocket and then he started to scour the ground, convinced the coin had fallen to the grass. Shaking his head, Mickey put his hand in his own pocket and after cautiously checking his father wasn't watching, he drew out a pocketful of change that caused Tom's eyes to bulge. Among sixpences and florins, the young gypsy separated out a thrupence and shoved the remaining coins back in his pocket. With one more glance toward the car, he positioned himself with his back to his father so as to block his view.

Mickey reached out and grabbed the youth's wrist, pulling his arm out straight and making him open his palm. He put the small, octagonal coin in his palm and rolled Tom's fingers closed over it.

"That's our secret" he cautioned. "Say nothing!"

Tom let out a pent up breath, convinced he'd lost the coin himself. He didn't know Mickey's father had palmed the coin away instead of placing it in his pocket and Mickey didn't dare tell the boy otherwise. It was an easy trick and more than once he'd used it himself to gain goods for free but today, for this boy, he didn't want the boy to get in any trouble.

"My name's Tom."

"Mickey" the gypsy responded. "Now get gone. Find me when tu has oil."

Tom tried to push his fringe out of his eyes as he made to smile at the gypsy boy. Without thinking, Mickey reached out and brushed the hair away for him and a brief smile touched his lips before he forced it away. He turned back to his da and saw him watching.

"Get out of here and get that oil" Mickey snapped, loud enough for his voice to carry to the black ford. "Don't tu go forgetting the curse that'll follow!"

For an instant Tom felt as though he'd been kicked, then he saw the pleading look in the gypsy's eyes and he understood. Though the comprehension didn't wipe away the hurt, he realised the boy had to be as cold as his father so with a quick smile, he turned and headed toward the road. He ignored the older gypsy and kept on until he reached the tarmac, then he turned left again and began to repeat the walk up the hill he'd made that very morning.

"Dinilo chava!" Jacky Ray muttered as Mickey returned to the car and began to find sticks to mark out where each caravan would stop. He didn't think the boy was foolish; just not used to gypsies. He watched him walking away from the meadow on the road and shook a daydream from his mind. If he didn't get the places set by the time the first family arrived he'd be in for a beating.

Chapter Six

Tom passed the graveyard once more and began the slog up the hill. His initial thought had been to call in at the small garage in Redford but as he forced one foot in front of the other, he started to think about cutting his journey short. He'd had to oil some of the large cogs that ran the great saw earlier in the day and the large vat he'd had to dip the small tin jug into was large and full; a milk bottle full wouldn't be missed and it'd half his journey.

Stepping off the road again, the young man began to slowly skirt his way back into the wooded area behind the farm he was approaching and made his way onto the edge of the common land that circled the old farmhouse. He wouldn't be seen by anybody as the land the farm hands worked was all on the opposite side of the road except for the one field at the end of the track. The field wasn't planted up, a dozen cattle would be his only spectators and they would ignore him just as they had when he had passed them on the other side of their field not an hour earlier.

There was a slight nagging feeling about his intentions; taking the oil was stealing. The boy's upbringing railed against the morality of the act and yet, if nobody would miss the small amount he was going to remove, was it still a crime? Tom considered leaving the thrupenny bit behind as payment but then he had the issue of finding change to stave off the gypsy curse. Each step that took him closer to the deserted woodsmen's camp took him a step closer to his quandary.

Gypsies were thieves, everybody said so. If Tom just took the oil, the gypsies would likely be blamed and yet, though the gypsies were the ones who wanted the oil, they were paying for it and Tom would be the thief.

It took almost half an hour for the youngster to reach the woodsmen's camp and he looked around as he approached the small wooden hut that sat beside the traction engine. The giant band that connected the saw blade to the steam powered behemoth had been removed and was nowhere to be seen and the engine itself sat and glared at Tom as he approached.

The camp seemed so quiet. Even without the hissing of steam and the whine of the saw, the camp always held a memory of the cacophony. It was the first time in two years Tom hadn't felt a ringing, singing sensation in ears. Aside from occasional bird song, the common was silent. It didn't help his mood.

Stood on the edge of the clearing, the teenager was utterly motionless as his eyes ranged across the broken bracken, the wood-chip carpeted dirt and the tidy stack of logs. Stubble of snapped grasses framed the work area, the pale, rigid stems pointing skyward at the periphery of the clearing.

Nervous and hesitant at the familiar place seeming so alien, Tom cautiously, quietly made his way around the side of the camp, circling the workspace to come behind the rudimentary shed where the equipment was stored against the elements.

A squawk and a flurry of motion; Tom toppled backward and hit the dirt hard as from between his feet a large game bird ran through his feet. As it escaped the interloper, the pheasant took to the skies screeching its distress with a warbling cry. The boy swore quietly to himself and grinned while he looked around once more to check he really was alone. Rolling to his side, Tom crawled to his knees and rose to his feet, brushing the dust and dirt from his clothes and continued his walk toward the shed.

Satisfied he had no audience, he came to the door of the hastily erected building and halted at the site of the hefty, rounded padlock that sat looped through the hasp and loop catch and the brief amusement at the bird startling him fell away in a long sigh. The youth hadn't expected the tool shed to be locked and it made a marked change to his thinking. It was one thing to take a small quantity of oil but to break into a locked store to do so was markedly different. The temptation remained but Tom was too honest to give the idea more than a passing consideration.

Stuffing his hands into his pockets, he continued past both the shed and the idle engine and continued over the rough ground toward the road. The common rose as he neared the tarmac he knew sat just on the lip of the lightly wooded area and he leaned forward against the incline. Once he was over the brow of the small hill Tom rested with his hands on his knees as he doubled over to catch his breath. After a moment, he stood upright and stepped onto the black-topped track and began the gentle descent toward the small village not even half a mile distant.

From the other side, Linch church was the first building of the village that would be encountered but coming in from Midhurst side, the garage was the first sign of civilisation Tom encountered. He crossed the roughly concreted forecourt and passed the oval topped petrol pump that had four red stars glued to its body like a soldier's rank. The rubber arm sat high on its rest as though raised in salute. Stepping between both pumps that stood sentry, Tom headed into the dimly lit workshop that had its shutter door raised for business and called a greeting.

A clatter of metal on metal sounded as the sole occupant, the owner of the garage, put his spanner down on the engine block of the

Land Rover he had been working on and peered around the raised bonnet to the silhouetted figure in the entrance.

"Robbie?" the mechanic asked.

Stepping a little further into the dingy building the youth shook his head "No Mr West, it's Thomas Quatrell, from the common."

Eddie West picked a rag off of the wing of the box like vehicle and wiped grease from his hands. "Thought you boys finished early on a Friday. Something wrong with that monster of yours?"

Tom explained he wasn't at the garage for the steam engine and then elaborated about the vehicle by the river in need of oil. He avoided mentioning that the owners were gypsies.

"Just a pint you say?" Still trying to wipe grease onto an oily rag, Eddie gestured with his head for the young lad to come further into the workshop and once Tom was stood beside him, the mechanic nodded toward the rear of his workshop. Just visible in the unlit area was a large drum with its push down lid off and resting against the side of it. "Help yourself to it. No charge but let the driver know if has trouble, I'll gladly look his car over."

With a wry smile at the irony of free oil, the youngster made his way into the dark, dingy area of the garage and spied out the large oil vat with the open top. The surface of the oil was a quarter of the way down on the interior and though Tom was wearing his working clothes, he tugged his rolled up sleeve as far up his arm as he could.

If he returned home with oil on his shirt there'd be hell to pay.

Holding the body of his shirt to his ribs and gripping the milk bottle in his right hand, Tom peered over the lip of the metal rim and swallowed nervously.

"Bleedin' heck lad!" Eddie West exclaimed, humour in his voice "You some sort of pansy? Give it here!"

Taking the milk bottle from the embarrassed boy, the mechanic didn't pause as he pushed the neck of the bottle down into the viscous liquid. Tom peered in, unable to see the bubbles gulping out of the glass as the oil fought into the bottle.

Feeling the need to justify his caution, the youth explained he didn't have many shirts and his mother wouldn't be pleased if he ruined one.

Eddie laughed quietly to himself and quietly muttered his understanding. "I'm right with you there. Once in a while I have to call in here in an evening and often as not, I'm not wearing my work clothes." He looked askew at the youth with the dusty, light brown hair and winked. "Think my wife likely has the same view as your mother."

Tom smiled without comment, waiting as Mr West wiped the surplus oil from the bottle and then wrapped a cleaner rag around the glass before handing it to him.

"Just remember, let them know if they need any work done on their car to come to me."

Assuring him he would pass the mechanic's message on, the youngster left the dingy garage and started his return journey. Initially Tom strode purposefully up the tarmac road but his eyes kept glancing to his right and the wooded paths that he knew led down to the river. Following the watercourse was a slightly longer route to take but with the summer sun shining down on him, he'd have the advantage of shade and a less arduous climb to the top of the hill if he detoured under the oaks and beeches of Woolbeding common.

Having convinced himself the scenic route had advantages, the young boy hopped up the small bank of pale, dusty dirt and rested his hand on top of the closest wooden post. Warily Tom squeezed through the narrow strands of wire that were strung just close enough together that however he passed through, he was almost guaranteed to snag himself on the metal barbs.

It was the work of a minute to release his trousers from the knot of jagged wire and quickly inspecting the damage, he knew it was wasn't overly noticeable but he frowned with the knowledge his mother would find the small tear regardless. He didn't relish the lecture that would accompany the discovery and started to toy with explanations which he rapidly discarded. The easiest option was going to be to sew the tear himself while he waited on the prepared stew to cook.

Tom halted his descent on the path and put his hand to his forehead as his memory waved a flag of surrender. He still had to finish the washing up he'd left first thing in the morning and he was going to have to relight the rayburn to heat their tea.

Glancing up through the dappled lime green leaves the youth located the sun and tried to gather his position relative to the road. Making a rough estimate of where the sun had been when he'd finished work and gauging where the sun would set Tom judged the time to be somewhere between three and four o'clock. It was going to be a close call to get home in time to prepare everything before his mother came home but it was manageable.

Squatting down amidst the twigs and stones at the foot of an established oak, Tom sat on the root stock of the aged tree and placed the bottle of oil between his feet. Unwrapping the cloth Eddie West had placed around it, the youth managed to stuff the neck of the bottle with the rag and experimentally, he tipped the glass bottle from side to side, eventually upending it to ensure the plug was firmly in place. Rising back to his feet, Tom began to jog down the track keeping a wary eye on the golden brown liquid as it sloshed within its container.

The path darkened as it descended where the trees overhung the route. There was plenty of light for Tom to see his footing clearly and he managed to sidestep the occasional rock that could twist his ankle if trod on. After a few minutes he felt the ground level out and the trees thinned as he passed from woodland back to open ground. The path rose up above ground level and the trunks of the trees drew closer together where they formed a crude but effective windbreak between the field to his left and the meadow to his right.

Slowing his speed, Tom slipped his way between the bore of two beech trees and dropped the two feet down to the meadow. It wasn't much of a short cut but he could see the tree-line at the bottom of the meadow and he knew it was there that the river marked the border between more wood and the meadow. Turning from the path he had been on, he moved diagonally across the meadow.

Though the water level was high for the time of year it was much lower than Tom had become accustomed to it being. He could still hear the burbling sounds it made as it churned over itself in a rush to be elsewhere. Closing on the noise, he slowed his pace again. This was one of the youth's favourite moments.

The water from the river could be heard running softly away and the sun was warm on his skin. Tom glanced around at his surroundings and smiled at the crimson bursts of petal where wild poppies were blooming amidst the long stems of grass and the yellow of buttercups and dandelions dominated the lower ground.

Trailing his fingers slowly through the high grass, the youngster plucked a stem of grass and tucked the stalk between his lips. Chewing it for a moment only, he drew it free once more and with his dirty fingernails, he scraped the grass seeds from the head of the stem so they gathered lightly in his hand, then blew them behind him where he had just been walking.

As the tiny grains fell into the crushed blades of grass where Tom's footsteps had made an impression, Tom bent down and plucked an almost unnoticed dandelion from the side of one of his boot prints. The wild flower had bloomed and faded and all that remained where the white wisps of star-petals as his mother called them; the seed of the flower ready to be sown on the wind. Lifting the ball-like head of the flower to his face, Tom felt sorry for the plant that it should be caught among the longer grass. Sitting beneath the longer stems, the dandelion had little chance of casting its seed into the air to be carried any distance as no breeze touched it where it was.

Tom smiled and whispered to the plucked plant. "Go and explore!" With a gentle exhalation, Tom blew the seeds from the stem of the plant and watched them dissipate; some falling to the soil a few feet distant but others caught in the minutest up-draught and carried high and to the west. With his back to the sun, Tom blew twice more until every seed had been released and chuckling a little to himself, he dropped the redundant stalk and turned back to face the river. The few minutes he had gained with his jog along the path had been lost by his delay in the meadow but he didn't worry about it. He'd enjoyed the moment and as happiness seemed to find him so rarely, Tom took the memory, wrapped it in wishes and tucked it away to savour later.

With a new found lust for life, the youth began to jog toward the edge of the meadow so as to follow the stream back to the gypsies' camp.

Chapter Seven

With his back pressed against the bole of the oak tree and cupping the bowl of his pipe in his hand, Mickey shifted himself on the damp grass and let his feet dangle over the edge of the river bank. The slope down to the water's edge wasn't so steep as to threaten a fall but it gave him a slightly elevated position to watch the youths from the camp playing in the water as they washed the grime and sweat from themselves after their long journey.

Letting a plume of smoke escape through his fingers, the young gypsy stared downward at the naked youngsters splashing in the river. His eyes were drawn as always to Paulo; the sixteen year old was well muscled in comparison to the boys surrounding him but his strength was gentle as he ducked his brother under the flowing water. Mickey locked his gaze on the bunched shoulders as the boy held Little Rob under for a few seconds before releasing him to rise coughing and spluttering.

As Mickey adjusted his position again, he jumped as hands covered his eyes, his reflexes halted as he caught the scent of rose oil. He raised his empty hand to his eyes and gently pulled Rosa's hands from his face. Keeping hold of one hand, Mickey kissed the back of it tenderly as the girl sidled down beside him.

"Tu shouldn't be here. It ain't proper." Mickey muttered quietly.

Rosa leant in toward him, resting her head against his shoulder so her hair cascaded down his chest. "Says who? Make me yours an' tu can say I can or I can't" she replied, a gentle mocking tone in her voice that belied her annoyance at their delayed marriage.

Reaching down, Rosa slipped her hand down the front of his loose trousers and she grasped him, squeezing firmly.

"Thinking of me?"

Mickey's cheeks flushed crimson and he whispered "Always" in her ear. The lie falling too easily from his lips. Decisively the youth wrapped his fingers around her wrist and drew her hand from the waistband of his trousers. "Eyes are on us."

Rosa shifted herself and sat heavily in his lap, looping her arms around his neck and she nuzzled against his neck. "Not now there's not; Stevo is carrying for your mother. Just tu and me here."

"And a dozen eyes watching from the river." Mickey added, looking over Rosa's shoulder as she kissed his neck. Watching the boys in the water, it was plain they barely aware of the promised couple sitting on the bank above them as they tumbled and splashed in the deeper part of the river.

"Then let's give them something to see" Rosa laughed. "I can feel you want to." Grinding herself against him, the girl stroked her fingers down Mickey's arms, feeling the corded muscles tense through the thin cotton of his shirt.

Worried and fearful, the youth looked among those washing and hoped for rescue. He knew it was the inevitable he postponed but as much as he loved Rosa, he was terrified. It wasn't the girl that he feared but being found to be less of a man than she both desired and imagined. Swallowing hard, he blinked back tears as they came unexpectedly to his eyes. There was no indication of his upset for his promised to be aware of, no interruption in his breathing, no heavy sobbing; Mickey simply felt the weight of the future resting on him and he bowed his head against her shoulder to subtly wipe his eyes on her thin shawl.

A voice called out loudly from the right of the oak the couple where leant against "Mickey! Raklo dihk ya."

Raising his face from the flowery scent on Rosa's clothes, Mickey turned his face to the voice and saw Gem, his eight year old nephew. Behind the youngster was the local his father had sent to get oil and behind him was a following of the camps younger boys and girls. In total there were ten children trailing behind Tom and Mickey could see the youth's discomfort.

"Amria! Les shee didikai." Mickey pushed Rosa from his lap and clambered to his feet. Despite the protests of his promised, Mickey ignored her and smiled at Tom, beckoning him forward with one hand and turning to glare at the children who all had either a stick or a stone in their hands. "Ga avree" he said to the youngsters in a firm enough voice to communicate his insistence but neutrally enough that none took offence.

Having told the entourage accompanying his nephew Tom was a friend and making them leave, Mickey ran his eyes over Tom and recognised the cut on his cheek and the weal on his arm as being part of his welcome. He apologised to the youth for the beating he'd clearly received and turning to Rosa, he sent her away that he could talk more easily with the gadjo.

Staring challengingly at Tom for his untimely arrival, Rosa squeezed Mickey's arm and pulled herself close to him. Pressing against him, she kissed her beloved hard on the lips and with a last glare at Tom, she swayed away from the pair making sure to tread lightly and she danced away as provocatively as she could. Mickey watched her go with an anguished expression on his face. Tom barely noticed the girl as he tried to keep his own pain hidden.

Staring at the ground in front of Mickey, Tom sniffed hard and fumbled with both hands at the bottle of oil in his hands. "I've got your money too, all of it." Tom blurted out hastily. "The man at the garage didn't want anything for it but..." he sniffed hard again and held out the oil. His lip quivered. "He said if you need anything more, just drop in."

Sensing Tom's distress, Mickey stepped into the gap between them and pressed his thumb against the cut on the youth's cheek and smeared the trickle of blood away. "I be sorry. I didn't think" the young man said. "We's none too welcoming for gadjos."

The small attention spent on him proved too much for Thomas and with a shudder, he coughed, his chest heaving. He doubled over, leaning away from Mickey and was sick on the grass, he dropped to his knees and began to cry. Wiping his eyes on his arm made no difference, no sooner had he cleared his tears than more appeared.

Careful to avoid the vomit, Mickey Ray crossed to the other side of the youth and he squatted low, placing a comforting arm on the weak youngster. His comments that people were watching had no effect on Tom and the gypsy scanned the distant faces that were still turned in his direction. One by one, as they made eye contact with the muscled boxer, the faces turned away.

"Tu should have walked on by Tom." Mickey hugged the youth and then leant across his body to place both arms across his back. "Come on, sit against the tree, ain't so bad."

Tom allowed himself to be led to the tree and he sat hunched forward as Mickey dropped down beside him. The gypsy grasped the local's wrist and pulled his arm out straight, turning it over to look at the red line that hadn't broken the skin but would show a bruise by morning.

"Did they hit you anywhere else?"

Wordlessly, Tom shook his head and sniffed again, slowly regaining control of his emotions. Lifting his eyes from the dirt, the boy caught sight of the naked young men cavorting in the water below him and he quickly lowered his gaze again, embarrassment causing his cheeks to flush just as Mickey's had a few moments before.

Mickey grinned to himself at Tom's shy demeanour but he quickly suppressed the smile in case Tom thought it to be at his injuries. "There were no need to return the money. Tu could have just passed the bottle to the first of us tu met."

"I didn't want your dad's curse following me." Tom said, his voice raw.

The tough gypsy pulled the boy toward him and shook his body as he laughed, "Da has cursed more people than you'd know and ain't yet seen any suffer for it!" Though he still hurt and he felt ill at ease among the gypsies, Tom felt himself slowly begin to chuckle with Mickey. The youth may be taller and stronger than anyone Tom knew but his presence was more of a comfort than Tom believed possible.

Digging his hand into his pocket, Tom finally managed to lock his fingers on the thrupence and he pulled it free, offering it back to Mickey. The gypsy hesitated, his eyes flitting from the coin to the face of the young man. He winked and whispered "Keep it miri rinkeni! For your trouble."

"Miri...?"

"It just means 'my friend' is all" Mickey lied. The gypsy scoured Tom's face for any hint the boy may have known different. Tom mistook the intense stare as condescension and turned his face away. Shaking his head and looking up into the branches of the oak tree, Mickey couldn't believe he could be so careless as to call the boy pretty even with no other ears nearby.

Tom sensed a change come over the gypsy as Mickey took his hand from his back and rose to his feet. Looking up into the tanned face, the dark eyes captured Tom's and he looked away again. An uncomfortable silence fell between them before Mickey said he'd see Tom to the road. Thinking it a step too far, Tom couldn't help himself but put his hand out to the youth that he might pull the boy to his feet. The hand remained stretched out, palm upward for an interminable time before Mickey finally took it in his own and with a little exertion, he pulled Tom to his feet.

It may have been Mickey's strength or Tom's slight build but as the youth suddenly found himself standing, he stumbled and fell forward. Mickey reached out to steady him and Tom landed between the strong arms of the gypsy, his face pressed against his chest. A hand lightly brushed against his hair then Mickey took a step back and with a slight rise to the corner of his mouth, the gypsy simply nodded once and turned away. He checked over his shoulder to see Tom was following and he skirted around the edge of the camp rather than heading through the centre.

The two youths didn't exchange any words as they passed by extravagantly painted caravans and Tom caught glimpses through occasional open doors of rich colours and tantalising smells of something cooking over open fires. Everyday sights, sounds and smells for Mickey were all foreign fare to Tom and though he made sure he kept pace with Mickey, he wanted to linger and experience the exotic surroundings in greater fashion.

For Tom, they were at the road all too soon. Barely fifty yards from the nearest caravan, they were out of hearing of any gypsy ears but both young men loitered in silence at the edge of the tarmac. Mickey held the milk bottle full of oil in one hand and the cool glass kept him rooted in reality; the bottle screamed of responsibility and commitment but Tom's presence whispered of impossible futures.

"I should get home." Tom muttered, his eyes on the grass of the verge and his inaction hinting that he didn't want to leave. Mickey grunted his understanding and he took a deep breath.

"Will you be okay?"

Looking up from the verge, Tom smiled sadly and nodded, not trusting himself to speak. He turned to walk away, then turned back. Hesitating just a few yards from Mickey, he clenched his hands into fists and steeled himself to leave. Biting his lip, he raised one hand and turned back to the road and began to walk away. He'd barely walked twenty yards when he gave into a compulsion and he looked behind him to see the gypsy still watching after him.

Mickey watched the young outsider walk away and felt part of him leave with him. Closing his eyes, the gypsy concentrated on his breathing and when he opened his eyes again, he didn't look up the road but turned rapidly and stared at the curved roofs of his home. Tightening his grip on the neck of the bottle in his hand, he let a breath out and headed back into his own world to seek out his father, he managed to take a dozen paces before he span on his heel and paused to watch Tom turn at the bend in the road and disappear from sight.

"Goodbye my friend" Mickey whispered as he stared where the road vanished from view.

Chapter Eight

The house was still lit by the late summer sun once Tom returned. Light speckled the local white bricks where it fell in dappled patterns as it was filtered through the branches and leaves of the stand of beech trees that lined the border of the garden. The lone laburnum a mass of hanging yellow flower sitting solitary in the centre of the largely untended garden.

It was close to seven o'clock and the youth retrieved the hidden key from under the earthenware pot that housed a cluster of late flowering violas and quickly unlocked the front door. The moment he made it through the door he hurried to the rayburn and lifted the heavy iron pan from the table to the hot stove. Glancing around he pulled a sour face as he unbuttoned his cuffs and rolled his sleeves up to attend to the washing up that had sat congealing in his absence.

Placing a kettle beside the stew to boil water he hunted out a wire-wool scourer from the cupboard beneath the sink and tipping the water that had been left to soak in the pan down the drain, he poked the wooden spoon at the dried porridge that clung stubbornly to the saucepan.

With a tea-towel in his hand, Tom retrieved the kettle and poured enough water in the pan to a depth of an inch and added some washing up liquid from the bottle on the windowsill. Most of the oat mixture came free with little effort but a black residue stuck to the bottom and he was forced to scrub at it until the last of the caked on mixture came free. Satisfied it was clean if not gleaming, Tom upturned the pan on the wooden draining board and left it to dry in the air.

After a quick check on the stew that had started to bubble reassuringly, the boy dashed to the staircase and pounded up the bare wooden steps to his room. He stripped his clothes off and scoured his chest of drawers for the clothes he would wear tomorrow. There was little difference in the new attire except the shirt and trousers where free of sawdust. Gathering his discarded clothes in one arm and the clean clothing in the other, Tom thudded naked back down the stairs. Dropping his clothes in a small pile on the kitchen floor, he unhooked the tin bath from the wall and set it on the floor between the stairs and the kitchen table.

It took one kettle of hot water and four kettles of cold to put a small puddle in the bath but it would suffice. With a bar of soap in one hand and a thin flannel in the other, Tom lowered himself into the lukewarm water. Scrubbing at himself the boy hurriedly sought to be out of the bath before his mother came home.

Satisfied he was clean as he was going to get, Tom clambered out of the tin bath and dripped on the floor as he reached for the threadbare towel he'd dropped just out of reach. Almost dry, he began to dress, his foot catching in the waistband of his trousers and threatened to tip him back into the bath as he overbalanced. A hand on the table provided enough stability for him to conclude dressing and feeling refreshed, he bent to the pile of work-wear he'd deposited on the kitchen floor and he dropped everything into the laundry basket that sat between the sink and the rayburn.

Tom dragged the bath to the kitchen door and tipped the water onto the stone path and watched it trickle away down the slope. With the bath lighter, he lifted it and hung it back against the wall. He made another check on the beef that was bubbling with the fury of Vesuvius, then drew two deep-bowled plates from the immense welsh dresser and began to set the table. After adding the cutlery, Tom slumped into one of the chairs and groaned.

With the back of his hand in the small of his back, Tom tried to stretch to relieve the tension he'd accrued through the day. It had been the first time he'd sat down since ten o'clock when the foreman had called for a tea-break and he'd perched on a log and eaten his sandwiches intended for lunch.

With the smell of the stew filling the small kitchen, Tom began to realise how hungry he was and as if reminded, his stomach growled with perfect timing. The clock on the wall showed it was half past seven, giving lie to the fact it was still losing ten minutes a day. It would only be a short while before his mother came home but there was enough uncertainty that he didn't want to take the risk of putting the vegetables on to boil just yet.

The vegetables! Closing his eyes and leaning across the table in defeat, Tom realised he still needed to pull carrots from the garden and cut some broccoli. Sitting back up and stretching with his hands behind his head, the youth was tempted to leave the vegetables for his mother but he knew her day had been longer his and she'd want to sit down just as badly as he would.

Staring vacantly out of the window, Tom raised his hand to his cheek and he let his fingertips lightly feel the raised scab that had already formed where the stone had cut him. The cut was slight and just from touch, he knew it had been a glancing impact that had just scratched his face like a bramble whipping across his cheek. He looked to his arm; the weal had lost its red, tender aspect and now simply looked like a graze but his fingers could feel the bump and he was sure it would darken by the morning. He rolled his sleeve back down to keep it from his mother's sight.

Putting his palms flat on the table, Tom pushed himself to his feet, his chair scraping backward on the ancient tiled flooring. Touching his cheek again, he smiled briefly as he remembered the gypsy smearing the droplets of blood away. Had it been a good day? There was something about the gypsy that tipped the balance and Tom decided it had been a good day. He laughed; he'd worked harder than ever on the milling machine with the boys jeering his efforts, he'd had his planned laze in the meadow spoiled and he'd been beaten with sticks and stones and yet it still seemed a good day.

Tom had gathered the carrots from the garden and managed to cut the broccoli without cutting himself. He was stood over the table with a small knife in one hand as the other held a carrot flat against the warped chopping board when the front door opened. Smiling at his mother as she paused, leaning heavily against the lintel, Tom stepped forward and took the string bag of shopping from her.

"Did you have a good day?" Tom asked solicitously.

Pale and breathing heavily, Mary Quatrell smiled at her only son and then broke into a heavy coughing fit. Tom turned hurriedly from putting the shopping on the table and leant support to his mother's slight frame as she struggled to remain upright. As the cough ceased, she drew a ragged breath and smiled reassuringly at Tom.

"It's okay" she wheezed, "Just that hill, it takes it out of me."

Walking his mother to the table, Tom sat her in the chair with the sink behind her and returned to the vegetables. He was reassured at her explanation but he couldn't help but worry about her; just as he was all she had in the world, she was all he had too.

"Maybe you should cut back on your hours." Tom said as he sliced the last of the carrots and slid them from the board into a small pan he had ready.

Mary smiled at her son's innocence. "Oh it's not so much. Every little helps." The reality was Tom's mother was in receipt of a widow's pension but even with that and Tom's income, they barely managed to meet the rent each month let alone buy food to eat. The sixty hour week she worked didn't provide any luxuries but she was a proud woman and took comfort that at least they had no debts to worry about.

Rising gingerly to her feet, Mary reached across the table for her shopping bag but turning back from the stove, Tom grabbed it first. "I'll see to that. You get your breath back, then I'll make you a cup of tea."

Taking the shopping from the bag and lining the items on the edge of the table, Tom smiled to himself as his mother dug into her pocket for her packet of cigarettes and with shaking fingers, she lit one and blew a plume of smoke to the ceiling. With the shopping away, Tom took an ashtray from the windowsill and placed it in front of his mother. He pulled his tobacco from his back pocket and put it beside her packet of Embassy, then turned to pour boiling water into the teapot.

"You should warm the pot first."

Tom smiled at his mother and chuckled. Every time she told him; every time he forgot. It was almost a ritual now. He scooped three spoons of tea-leaves into the pot and stirred it once to encourage diffusion. He couldn't make a pot of tea without the memory of an old physics lesson coming back to him. He'd explained Brownian motion to his mother so often and so thoroughly that neither of them could make tea without the conversation coming back to them both.

Behind the youth, the lid of the saucepan of vegetables began to chatter to itself as the steam pushed it up repeatedly. Tom ignored it as he lay the tea strainer on top of one of the cups but his mother caught his eye and he left the teapot to attend to the pan. She always chastised him for not letting the tea steep; he tried to counter the weakness by using less milk but Mary Quatrell was a stickler where her drink was concerned.

Angling the lid to release some of the pressure, Tom turned back to the teapot and his mother quickly halted him.

"Give it another minute Thomas." Mary said, her smile a small part of the regular lecture. Tom nodded and still standing, he rolled himself a cigarette and lay it beside his plate for after their meal. Glancing at his mother for permission, he received a small nod and he picked the china teapot up and swirled it theatrically in the air before pouring it through the metal strainer while he held the lid in place. With two cups poured out, he put the pot on the rayburn to keep it warm; his mother always had a second cup.

Mary raised her cup delicately, gripping the small handle between her thumb and index finger; Tom gripped the bowl of his tea in both hands and with his elbows resting on the table he brought his drink to his lips.

"Did you have a good day?" Tom's mother asked.

After a brief hesitation while he considered the arduous teasing the morning had brought, then the beating the children had given him, he smiled as he remembered the raw tone of the gypsy boy's voice and nodded neutrally but with a hint of smile on his face. "We've gypsies down by the river, just past the bridge." Putting his cup down, Tom stood and turned back to the stove. "They weren't there this morning but they'd appeared when I came home."

"That's all we need!" Mary sighed. "If they come to the house, don't even answer the door. Nothing but thieves and tricksters the lot of them."

"They didn't seem so bad. I mean, I only spoke to one of them but they seem pleasant enough." As Tom spoke, he subconsciously rubbed at his arm where the swollen flesh was barely noticeable. "They've got a car but most of the caravans are pulled by horses. Oh Mum, you should see the caravans. They're painted in really bright colours, it's like a circus stopping in town."

"Don't be fooled by the glitz and glamour, those Irish aren't people you want to be mixing with." Tom's mother stubbed her cigarette out in the ashtray and tried to suppress a cough that kept trying to surface. "We may not have much but we're a respectable family."

Whatever Mary was going to say next was lost as the constrained cough won over and her face turned red as she tried to draw breath between the hacking, rasping bark that doubled her over.

Tom clattered the saucepan he was spooning carrots from back onto the rayburn and hurried to his mother's side just as she recovered her breath. "You should see a doctor Mum."

"I'm fine" she said, wiping her mouth with a handkerchief and folding it over to hide the blood stained cotton. Stuffing the white square back into her pocket, she smiled weakly at her son. "I've probably been smoking too much today, it's been quite hectic at work."

Dubious, Tom returned to dishing up the stew and slipped a full plate in front of his mother, returning to the rayburn to serve his own, he called over his shoulder. "They're not Irish anyway, they look foreign."

"Romany!" Mary muttered, nodding to herself. "They're a little better." She gathered a spoonful of stew and steered it to her mouth, blowing gently over it to cool it. "Don't see as many as we used to, time was they passed through the town every year. At least they make a pretence of earning an honest living." She nodded at the large copper kettle sat at the foot of the rayburn. "They mended that big kettle for your father once; you can hardly see the join. Never really trusted it since but it's a pretty thing."

Sliding into his chair with his plate threatening to flood over the rim, Tom glanced at the oversized kettle. He'd almost used the massive pot when he'd filled the bath but he hadn't been convinced he could lift it when full.

For a few minutes, mother and son ate in silence sat opposite each other. After a short time, Mary asked "What did you have planned for tomorrow?"

"I'm probably going to go to the library" Tom replied. "Miss Corbett said the new Narnia book should come in this week." Tom mopped his plate clean with a chunk of bread torn from the loaf his mother had brought back among her shopping. "Are you finished?" Tom looked at the half empty plate of his mother's and frowned. She was sat back looking pale and though he knew she always complained he gave her too much to eat when he cooked, he had deliberately cut back tonight.

With a forced smile and pushing her plate away from her, Mary apologised. "I had a very late lunch, sorry."

"Well I'll see to the washing up. You head into the sitting room and tune the wireless in." Tom grinned, "I think Dan Archer and Walter are going to have a head to head tonight."

Clearing the table and transporting the saucepans to the sink, Tom didn't see his mother leave the room but once he had managed the washing up, he moved into the living room to find his mother asleep in her armchair with the radio sat in silence on the table between her chair and his. He considered waking her but decided she needed the rest.

Tom crossed to the window on the far side of the small room and he drew the thin curtain closed. He lit the paraffin lamp on the mantle and turned the wick to generate more light. The glow through the white glass glinted against the silver frame beside it. Lovingly, Tom stroked the glass and stared damp eyed at the black and white images of his father. There was a photograph of himself as a small child being held in his father's arms and a second, smaller picture of Martin Quatrell in uniform. In the facing frame was a coiled loop of hair and as always, Tom had the urge to pry the frame open so he could simply make contact with the father he barely remembered.

Sighing hard, he turned to look again at his mother. He crossed the room and draped her with her crocheted blanket, then curled himself up in his chair beneath the mantle, drawing his feet up beneath him. From the small table beside his chair he picked up the battered copy of The Hobbit he was reading; he knew so much of it by heart but he loved it. It wasn't the words or the story but as he read, he could just remember his father's voice reading it to him before the war.

Chapter Nine

Midhurst was a quiet town with only a handful of people on the High Street. Mickey had been to the stream that fed the river having walked most of the town shortly after the sun had come up. He was on his way back to the camp and was at the top of the hill when he caught sight of a small group of youngsters ahead of him. Ever wary of the attitude of locals, he was content to loiter behind as they progressed up the walled, narrow lane that led out along the main road through Midhurst.

The party in front of him appeared to be a mix of ages. Despite slowing his step he was gaining on them and he judged the youngest of the five boys to be in his early teenage years and the oldest was maybe just sixteen. They were loud and obnoxious but it wasn't until he saw them turn from the road to head down the lane he himself was heading for that he realised their noise was focused on a youth a dozen yards ahead of them.

As he drew closer he recognised Tom to be the centre of their attention and words began to become audible from the gang that were clearly taunting him. Mickey could feel his ire rising and as much as he didn't want to get involved, the apparent bullying was something he felt an urge to deal with. Mickey didn't recognise the hypocrisy in himself, many times he'd used his strength and position in the family to belittle others.

Tom was a few hundred yards down the Petersfield road when the bullies changed tack; instead of calling him names they gathered around him and the first punch was landed to the accompaniment of laughter. The blow landed hard against the youngster's chest and was just off centre causing him to spin with the blow. The books clutched in his arms fell to the ground and Tom bent down to gather them back up just as the oldest of the aggressors kicked him in the stomach.

Rolling onto his back with his arms wrapped around his midriff, Tom cried out for them to stop but it only spurred them on. Engrossed in the beating that was only just beginning, nobody noticed Mickey catch the stationary group up.

The fourteen year old hit the ground holding his side where a southpaw blow struck the area where his kidneys were. Mickey stepped forward to face the four remaining teenagers and squared up against the largest of them.

"Tu like to fight?" Mickey asked, "Come fight me!"

Mark Trent wasn't the oldest of the group but he was the tallest and carried enough weight to appear imposing. As the gypsy stared into his eyes challengingly, Mark grinned and raised his fists. A fast punch connected with his jaw snapping his head back then a second blow boxed his right ear causing him to wobble on his feet. Swinging a wild arm he almost caught Mickey's cheekbone but swaying back without moving his feet, the gypsy brought his right hand in low and hit the stomach hard with a rising force.

Rising onto his toes with the force of the punch, Mark felt himself angling forward as his stomach muscles tried to make him double over. He held himself almost upright but a hand grasped the back of his head and pulled his unresisting face downward where it met the rising knee of the gypsy. Blood spattered Mickey's trousers as Mark's nose broke. Clutching his hands together, the wild eyed traveller brought his hands down like a hammer at the top of Mark's shoulders and the boy was unconscious before he hit the gravel of the pavement.

The three remaining youths hesitated for a moment then charged the gypsy like a wall. Sidestepping the closest assailant, Mickey put himself behind the prone figure of Mark. Two moved to circle their still friend but one leapt the body to meet a backhanded blow that sent him reeling into one of his companions and they both tumbled to the ground.

The last approaching threat came in from Mickey's left and as he turned his attention to the youngest of the group, he watched the scared and nervous face suddenly smirk; a slight flicker of eye movement and Mickey understood the new confidence. He turned on in time to see the first person he'd disabled lunge at him. The traveller didn't pull his punch and the single right hander he landed on the jaw of the boy spun him on the spot and he fell almost on top of Mark.

Two of the downed youths were untangling themselves and preparing to rise as Mickey realised he had a pain in his side. Glancing down for a moment he noticed blood seeping through his shirt. The initial confusion faded as he saw one of the boys snatch up a dropped pen-knife that the last attacker had dropped. The blade was small but it had been enough to cut Mickey's flesh.

Two of the group were out of the fight, both lying still and oblivious on the ground but Mickey had the youngest behind him and two before him. Unconcerned about the cowardly thirteen year old behind him, the gypsy locked his eyes on the boy with the knife. Reaching to his hip, Mickey drew a sheath knife with a wicked-looking eight inch blade and held it to his side where it caught the sun. Grinning challengingly, he took a slow deliberate step toward the two he perceived as the greater threat and they retreated warily.

"Me friend and meself will be getting gone now." Mickey

moved toward Tom who was sitting on the road holding his stomach, his eyes wet with tears. Drawing up beside him, Mickey stood between Tom and those of the gang still standing. Tom sniffed and scrabbled across the tarmac gathering up his library books. The gypsy paid his friend no attention, cautiously watching as the trio tried to bring their companions back to consciousness.

With Tom ready, the pair backed away from the scene of the fight. As the distance between them increased, Mickey alternately looked ahead, then turned back to ensure there was no possibility of pursuit. After a hundred yards he returned the knife to its sheath and fastened the securing press-stud to hold it in place. He put his hand under his jacket and pressed it to his shirt; his fingers came away bloody.

"They cut you?" Tom blurted out, horrified at the sight of the crimson stain on his rescuer's hand. "I'm sorry. I..."

Mickey saw Tom tremble at the sight of the injury and as his words dried up, the gypsy smiled at the youth. "Be Khushti. Just need patching up is all." He reached out with his clean hand and tousled Tom's hair. "Tu? Is tu fine?"

Ignoring the pain in his stomach and the dazed, throbbing headache, Tom nodded once but his sadness was apparent. "I'm used to it. It's not the first time." Tom paused then added "Thank you though." He grinned momentarily. "I've never seen anybody fight like you did. That was incredible. Punch, punch, punch" The youth mimed Mickey's actions, then dropped his hand back to his side with a sigh. He looked to where the gypsy's coat flapped open where he walked and saw the dark stain had grown in just the short space of time since they'd left the gang behind.

Although the gypsy was walking confidently and was as alert as ever, Tom noted his face was a little pale and his fingers seemed to be trembling slightly. "My house is just up here" Tom said, pointing up a lane that was overhung with trees. "Let me see if I can do something for you; you can't walk all the way to the meadow bleeding like that."

The two boys crossed the road and began to head up the small incline toward Tom's solitary house without discussing the option any further. Mickey had a fear of houses having never been inside one before but he understood that Tom was right that he needed to see to the stab wound as soon as he could. As they came out of the shadow of the trees, Tom moved in close to the gypsy just in time to be a supporting shoulder to his weakening saviour.

Mickey sagged noticeably and leant heavily on Tom as they reached the gate to the house's garden. It wasn't simply blood loss that was his enemy, the brick structure instilled a terror in the gypsy he had never anticipated. "What about Familia?"

Understanding the poorly phrased question, Tom explained his mother would be at work. "I've no brothers or sisters anyway and my father... well, my father died in the war." Expecting the usual sympathies that such a revelation usually invited, Tom was surprised when Mickey ignored the comment about his father's death but instead expressed shock that Tom was an only child. He didn't understand the gypsy's muttered reply that everyone needed brothers.

Once inside the house, Mickey kept gazing at the kitchen window, the low ceiling and close walls seemed to be squashing in on him and he had to keep his eyes focused on the vista outside. Swallowing hard, he let Tom sit him in the chair, then he leant back so as to ease the pressure on his wounded flesh.

Mickey made a comment about how dark it was inside and Tom glanced around the kitchen in puzzlement. Looking back to the gypsy he watched as his friend's eyes rolled back in his head and Mickey's hands unclasped and fell from the table as his slipped into unconsciousness.

"Shit. Don't you die on me!" Tom dropped the mug of water he'd been filling into the sink and paid no attention to it as it broke against the enamel bottom. Dashing across the room he tried to wake the eighteen year old by shaking him and shouting but even though he managed to elicit responses from the boy, they were at best drowsy and vague. Using all his strength, Tom managed to pull Mickey from the seat and draped him awkwardly across the kitchen table. He manoeuvred him as best he could until eventually the gypsy was laid on his back with his legs hanging over the lip of the table.

Hesitant and unsure quite what he needed to do, the scared youth managed to pull Mickey's arms from his coat while still leaving the clothing underneath him. Trying to pull the shirt up wasn't working so he unbuttoned the cotton cloth and pulled it open to expose the wound. Blood glued the fabric to the wound and Tom winced as it eventually parted wetly. Ignoring the muscles of Mickey's pectorals, Tom was stunned by the muscles of his stomach. He'd never seen the definition of the abdominals, even the woodsmen he worked with didn't look as sculpted as Mickey.

Pushing his hair from his eyes, the boy put the fingers of both hands either side of the injury and tentatively squeezed the skin from each side simultaneously. The cut opened and Tom saw it was only slightly more than half an inch wide. A trickle of blood oozed from the cut and ran slowly down the side of the youth's flesh just below his lowest rib.

Had Tom not passed his eleven-plus he wouldn't have known much anatomy but fortunately, his grammar school had covered enough that he was able to gauge the blade had entered below the lung and though he kept his fingers crossed, he was almost certain it had cut in just above the liver.

Turning from the prone figure on the table, Tom returned to the sink and took a new cup from the draining board. With the cup in one hand, he picked up the bottle of disinfectant from the windowsill and poured a small amount in the bottom of the cup. Moving to the rayburn he added an inch of water to the brown liquid and returned to Mickey. Passing the sink he snatched up the dishcloth and then, pausing by the table he worried about permanently staining the cloth. With a shrug, he discounted his concern, his mother's upset didn't really factor into things given the situation.

Carefully Tom washed the area around the wound until the cut was visible as nothing more than a red-lined tear in the skin. He was cautious not to part the flesh and start it bleeding again and he considered sewing the skin together but decided against it. It wasn't a large wound and it would likely heal on its own given the opportunity.

Squatting down at the sink a small tin of basic first aid was found and a large wad of dressing was pressed against the injury. Tom struggled to bind a bandage around Mickey as he had to lift him from the table and hug him close with one hand while he passed the crepe strip under his shirt and pulled it taught three times to ensure it wouldn't work loose.

Satisfied he had done all he could, Tom tried to think how he could wake Mickey up so he could get at least a cup of tea in him to replace the blood he had lost. He was still considering this when the gypsy groaned quietly and tried to raise his head.

Laying a hand gently on his chest was enough for the boy to keep Mickey pinned down and he advised him to move slowly so as not to open the wound. Tom took his hand back and quickly moved to the kettle on the rayburn. He thoroughly rinsed the teacup and poured from the stewed tea that sat in the pot resting on the cooler part of the hob. Turning back he found Mickey sitting up and trying to clamber from the table.

"Stay there a moment, drink this." He thrust the teacup into the youth's hands and Mickey drained the lukewarm drink in one go and passed the cup back. "Another one?"

When Mickey nodded, Tom poured the last of the dark brown liquid out and gave it to the gypsy but told him to wait a moment. Opening the larder he grabbed a bag of sugar and poured a small amount equivalent to a tablespoon into the tea and stirred it with his finger while apologising all the while.

Carefully Mickey made it to the chair and when he was given the cup, he drank more slowly and over five minutes, he could feel himself becoming more aware. He put the empty cup on the table and smiled his gratitude but he said nothing of his thanks.

"You've lost a fair bit of blood" Tom said. "The top of your trousers are soaked. Stay there a minute." Tom ran from the room and thudded up the stairs. He was only gone a couple of minutes but by the time he returned to the kitchen the gypsy was nowhere to be seen. Panic evaporated as he noticed the door to the living room was open and he crossed to the doorway. Mickey was standing by the unmade fire with his fingers resting on the mantelpiece.

"Your da?" Mickey asked.

Tom moved into the room and stared at the photograph Mickey was looking at and quietly confirmed it was his father.

"That prikasa, narky!" Mickey pointed to the lock of hair under the glass. "Can't be doing that." The gypsy stared with alarm at Tom, true concern clear in his eyes as his agitation grew. "The mule, the spirit of the dead... you can't be keeping them! You own the part, you own the whole." Mickey looked around the room fearfully as though expecting the spirit of Tom's father to appear.

"It's all my mother has of him, it's just a love token." Tom blinked hard, he wasn't going to cry but as always, mention of his father's absence hurt.

"It's bad" Mickey restated. "Tu keep nothing of the dead."

Frustrated at the gypsy's superstition, Tom shook his head. "It's only a bit of hair."

"Hair, nail, it's all they needs to control you. The living don't give it up and the dead shouldn't neither." Mickey reached his hand out to snatch the picture frame down and destroy the lock of hair but his own fear prevented him from touching it. He swallowed hard and just stared petrified at the keepsake. Mickey jumped as Tom put his arm on his shoulder.

"Even if you're right... he wouldn't ever hurt us."

Mickey wasn't entirely convinced but he allowed himself to be mollified and let Tom steer him to the armchair by the fireplace. He knew he wasn't communicating the Romany superstition as well as he should; it was partially a language barrier but also, Mickey found it hard to explain himself in his weakened state. The Familia had rules to live and die by and though they varied from one Romany group to another, all agreed you kept nothing of the dead. The lock of hair from Tom's father unsettled the gypsy more than anything else could.

Putting the clothing he had brought downstairs from his bedroom in Mickey's lap, Tom sat on the arm of his mother's chair. "They should fit you well enough, they're big on me."

Lifting the shirt from the top of the pile uncovered underwear and a pair of trousers." Whose are these?" Mickey asked with concern he already knew the answer. When Tom admitted they had belonged to his father, the gypsy pulled a face and held the pile back to the young lad. "I can't be wearing them Tom." He put his hand above the youth's knee and gently squeezed his thigh intending the gesture as an apology.

"More superstition?"

With an embarrassed grimace, Mickey nodded. "Something like that!"

Tom nodded, not really understanding. He deposited the clothes behind him in the seat of the chair and asked how the gypsy was feeling."

"Weak" the youth replied. "I'll be khushti. You did good." Putting his hand to the wadding under the bandaging he asked how many stitches he had. His brow wrinkled as Tom explained he hadn't tried to put any stitches in. He was reassured when the size of the wound was described but he did comment he'd put a couple of stitches in himself when he got back to his vardo.

Mickey gripped the arms of his chair and levered his weight onto his feet as he stood. Though a little unsteady, he felt stronger already. When he told Tom he needed a pint of stout, the youth thought it was a joke but the gypsy knew he needed the iron from the dark liquid. There was no comprehension of its content but as a boxer, he had been told often what foods and drinks were good after a bout.

Once he understood it wasn't a joke, Tom headed back into the kitchen with the gypsy following him and began to hunt the shelves of the larder until he came across a dusty bottle of Guinness tucked at the very back of the walk in cupboard.

"Will this do? It's been here as long as I can remember." He held out the heavy black bottle and then added "This might actually be my father's too. Does your superstition allow that?"

Mickey took the bottle without offering an answer. Tom turned to the drawer beside the sink and located the bottle opener and was just looking for a glass when he turned at a bang behind him. The gypsy had the metal cap of the bottle resting at an angle on the edge of the table. The sound had been his thumping the bottle to pry the cap off against the wood. The youth flinched as he noted the scoring on the wood and he knew his mother would tell him off. He was about to speak and hold out the bottle opener when Mickey again thumped his hand on the top of the bottle and forcibly prised the cap from the bottle.

Staring Tom in the eye, the gypsy raised the bottle and putting the lip of the neck to his lips, he tilted the bottle upward. Despite the frothing of the dark liquid, Mickey swallowed fast and raised the bottle until it blocked his gaze where it obscured the line of sight between the two teenagers. With two thirds drunk in one attempt, Mickey paused and lowered the bottle. "Tastes fine." He raised the bottle again and drained the last of it.

Tom took the empty bottle back and managed to make no comment as to how quick the young man had drunk it.

"I'll be getting on" Mickey said. "Was only dihkin your town."

"Dihkin?"

The gypsy hesitated and ran through the words in his head to find the closest to his intent. "I were... looking, dihkin; seeing what was and what weren't. Best I was avree." Mickey stepped in close to Tom and put his hand on the smaller youth's shoulder. It wasn't the gypsy way to thank people for small deeds, nor were the men of the Familia ones to show emotion but Mickey moved his arm behind Tom's shoulder and pulled the boy toward him. His one armed hug was a slight affirmation of the gypsy's gratitude but for Mickey, it was a big deal. Saying nothing more, he parted from Tom and stepped to the door.

Tom called after him that he should walk him back to his camp in case he collapsed on the way but as he turned the door knob, Mickey looked over his shoulder and assured his friend he'd be fine. Opening the door, he moved out into the sunlight and though Tom only saw him as a silhouette, he saw the gypsy nod to him before he closed the door.

Alone in the kitchen, Tom looked around the small room. Dirty footprints marked the tiles and blood stained both the floor and the table where the injured gypsy had bled. It wouldn't take long to clean up the small traces of the gypsy but as he looked where Mickey had opened his bottle of Guinness he saw the lip of the table had teeth marks from the concertinaed cap and the edge had a slight splintering to it. Tom chewed nervously at his lip and tried to think of a way to either hide the damage or explain it away. Sighing gently, he picked up the bottle cap and headed to the dustbin with the easily disposable evidence.

Chapter Ten

The sun was high in the sky by the time Mickey had made it to the bridge near the meadow. He was puffing hard, blowing his cheeks out with every slow step. The fight hadn't taxed him but he was suffering from blood loss and without looking, he knew the padded bandage the youth had fixed to his side would be a dark red from the little exertion he'd made.

The gypsy wanted to examine the wound but knew better than to poke at it. The domed vardo wagons and the bivouac style tents the older children had built were visible from where he stood and he took a long deep breath before pushing himself from the wall he had been leaning against. The last three hundred yards were an effort but Mickey wandered back into the camp relatively unnoticed.

Few of the men were present having headed in all directions to find employment of some nature. There would be legitimate work to undertake as well as opportunities to exploit. Casting his eyes around the camp he noted a number of the older boys must have gone with their fathers and brothers.

Heading to his family's caravan Mickey acknowledged half a dozen of the women and the young children with nothing more than a nod. There was nothing to be said, he smiled when somebody smiled at him but otherwise his face was stone, his lips thin and tight as he slowly sucked air in through his nose, hiding his discomfort in feigned arrogance.

Finding his mother absent was a mixed blessing. The young gypsy hadn't wanted to explain the cause of his injury but he knew she was the best with a needle and thread. Hesitating for a moment a few paces from the steps that led into the curved wooden wagon, Mickey made his decision and swiftly ascended the steps and pushed the door open, ducking as he entered.

Without waiting for his eyes to adjust to the gloom of the interior, the boy turned to his left and stepped to the side of the door, his hands running swiftly over the shelving built into the niche just inside. As his fingertips lightly touched the tanned leather of a small purse, he gripped the brown, flat pouch and brought it to the light.

Flipping the purse open he scanned the content and saw beside the needles and narrow blade two spools, one of catgut and one of cotton. Closing the leather wallet with a clap, he pushed it into the pocket of his trousers and stepped out of the vardo. On the top step he wavered as the light disorientated him and he had to check his balance by gripping the rail of the door.

Mickey carefully made his way down the steps and pulled the door shut behind him. He paused at the foot of the stairs and sat on the bottom rung of the foldaway steps. Thinking through possibilities he had to accept he was going to struggle to sew the wound himself but he needed somebody he could trust to say nothing in his da's presence. The last thing he needed was a lesson from his belt about letting himself get stabbed.

Two young girls with dirty faces laughed and he turned his head to see them burst around the side of the caravan and skip away toward the river. As he identified one of the seven year old girls as being a sister to Rosa he called after her.

"Ghel! Daisy, kaj ya phen?"

Both girls stopped in their tracks and giggling to themselves the taller of the two nudged the other.

"Which one?" Daisy asked with a cheeky expression on her face that caused her companion to snigger and turn her face from Mickey in case he was angered by her friend's cheek.

Mickey said nothing more but raised his eyebrows and stared intently at his future sister-in-law. He knew she understood exactly who he meant and he wasn't about to humour the youngster.

Grinning back at him with a defiance he recognised only too

well from her older sister, Daisy eventually laughed out loud and said "Rosa shee kulath pani nevi." She grinned and along with her friend, they dashed from the small clearing in front of Mickey's caravan, darted around the car and out of sight behind the brightly coloured wagon of the Keast family.

Mickey heard the horses snicker and whinny and imagined the girls weaving between them. If he had the energy he would have headed after them and reprimanded them for worrying the horses. As it was he rose slowly to his feet and headed toward the river to find Rosa. He hoped she would be easy to find, he didn't cherish the idea of being seen near the river in case the women were washing their unclean items. He shook himself as a chill ran down his spine.

Choosing not to appear furtive, the young gypsy walked to the edge of the camp and walked the invisible boundary of the tents and vardos whilst keeping a roving eye on the line of trees that denoted the river's edge. He caught sight of the older mothers and wives downstream and began to navigate his way upstream while keeping a fair distance from the water. Passing the clearing where he'd first met Tom brought a smile to the gypsy's face and fifty yards further on, the trees grew denser and he could make out a splash of red through the leaves of the bushes.

In retrospect Mickey wanted to kick himself. It should have been obvious that Rosa would be gathering drinking water upstream.

Nobody would drink from water that blooded cloth had been washed in.

Closing on the swathe of red that intermittently flashed through the leaf, Mickey became a little more circumspect in his approach. He was almost certain the fabric he had glimpsed was Rosa's skirts but he didn't want to find he was mistaken in case his confidence was misplaced. As he covered the last dozen yards he heard the woman start to sing and he recognised the lilting tones of his fiancé.

Grinning to himself he echoed the last lines of the refrain and heard her fall silent. The bush parted and a round face framed with long, dark hair peered through the gap. Rosa grinned as she caught sight of her rom and she beckoned him forward.

The smile dropped from the boy's face as he realised she thought he was there for another reason. Approaching slowly, he began to talk before he reached her in order to quell her passion and steer her from her intended seduction.

"Been looking f' tu" he began and immediately knew it was the wrong start to the conversation as she stepped from the water. Her skirt was rolled high and thighs and calf were exposed, water droplets clinging to her skin where she had waded into the deeper waters.

Rosa grinned and instead of lowering her skirts she reached down and raised the hem higher. "Found me now!" Keeping herself from the view of the rest of the camp by careful positioning among the bushes, she stroked a thigh with a free hand. "No niamo neither!"

Swallowing hard, unsure how to steer his promised from her intent he looked left and right and saw she was right; there was no sign of Stevo. "Can you stitch a wound and say nothing of it?" Mickey blurted out.

The hurried words were more effective than he had thought as Rosa's lustful looks switched to outright concern. Dropping her skirt she hurried toward him and asked what had happened.

Briefly the muscular youth outlined the barest detail of the circumstance that had caused him to be stabbed and as he raised the side of his shirt to show his bandaged side, his fiancé dropped to her knees in front of him and knocked his hands away. Tentatively she raised the cotton shirt and gently probed the area around the wadding tied to the incision.

"This not well done" she muttered, her fingers touching the bandage that was crimson with Mickey's blood. Looking beyond her rom toward the camp, the young woman took in the few people at the camp outskirts and rose to her feet unsatisfied with how exposed they were to prying eyes. It said a lot of her nature that she would happily lay with him in full view but wouldn't tolerate a weakness being seen by the Familia.

"Arter me!" Rosa ordered and dropped Mickey's shirt back

down. Saying nothing more she retraced her steps to the bush and stepped through out of sight except for the repeated glimpse of her red cotton skirt.

Resigned to trusting her, Mickey followed her and pushed through the bush to find a small bank at the edge of the water. Rosa was standing in a still pool of water where the river had forced a cutting in the bank over the years. The water rippled gently against her knees and she slapped her hand on the grassed bank before her.

Understanding the indication from the woman, Mickey lay himself down on the grass sideways to Rosa and close to the edge of the bank. With the riverside as an improvised table, she again pulled at his shirt and dragged it up his body to expose him from breast to waist.

Deliberately and with a neutral expression on her face she placed a hand on his chest, lowered her face to his muscled stomach and kissed his abdominals. Then as though she hadn't done anything, she slapped his chest and glared at him.

"Dili chava! A feckin' Gadjo!" Rosa cursed.

"There were six of them" the youth retorted, both annoyed and embarrassed.

"Only six? Maybe you're not the rom I thought you to be." Rosa suddenly smiled and as she lowered her eyes to the bandage Mickey could hear her chuckle quietly. Despite himself, he couldn't help but smile. With great tenderness, his fiancé unwound the bloodied strip of material that had been bound tight to the injury and examined the sight of the stabbing.

"Needle?"

With a groan of discomfort, Mickey Ray tried to extricate the pouch from his pocket but as it became clear it wasn't easy to draw out, Rosa pushed his hands away and dug into his pocket herself. Once her fingers fastened on the leather she drew the slim package from his trousers and folded it open on his chest.

Threading the needle she prodded the thin red line of the cut causing it to bleed again. "Ain't much of a cut" she said frowning. "May not even scar."

"It's bled a lot."

"Iffen you jilling to ga wi' no stitches, course it bleed." Rosa gripped the edges of the wound and pinched the sides together as she punched the needle through the skin and pulled the thread through the flesh. "Tu dinilo! Sar san?" The dark haired girl grinned at him and then looked back to her sewing, pulling a second time to form a loop of cotton and pushing the steel tip through the skin again. In a short time she had three tight stitches holding the flesh together and asked once more if he was okay.

Mickey nodded "Arvah." Rising slowly to a sitting position he managed to shuffle backward against a slim birch while he pulled his shirt back down to cover his body.

Rosa stood up straight and raised her hands to tie some of her hair back in an improvised pony tail. Her hair was the pretence, she knew well enough how to flaunt her body at the boys. As the girl pushed her breasts out toward Mickey she glanced down and glared at him. The young gypsy boy was paying her no attention. Mickey was consciously looking in the opposite direction.

Chapter Eleven

Tom was sat in his chair in the living room with one of his library books in his lap. The book was open but Tom was staring at the photo-frame and lock of hair encased with the frozen black and white image. The story wasn't holding his attention and the previous two tales of Narnia had. Much of it was to do with the character of Prince Caspian.

The boy found it hard to shake the memory of Mickey, the gypsy who had come to his aid. Tom had unconsciously bound the gypsy and the Prince into one imagined character. Despite the elegance of Lewis' description, his own mind conjured the face and figure of the young man and dressed him as Caspian.

Stories had been the youth's escape from an early age when as a child his world had been upset by his father's death. This was the first time he had not fallen between the pages of a tale and been lost to the world. Unable to turn off the events of the morning, Tom kept revisiting both the fight and the dressing of Mickey's wound.

There was something about the strong, blunt traveller that attracted the teenager but he couldn't understand his own fascination. In the story he was trying to read, the Prince had a nobility and a sense of righteousness that Tom found compelling. What he had recently been told of gypsies was anathema to his conjured image but still he couldn't dispel the idea of Mickey as the Prince.

With a long, drawn out sigh, Tom lifted the book, closing it on the home-made bookmark and leaning over the high arm of the chair he was sat in, he laid it gently on the floor. He sighed again and pulled himself out of the deep chair by the armrests. Standing despondently, Tom slowly crossed the threadbare carpet to stand again before the fireplace and rested his fingers on the mantelpiece.

Thoughtfully, the youth let his eyes linger on the photographs and his attention kept being drawn back to the lock of hair that had so concerned the gypsy. Instead of firing the pained smile the images used to, Tom frowned as he tried to shake off the fearful expression on the eighteen year old's face.

Tom liked to think he wasn't superstitious but he had to acknowledge during his first meeting with the gypsies, the curse he had been told may follow him had been a strong motivator. Had it not been for the fact his mother would notice and be hurt by it, Tom was tempted to put the lock of his father's hair out of sight.

With a shake of his head, the boy turned away from the framed pictures and glanced around the living room. He'd lived in the same house his entire life yet suddenly the room seemed darker and smaller. Cosy had become cramped; alone had become lonely. Tom knew he must have had friends visit when he was younger but it had been so long ago. Today he was seeing his home as Mickey must have seen it.

When he'd been in the library, Tom had tried to seek out books about gypsies but he'd not found anything he could consider informative. Miss Corbett had asked what he was looking for and although she couldn't point him to any texts, she was a wealth of knowledge about the Romany community. He'd learnt a lot and it was the concept of living a life in the outdoors that had fired his imagination.

To the gypsy, Tom's home must have seemed so claustrophobic. A life under the stars and only moving under cover to sleep. An envious feeling crept into the teenager's soul; he knew he was romanticising the gypsy life but he was seeing the walls of the room draw closer by the moment.

Bending down to pick his book up from the floor, Tom decided he'd read in the garden. Though his job had him outside all day, he usually delighted in hiding away inside on his days off. Since his encounter with Mickey he felt a need to rest in the sunlight for a short time. He knew the reality was a desire to visit the gypsy camp but he felt a little discomfort about actually doing so.

Miss Corbett had told him a Romany camp was a very closed community but they accepted visitors under a specific set of circumstances. As all the reasons she outlined for gypsies to permit him to enter the camp involved finances, Tom couldn't think of a way to do so; his money was hard earned and not sufficient for him to pay for any of the services the librarian had told him of. Even knowing that, he kept imaging having his palm read by one of their fortune tellers.

The youth wished it had been him who had rescued Mickey from the local boys rather than the other way round. The gypsy would be in his debt then and he might be able to get his fortune told for free.

Passing from the living room into the kitchen, Tom paused and with a smile on his lips, he ran his fingers across the wooden top of the table Mickey had been laying on. The smile faltered as he again caught sight of the slight damage caused by the bottle cap being prised off against the lip of the table.

Tom jumped as the front door opened unexpectedly and his mother appeared in the doorway. Even with the sun behind her Tom could tell she was exhausted as she sagged against the frame of the door. Skipping forward, Tom put his hand out and helped his mother over the step.

"That hill is going to be the death of me!" Mary wheezed. She managed a smile at the gentle ministrations of her son as he pulled a chair from the table and helped her lower herself onto it. "Thank you Tom. I wish we lived closer to the town."

Moving back from the table, Tom leant against the sink and returned his mother's smile. He would happily have moved even further away from the town if he had his way but he had to acknowledge the walk certainly took a lot out of his mother.

Though Mary Quatrell was still a few years from forty she looked a decade older. It wasn't simply the distance that wore heavily on her, the last five hundred yards was uphill and though Tom barely noticed it, his mother was increasingly struggling with the steepness.

It was apparent that his mother was tiring more easily than she used to and as Tom stood, his mother began to cough hard. Clutching at her chest, Mary eventually leant back and tipped her head so as to gaze at the yellowing ceiling.

"Don't look so worried Tom" she said as her son began to move toward her. "It's been a long day already and I think I'm coming down with something."

Despite her assurances, Tom couldn't help but be concerned. Wondering how he hadn't noticed before, he noted his mother seemed to have lost a lot of weight recently. Pinching his lip between his fingers he watched as Mary pulled a cigarette packet from her pocket and proceeded to light one.

Blowing a cloud of smoke out slowly, Mary asked if there was any tea in the pot. Reassured at her even tone of voice, Tom relaxed and shook his head, then told her he'd make a drink for her. Turning away, Tom didn't notice his mother take a handkerchief and wipe a trace of blood from her lips. She frowned with concern as she looked at the tell-tale stain on the cotton and then raised her eyes to stare at her son's back. Screwing the handkerchief up, Tom's mother thrust the small square back into her pocket and started to chew nervously at her knuckle.

"Are you feeling any better now?" Tom asked as he pulled his chair out and sat at the table opposite his mother.

"I'm fine" Mary responded with a forced smile. "I think I might stop smoking for a bit until I've shaken off this cold though."

Tom grunted his agreement and nodded slightly. He personally thought it was more likely to be influenza than a cold but he knew better than to argue about anything remotely medical with his mother. Her job at the hospital gave her a much better knowledge than his own.

Mary Quatrell frowned suddenly and her fingertips skated over the grain of the wooden table to the edge. "What happened to this?" Her fingernails picked at the splintered wood.

Pulling a face, Tom apologised. "I caught it with a tin earlier. I tried to push it back but..."

A gentle chuckle came from Tom's mother as she looked at the worried expression facing her. "Just be a bit more careful!"

Unable to help himself, Tom let a little laugh out. He'd been so worried he would get in trouble that the absence of a rebuke caused all the pent-up tension in him evaporate. He rose from his chair and walked around the table to stand behind his mother and draped his arms over her shoulders, wrapped his arms around her neck and hugged her tight. He bent down and wordlessly kissed her cheek.

"It's only a table sweetie!" Mary reached up with her hand and patted his arm. She asked him if he'd eaten yet and he said he'd grabbed a sandwich. Promising him a cooked tea she queried if he had anything planned for the afternoon.

Not wanting to say an outright lie, Tom told his mother he was considering walking down to the river with his new book and relaxing for a few hours.

Releasing her hold on his arm, Mary let go of her son and watched him move around the kitchen to put the kettle over the heat of the rayburn where it rapidly began to reboil. "You might want to just sit down near the pub instead, there's those tinkers in the meadow don't forget." With concern for her son showing through, she added "Gypos can be a brash bunch, the older ones aren't so bad but the younger men are always spoiling for a fight."

Spooning tea-leaves into the pot, Tom acknowledged the warning but silently he thought his mother knew less of the gypsies than he already did. He'd made his mind up to spend a few pennies to have his palm read and though he wouldn't worry his mother with the information, he didn't intend to tell her his plans.

Having made his decision, Tom's stagnant mood was beginning to lift as he added water from the kettle to the pot. He was feeling good about the afternoon now he had settled on a course of action and the thought he may again bump into Mickey caused a light euphoria to envelop him.

Though he barely knew the youth, he was one of the few people to act as a friend in the seven years since Tom had passed his eleven-plus and left his childhood friends behind. It was a good feeling not to be judged by his peers and despite the fact Tom knew Mickey would move on with the rest of the camp, he hoped to spend some time with the young man while he could.

Chapter Twelve

As the young gypsy turned his face to Rosa, she slapped him hard and pouted. "When we gonna wed Mickey?"

The gypsy smiled at her and looked up into her face with soft eyes. He felt great affection for the young woman and hated to see her suffering. Reaching toward her he took her hand and clasped it in his own, bringing it to hold it tight to his breast. "You know I don't want us to share my da's vardo. Wi' the coin me won... won't be long."

"Tu said we'd see at Appleby and nothing." Rosa pulled her hand free from Mickey's grip. "Even Daisy be promised; like she'll puterdea o'er her rom afore I."

Mickey felt as though he'd been slapped. Rosa could swear as well as any but painting the image of her young sister straddling a man felt wrong to the gypsy. It wasn't like Rosa to be so blunt and he knew it was a sign of her frustration; he could plainly see the hurt he was causing her. It was true most of her friends were already carrying babes in their arms and the guilt of how he was treating her pained him.

"Stow!" He stated.

Rosa turned a stern face to him and glared coldly. "Stow?"

Mickey swallowed hard and swinging his boots into the river, he again reached for her and clasped both of her hands. Pulling her close, he wrapped his legs around hers so she couldn't pull away easily. "Stow! Me gabli will gain us a grast an' a vardo when we get there, then we can wed."

As her heart leapt Rosa felt tears in her eyes. The Stow market was barely three months away. A horse and a caravan? Even Kizzy with her two sons didn't have her own horse and wagon. Draping her arms over Mickey's shoulders she hugged him tight. "Chachimos? Vortimo?"

Pressed against her breast, Mickey nodded and though he was nervous of his commitment, he grinned unseen at her delight. "Arvah Rosa; truth!"

Rosa threw herself backward into the river, pulling Mickey from the bank so they both splashed into the cold water. The two gypsies laughed together though Mickey's pleasure was from the small happiness he had given his fiancé. For himself, he was trying hard to be happy but it was a two-edged sword. It hurt that he must be who his Familia needed him to be rather than who he felt he was.

Making his future was not a choice, it was an obligation but, of all the girls in his life, only Rosa was able to make him smile. There was a sense to it. From a practical perspective, the sickly horse Mickey had bought in Appleby would be in good health in time for Stow. He wouldn't earn as much profit as he would if he waited for the next Appleby horse fair but with that almost a year away, Rosa would be the oldest unmarried girl in the camp. He couldn't do that to her.

Mentally adding up the coin he had put aside and the price he could expect for the horse he owned he knew he was close to providing all he had promised Rosa. Still he had a growing feeling of unease.

A gypsy was ever practical and his marriage to Rosa would put him in a strong position to eventually take over from his da as the Rom Baro; the Big Man. Was it what he wanted? He didn't know the answer to that but his father had shaped him as much as he could to take on the role in time. There was no doubt he was physically the strongest in camp and he had a thorough understanding of what was required as the leader of the Familia. All he was lacking was children of his own and the respect that would only come with age.

Children. Mickey quailed at the thought. It was to be his lot in life, he knew that. He loved spending time with the boys in the camp, especially teaching them to fight and he'd even taught a number of the youngest how to set a trap and skin a rabbit. There was no concern in his mind about raising a family, his worry was fathering babes in the first place. The young man could acknowledge he loved the girl with him but he was unsure if even her wiles could cause him to rise to the occasion.

Holding Rosa in his arms, he swayed lightly with her, both of them knee deep in the river. The young girl had tears on her cheeks as she hugged herself against her man; *her man*! She didn't sob or wail, she was content at last. Rosa had set her sights on Mickey when they were both very little and for the last decade she had actively sought every advantage over the other girls in the camp.

When her da had told her they had reached an agreement with Mickey's da, Rosa had been overjoyed but as the years had ticked by and she'd seen her friends become wives and mothers she had begun to doubt. Come October she would finally have the status that she knew was her due.

Even before the two of them had been promised Rosa had been working hard on the elder mothers to both bring them to her side and to learn all she could from them. It had taken years to learn about all she would be required to do. She understood everything that was expected of her and the old women clearly favoured her over other girls. It may be a man's strength that ruled the Familia but it was the women that ran things.

There was only one thing Rosa still needed to learn and she knew that was something she couldn't manipulate. Her father's mother was the best at brewing a good ale and she wasn't going to share her secrets until she was ready. The young girl had spent a lot of time with her puri-daj but the paternal grandmother refused to be rushed. She would share her knowledge in her own time and not before.

Though frustrated, Rosa knew when the time came, she was the only true choice to be given the recipe. Already she was allowed to enter the vardo that was used exclusively for the brewing and bottling.

Mickey eventually managed to extricate himself from Rosa's embrace but even then, he didn't get far. With her hands gripping his elbows firmly, the young girl moved in toward the youth and tilting her head, she angled herself to place a kiss on his lips. Without showing any deliberate reluctance, Mickey permitted a chaste kiss, then attempted to draw back but Rosa had other ideas. Reaching her hands to his head, the girl held his head steady as her tender kiss evolved with her passion and she pressed herself against him.

Fearful of pulling away, Mickey allowed himself to be kissed and despite not sharing her passion, he forced himself to moan and respond with feigned enthusiasm that mirrored Rosa's apparent ardour. When the young woman raised a leg from the water to wrap it around the back of his thigh, Mickey swallowed hard and managed to break away from the kiss.

Not content to let what she perceived as Mickey's chivalry win, Rosa dropped her foot back into the water, put both her hands to his chest and gently pushed him backward until he felt the bank against his lower back. With nowhere to retreat to, he could feel Rosa grinding against him. The worry lasted a moment only before the girl steered Mickey away from the bank and caused them to swap places.

"Lift me up" the young gypsy whispered into his ear and with a little relief, Mickey put his hands to her waist and raised her from the river to the bank with an easy lift.

Relief faded as Rosa wrapped both her legs around him and with her heels, she pulled him toward her, locking her feet behind him, preventing his escape. She put her hand between them, tugging her raised skirt to remove the thin cotton barrier between them, then her hands reached to the top of his trousers, rapidly unbuckling his belt and she began to fumble with his buttons.

"Want you Mickey Ray, want you now!" Rosa growled.

From the other side of the bush a young male voice called out "You there Mickey?"

"Amria!" Rosa said, the curse filled with rage. "Me muller pesho dilo cheeb! Armaya!" The curses and threats rolled from Rosa's mouth as she ranted quietly in Mickey's ear.

Though sympathetic to Rosa's feelings, Mickey's relief was palpable as the girl took her hands from his trousers and she tucked her skirt back over herself to appear more respectable. The anger on her face broke as Rosa caught Mickey's amused expression and she tried not to laugh with him as the young man giggled as much with gratitude for the intrusion as at her tirade of abuse spat with venom beneath her breath.

Allan appeared through the bush that had hidden the pair from sight of the camp and though the ten year old understood he had interrupted Rosa, the smirk on Mickey's face reassured him. With the young woman still glaring at Allan, Mickey asked the youngster what he wanted and the boy explained there was a gadjo in camp asking after him.

Puzzled but hopeful, the gypsy frowned and asked Allan to describe the outsider but the boy shrugged and explained he hadn't seen him, he'd only been told to find the youth.

Calling over his shoulder that he'd found Mickey, Allan gave his hand to the older gypsy and helped him climb from the river onto the bank. Rosa made space on the bank for her betrothed and stood wringing the river water from her skirts. She was well aware of the young boy staring at her slim legs and pretending not to notice his eyes on her, she pulled her skirts higher to expose her thighs.

The youngster coloured but was unable to tear his eyes from the sight before him and he licked his lips as he hoped she would lift the hem a little higher. The boy jumped as the bush behind was parted again and a girl in her early teens emerged with the outsider in tow.

Mickey looked up at both newcomers and ignoring the heavy-chested teenage girl, he inclined his head to acknowledge Tom's presence.

"Tom! Is there problem?"

Chapter Thirteen

Tom found the situation he was in extremely intimidating. Just arriving at the edge of the camp had caused a dozen malevolent pairs of eyes to settle on him and he was sorely tempted to keep walking as though he was just passing by. He may have done just that if a voice hadn't called out to him.

Though he didn't know the meaning of the word, Mickey's father had addressed him as 'chav' earlier and though he spoke no Romany, Tom had a good ear for languages and he'd identified the term as being specific to him. At the sound of the word coming again, the youngster had turned and seen Jacky Ray striding past an immense piebald horse toward him.

Nervous but too fearful to ignore the man, the teenager had waited as the muscled man in forties kept walking toward him. A dozen paces from him, the gypsy leader halted and rattled out a sentence so fast Tom only managed to identify the word oil. A coin was flying toward the boy, thrown by Jacky Ray and it was more luck than judgement that had Tom snatch the dark brown coin from the air.

Opening his fingers, Tom looked down into his hand to find a large penny given as a reward for his fetching oil the evening previous. He smiled and looked up to thank the man but he was already walking away. Hostile eyes still surrounded him but the number had lessened once it became apparent the youth had dealings with the gypsy.

"I was looking for Mickey!" Tom shouted after the man. Wincing as all the eyes turned back to him again, the boy wished he hadn't shouted. Jacky Ray halted in his steps, bringing his raised foot down with exaggerated deliberation.

Very slowly Mickey's father turned, his eyes were lowered and peering at the gorgio boy from under his thick eyebrows, the man slowly raised his face to stare at Tom. The man said nothing for a moment, simply holding the boys stare and gauging the youth before him. With a brief glance to his left, then looking to his right with no hint of haste, he gestured to a group of three children whose ages ranged from ten to thirteen and beckoned them to him.

Allan, Ruby and Dinah stood in silence as Jacky Ray spoke to them; from time to time one or other of them would turn their head to look directly at Tom and eventually, the conversation was over. Jacky Ray straightened up from having bent down to the children, nodded his head once at Tom, then he turned and strode away to disappear behind one of the colourful wagons.

One of the girls quickly headed away in the opposite direction than the man had taken and the boy and girl left behind walked toward Tom.

Ruby was wary of the young man but was not going to show any concern. Despite being thirteen, the brown haired girl managed to communicate her disdain of the outsider and Allen effected an arrogant swagger that should have been comical for a ten year old but Tom couldn't help but be aware the boy may be half a foot shorter than he himself was but he was better muscled already. There seemed little doubt that in a fight, Allan would walk away the winner and extremely quickly.

"With me!" Allan barked and made to move away. In itself the order was sufficient but Allen gave the lie to his age as he turned back and with a modicum of uncertainty he gave further explanation that Tom should follow him.

The girl rolled her eyes and shook her head. She muttered something too low for Tom to catch but the boy pulled an annoyed face that suggested he had heard her. Ruby said nothing more but pointed ahead for Tom to follow after Allan. Trying his most disarming smile on the girl caused her to raise her eyebrows and shake her head to herself again. She walked after Allan and Tom finally followed behind.

"Are you taking me to Mickey?" Tom checked as they passed through the large number of caravans and he found himself among a collection of tents. In some instances the tents were elaborate wooden frames with canvas draped over them but mixed in with these were others that seemed to be little more than a fabric stretched between posts that did nothing more than create a vague impression of a roof with no walls.

The young girl Tom had gathered was Ruby nodded and said something the boy didn't understand. From the left of them, the other girl reappeared, spoke briefly to Allan and the group veered away from the main body of the camp and headed directly toward the river.

Ruby and Dinah were talking quietly among themselves. Dinah was whispering fast and she was grinning the whole time and as she told Ruby whatever it was she was saying, Ruby's mouth fell open and she clamped her hand over her mouth. Dinah started to giggle and Ruby tried hard not join her. The girl turned back to Tom and he could see a sparkle in her eyes that unnerved him and smirking to herself, Ruby uttered half a dozen unintelligible words to him that caused Dinah to laugh out loud before she too forced her mouth closed.

Tom was beginning to get worried. Something was going on

that he wasn't privy to and he had a feeling it wasn't going to be good news. It was too late to rethink his current course of action but a dread began to rise in him.

The boy leading the way was a couple of yards from where the river's edge must be when he called out Mickey's name.

Tom heard a woman's voice muttering something and though he knew none of the words, they dripped with vitriol and he saw Allen's steps falter for a moment before he hesitantly pushed his way through a bush and vanished from sight.

Stopping where he was, Tom had an overwhelming urge to turn and run along the river's edge until he came to the bridge, then he could get back on the road and be home in half an hour. Closing his eyes and taking a deep breath, he felt something brush against his hand. Opening his eyes, he looked at his hand and realised Ruby had gripped his palm and somewhat reassuringly, she winked at him and gently pulled him forward the last few steps to the bush. She let go of his hand, parted the bush and the pair of them passed through the foliage to stand on the bank of the river.

Tom let a pent-up breath out as he caught sight of Mickey, then a moment later, he noticed the beautiful woman with the bare legs beside him. Tom coughed and turned his back as Mickey asked if there was a problem and the woman laughed.

"I... erm... sorry, I didn't mean to..." Tom's apology generated laughter from everybody present except Mickey who spoke sharply to Rosa and the three children.

Allan was entranced by Rosa but he flinched at Mickey's angry reprimand and he turned to find Dinah was trying not to laugh and to pretend to be chastened. The boy and the girl retreated and headed back to the camp but Ruby loitered a moment. The young teenager ignored Mickey and his girlfriend and she lowered her eyes to peer up into Tom's face. Batting her eyes, she spoke confidently to Mickey but didn't take her gaze from the young gadjo.

Tom felt Ruby take his hand again but this time, she clasped it in both hands and smiled at him.

"Dordi! Ruby!" Rosa snapped at the young girl and instantly the smile dropped from her face and she scampered away to chase after her friends. Rosa looked from one young man to the other and Tom could feel the woman didn't welcome his interruption.

Attempting to brush the excess water from himself, Mickey asked Tom why he'd been looking for him. Keeping his eyes from Rosa, as much to ensure he didn't stare at her legs as to avoid her harsh glare, the youth spoke softly and with hesitation as he managed to explain he was hoping somebody could read his palm.

Rosa snorted "Tu could have asked anybody that!"

Misunderstanding her meaning Tom asked if she meant all gypsies could see the future. Mickey laughed and Rosa tried hard not to. Muttering a curse and an offensive word under her breath the girl rolled her eyes and explained he could have *asked* anybody, they would have taken him to Sara and she would have read for him.

"I'm sorry." Tom said, his eyes wide. Though he could understand Rosa's words he had to listen hard as she spoke so fast. "I didn't know who to ask."

Mickey moved forward to the boy and wrapped an arm around his shoulder and soaking the boy's shirt as he pulled him under his wing. "Don't to be thinking palms though... Sara is stronger with a deck." Turning Tom so he was forced to face Rosa, the gypsy let his disarming smile charm the pair of them. "This the didikai that bandaged me."

Rosa kept her tongue for a moment as she assessed the boy before her. He failed to impress her; he was slightly built and shorter than her beloved but most of all, he seemed small inside. Tom's eyes didn't meet hers and he fidgeted nervously as he was studied.

"Tu should've made stitches."

Unsure how to take the woman's flat emotionless tone, Tom quietly muttered he didn't know how, adding he'd never treated a stabbing before.

Rosa took a deep breath in and then slowly let it out. "Tu should learn." The gypsy girl saw a mix of fear and dread in the young boy's face and despite her initial hostility, she suddenly grinned. She hadn't planned to but the youth was so tense she had a mental picture of a young fawn in the meadow that had sighted the hunter and suddenly known fear. The boy had a sweet quality of an innocent gypsy babe despite his years and though she wouldn't forgive him for his appalling timing, she suddenly saw him as the younger brother Mickey didn't have and it explained a lot.

"Come here!" Rosa called to Mickey crooking her finger to the taller youth.

Curious and slightly apprehensive, Mickey did as directed, letting his arm slip from Tom's shoulder. When the girl also beckoned him, Tom glanced first at Mickey, then when he received no warning glance, he moved forward slowly. Rosa sat on the trunk of a fallen tree and patted the bark beside her to indicate Tom should sit beside her.

With Mickey standing before her, she spoke tersely to him in pure Romany and the youth pulled his shirt up and turned to expose the bandage Rosa had retied around her stitching. Swiftly, Rosa unbound the strip of linen and grabbing Tom's hand, she made him poke and press at the site of the wound.

Tom could see how simply she had worked and it was apparent he could easily have managed the stitches himself but he couldn't bring himself to admit it was less the practical side of things that he'd had issue with and more the idea. He was as good as certain the gypsy wouldn't have cried out but he knew it must have hurt to have a needle pushed through the flesh and Tom understood his own limitations. The young man wasn't somebody who could inflict pain on another whatever the benefit.

As neutrally as he could, Tom nodded and acknowledged he hadn't done as well as he could have. He watched as between them, Mickey and Rosa re-wrapped the bandage and tied it off. A loose thread hung at the point the strip had been tucked beneath itself and Rosa leant forward, biting the stray fibre off with her teeth. She stroked Mickey's chest beneath his shirt and placed a kiss on his stomach that caused Tom to flush crimson and to look away.

When Rosa noticed Tom's embarrassment she laughed and pulling away from the muscled gypsy, she punched the youth beside her hard on the shoulder. "Maw! Tu gorgios is funny."

Despite not catching every word, Tom understood enough to know she was amused at his prudish behaviour. The girl's laughter was infectious and though he cringed a little at her comment, he couldn't help but chuckle along with her and Mickey.

As the humour died away, Tom realised he was relatively content with the two gypsies. The camp and the inhabitants were intimidating but sitting just out of sight with Rosa and Mickey felt natural enough that he suddenly realised it had been years since he had laughed with people his own age. Nearly a decade had passed since he'd found himself in the company of anybody who didn't seek to humiliate, tease or punch him. Even though the girl wasn't welcoming toward him, she wasn't openly hostile.

Rosa looked askance at the boy beside her and from under her fringe of hair, she switched her sight-line so her eyes rode upward to take in Mickey too. It was obvious the boy from the small town was very much the loner by his behaviour and the fact he had visited them without an army of friends. It didn't take long for her to appreciate Mickey was also a loner but in his case, it was an imposed loneliness.

Jacky Ray had four daughters and only the one son; he'd been grooming Mickey for many years to be a rom who was both feared and respected. Everybody liked Mickey but there was nobody he could truly be himself with. Rosa felt the teeth of jealousy bite deep as she conceded the young boy was subverting her interests. Though she'd spent a long time seeking to share the gypsy's bed, she had spent a longer time sharing his life.

Mickey's eyes were fastened on the young boy and a momentary fear touched the girl as she glimpsed something more than the beginnings of friendship. She shook her head and fought the urge to laugh out loud. Mickey being '*she'chrone*' was beyond imagining.

Rosa steered the pair back to the original reason for Tom appearing and ruining her fun. "Why tu want to know your future anyways?"

Thinking hard about what it was sensible to admit, Tom eventually explained his life didn't seem to be heading anywhere and he felt like it should be.

"What does it matter?" Rosa asked. "Tomorrow is tomorrow. Today tu smile, laugh, eat and dance!"

"Precious little of that" muttered Tom half under his breath.

Mickey leant forward and slapped a strong hand on his friend's shoulder. "Come on then, let's see what Sara can tell you." The gypsy winked at Rosa and leaving her sitting alone with her thoughts, he helped Tom to his feet and walked him back toward the camp and the ofisa of the fortune teller.

Chapter Fourteen

The tent was cramped and dingy inside but Tom noted to his surprise it was exceptionally clean. Though the floor was nothing more than dry soil it had been swept so thoroughly he could imagine treading through it and not even dirtying his feet.

Mickey and Tom had been made to wait outside for the best part of five minutes before Sara had permitted them to enter. Once he stepped through the canvas flaps of the entry, Tom had felt both delight and fear. The interior of the ofisa was strewn with fabrics of the most lustrous cloths and the colours the candles illuminated were rich and brighter than anything he could remember seeing away from the wild-flowers of a meadow.

A small table sat near the entrance with a single, empty wooden chair waiting for him. At Mickey's insistence, Tom sat in the seat and swallowed down his nervousness. Opposite him on the other side of the table, beyond a pair of yellow candles that were placed to the sides, a figure sat in the shadows. He could see the aged, liver-spotted hands of the Drabani; the fortune teller.

The old woman leant forward and the gold coins sewn to the hem of her headscarf caught the light, glinting in the dark like cat's eyes. Her hand opened on the silk that covered the wooden table and she reached out, placing her hand palm up between the candles. Tom looked to Mickey for guidance.

"Cross her palm with silver." Mickey stated coldly. The gypsy dug in his pocket and produced a sixpence; he placed it firmly between Tom's thumb and forefinger, turned his hand over and guided him so Tom ran the small coin from side to side then up and down the woman's hand. He then indicated Tom should place the coin in Sara's hand.

As the coin was released, Sara cackled as she closed her fist on the coin. "Ah Mickey, sastimos!" She reached forward, grasped Mickey's wrist and twisted his arm so his palm was turned upward and pressed the coin back in his hand. "Hush! Tu tell no-one!"

The surprise that registered on Mickey's face told Tom this wasn't a normal event and he felt an added pressure not to do or say anything that might embarrass either of them.

Tom put his hand out on the table expecting the fortune teller to take it, turn it over and begin the reading but she made a hissing sound as she blew through the gaps in her teeth. "Kek, kek tu!" She laughed again and produced a square of green silk that resembled a covered brick. Slowly and reverentially she unwrapped the package by folding open each side of the silk as though opening a present with the greatest of care.

With the fourth and final corner of the material pulled away a deck of cards was revealed. The pack was larger than any Tom had seen before and despite their apparent age, they were only slightly yellowed where they would once have been white. She raised the cards from the table and swiped the silk away swiftly to deposit the deck on the table a little in front of the boy. "Chin."

Mickey leant over Tom's shoulder and whispered for the youth to cut the deck. Reaching out, Tom split the pack into two piles and glanced back at Mickey to find the young gypsy was still leaning over him but his eyes were on the table, his eyes brightly reflecting the flames of the candles. He seemed genuinely interested in what was transpiring. Catching Tom's attention, he grinned, his earnest, rapt attention apparent.

Looking back to the old woman, Tom noticed the deck had been put back as one and Sara was staring at him. "What would you know?" Sara asked, her words clearer than most gypsies Tom had encountered but she had a thick accent he couldn't place. "Would tu know of love? Money?" Pausing for effect, she then added "Death?"

There was a hesitation as Tom considered the question. He licked his lips before he answered "Just... what the future holds."

Tom knew it was a very vague answer but he hadn't given a lot of thought to what he would say.

"Just?" Sara smirked. The humour was lost on both Tom and Mickey. Smiling to herself, the woman dealt out a nine card spread of her tarot; the layout appeared to be simple as it was a straightforward three by three square that she lay upon the table between the candles. "This will give us past, present and future."

"I already know my past and present." Tom frowned. He recoiled involuntarily as the old woman grinned her gap toothed grin at him.

"We shall see" she said, quietly amused at the stock answer she always received.

Sara reached her hand to the top row and turned over all three cards and peered intently at them. The Bacchus tarot she used was an original deck nearly two centuries old that her great grandmother had gifted to her almost forty years previous. Even the regular use over the decades hadn't dulled the images and the ten of Swords, the Moon and the five of Coins stared up at her.

Mickey looked intently at the formation. He didn't have any great understanding of reading but he had seen La Lune card before. It had been upside down when it had last appeared for him and Sara had told him it referred to his confidence.

After a brief pause, the old woman raised her eyes to Tom and spoke with conviction. "Tu has had a hard past; you've known loss an' it took a long time for tu to find a place in the world. Much of your past has been difficult and you has worried much."

Accepting her words with a nod, Tom thought of his father and he knew everything the woman claimed was true but he was also aware of how vague her words were. He watched again as the woman turned over the next cards and he was surprised to see all three cards had people drawn on them, he took a moment to translate the Reine de Coupe, Valet des Epee and L'Ermite. Though he wasn't entirely sure about Reine, he thought from the images he had the Queen of cups, the Jack of swords and a Hermit, though the hermit looked a lot like a monk to his mind.

"Hmm! Unusual." Sara said. Her fingers lightly ran across the face of the cards, a gentle touch that didn't disturb the arrangement. "This is now. You know much but always want to know more. You know some things without knowing them. Also... you seek... this is the Hermit, the Hermit seeks but... for tu, it is not knowledge."

Tom expected more to be said but he was taken unaware when careless of the already upturned six cards, Sara hurriedly turned over the last cards and then sat back, drawing her face away from the light.

Face up were the last trio of cards that indicated the future of the local boy. Two sevens and a three. The seven of cups, the seven of swords and the three of swords. The cup card was upside down, inverted.

"You will know pain."

Mickey looked down at Tom as the youth peered intently toward the card reader in the shadows. Her face was unseen as he waited for her to elaborate, she slowly drew her hands away from the candlelight. Mickey hesitated, he wanted to ask more on Tom's behalf but he didn't want to interfere in the reading. All his life Sara had been friendly outside of her tent but when she was inside her ofisa she was taciturn and there was a strict code of behaviour.

The pause stretched out painfully and finally, Tom broke the silence and asked to know more of the pain the cards spoke of.

"The cards do not say" Sara stated, brooking no further discussion then elaborated of her own choosing to add "It will come soon but much is unsaid."

Tom turned to Mickey, his face showed a hint of worry but mainly, he came across as puzzled. The expression on the face of the gypsy beside him was not encouraging as Mickey's brows furrowed and he shrugged at the unasked questions it was clear Tom had.

Sara did not move from the shadows but said "Tu both shall go now, nothing more to know."

Squeezing his friend's shoulder, Mickey gained his attention again and inclined his head to Tom to indicate that they should leave. Quietly but with reluctance, the boy stood and followed the gypsy out of the tent into the harsh light of the summer sun.

Inside the tent Sara let out a deep sigh and her hands scooped up the first six cards with practised ease and returned them to the deck. She stared down at the three last cards that indicated the boy's future and shuffled forward in her chair, leaning her elbows on the covered table and resting her head in her hands. Taking in the detail of the three cards the aged woman let her eyes run over each card and she felt the weight of the world on her as all her years suddenly bore her down.

The suffering the swords indicated was a harsh combination that told her pain was an understatement of what the boy was going to face but she worried about the inverted cup card. The card represented fantasy and dreams and with it upside down, it could mean either the young man would choose a practical future or... his dreams and fantasies would be swept aside.

Though she knew the coming days were going to be hard on the gadjo, Sara wondered at the uncertain nature of the cards. Pushing the cards away from her she quickly spread the pack of cards before her and separated the major arcana from the deck, she quickly shuffled the light deck and sat them face first in front of her. Focussing her thoughts on the youth she turned over three new cards and interlocked her fingers under her chin as she studied the intricate faces of the cards before her.

The Flemish cards before her told her more than she had wished to know but as much as she had expected. Le Monde, La Foudre and L'Amour.

Mickey Ray hadn't had a reading from her for six years, two months and eight days but she remembered every card she had turned over in her life. The boy had a secret and from the reading she had just made, she knew trouble was going to come to both youngsters.

Leaning back in her chair again, Sara reached beneath the table, lifted an open bottle of sloe gin and took a mouthful. Where the two boys had left her ofisa the flaps of the tent hadn't fully closed, an occasional breeze caused the vertical creases to flutter. Sara let her mind drift while her eyes locked on the slight rippling material.

"Kek Lashav me chavas, kek lashav" she muttered under her breath and took another swig from her bottle.

Chapter Fifteen

Rosa finished collecting the fresh water upstream of where the women would attend to marime details. The order water in a flowing river was used was one of the strictest rules a camp had and there could be no variance. The first water was for drinking and cooking, next the men were permitted to bathe; further down the river the men's clothing could be washed, then certain cooking utensils. Away from the sight of the men, the remaining impure, unclean or marime washing was undertaken.

With both the old, metal jerry cans filled with water, Rosa gripped a handle in each hand so as to balance herself and she struggled back to the camp to provide water to her own mother and to gift the second to Mickey's.

Approaching the camp, the young woman stopped in her tracks as she caught sight of Mickey holding the flap to the ofisa open to allow the gadjo out. It was apparent even from sixty yards distant the reading hadn't gone well. Tom seemed bowed under the weight of his revealed future and her fiancé looked troubled.

Setting the heavy cans of water down and rubbing her palms to ease the cramp that was trying to lock her fingers into a set shape, she shook her head to herself. The future would come whether it was known or not and Rosa couldn't understand why anybody would think knowledge of it could be a good thing. If a reading told of good news, the delight in the surprise would be lessened and if it spoke of bad news, the recipient would sour the time between the reading and the event with worry.

Rosa lived by the words she had told Tom and she was frustrated that men never listened to her. Tomorrow would look after itself; today should be lived.

As she watched the two young men she felt a stab of envy as the pair embraced briefly, broke apart and then began to walk away from her at an oblique angle. Taking the water she carried to the vardos of her and Mickey's family took precedence over following the two youths but Rosa made a mental note to speak with her rom about hugging any man where people could see. It was a weakness and he wasn't to be seen as being weak by any in the kumpania.

Tom let Mickey lead him away from the tents and caravans without giving much thought to where they were heading. His thoughts were deeply bound in his memory of the reading. The past and present were accurate but potentially vague enough to have been pure speculation. It was true he had experienced loss and had a hard past but eight years on from the end of the war, so many people could say the same.

The woman's reading of his present was complimentary and he'd immediately recognised himself in the description. The more he considered it though, the more he wondered if she had simply gauged his education; it must be true she could tell a grammar school boy from one who was not.

It had been the telling of his future that disturbed him. 'You will know pain'. Try as he might, he couldn't shake her words. Had they been wrought in iron, heated and branded on his flesh he wouldn't have forgotten the words any slower. Her tone and seeming reluctance to speak the meaning of the three tarot cards stayed with him as surely as the words themselves.

There had been no indication of where the pain was to come from, nor did she indicate any time-frame. The moment he had stepped back into the light of the outdoors, he had deflated and if Mickey had not placed his arm around him, Tom knew he would have dropped to his knees and vomited in the dirt. Even minutes later as the gypsy had steered him into the woods he could feel his muscles tremble as they sought to fail and drop him to the ground.

Mickey worried for Tom; the boy was clearly struggling and his thought had been to take him from the sight of the Familia. Maybe it was a selfish act to permit the boy privacy to weep as a woman but he hadn't actively thought of himself. The youth needed seclusion and Mickey was determined to provide it. There was a good likelihood Mickey would have been challenged of his friendship with the upset gadjo but that hadn't been his motivation.

Once in among the trees of the ancient broad-leaf forest he continued to take Tom deeper into the wood that bordered the river. When he was satisfied they were a sufficient distance from the camp, he manoeuvred the teenager toward a stump of an oak that had been cut many years before and was only now beginning to darken and split with age.

The low stump was large enough to permit Mickey to sit Tom down and then perch beside him. The gypsy didn't want to discuss the reading he had just heard as he could think of nothing to say. Sara's readings for the locals were always made in the same vein. The old woman would never lie whether she read cards or as was more common, read their palms. Every reading he had been present for had mixed bad news with good; he'd never heard her issue such a simple and succinct telling.

It wasn't part of Mickey Ray's nature to offer physical comfort to the men in his life; if he had tried the effort would have been rebuffed but Tom was very different. A gypsy didn't express emotion like the boy sat beside him. A gypsy was mentally strong and emotionally stable, a gypsy didn't cry in public and rarely in private. Life was harsh and the measure of the man was reflected in how he dealt with hardship.

Mickey was unable to distance himself from the trembling and angst ridden youth. For the third time in a short history the gypsy broke with his public persona and put his arm across Tom's shoulders and silently held him close. He lowered his head to try and peer at the face of the teenager where his hair had fallen forward to hide his expression. He saw tears drip from Tom's nose and chin and reaching his hand out, he lightly touched his chin and tilted his head upward.

Wet cheeked, Tom glanced fearfully to the gypsy then hurriedly lowered his head again as soon as Mickey took his hand away.

"Only words lad" Mickey said quietly. "Not something tooti be worrying on."

Between sniffs that threatened to become a torrent of tears, Tom managed to tell the gypsy he couldn't help but fear the words. "I'm not good with pain. I should never have come."

"Future's a drom t' ga in the dark" Mickey whispered.

Tom laughed but stayed with his head bowed. "That may be the greatest advice ever Mickey but... I have no idea what you said!"

The humour cut through the sadness and the gypsy took his arm from around the boy's shoulders and clasped his hands together between his knees. He chuckled to himself and explained. "Only saying you got to walk your own path; if your future is lit and you can see your way... ain't your future no more." Bringing his hand up, he stroked Tom's hair and smoothed the hanging fringe back. He touched his fingers to Tom's cheek and guided his face to make the youth look him in the eye. "Future's dark for a reason. Sara can light a candle but it don't chase away the shadows, just shows you the next steps."

Tom gazed into the depths of Mickey's dark eyes and lost himself momentarily. The urge to admit he had only sought a reading of his future to create a reason to find the eighteen year old was strong. There had been no lie or evasion but Tom felt dishonest in not telling the young man everything. Dark eyes looked back at him, they grew in his vision and it was only as he felt his lips touch Mickey's that the youth realised he had leant in and kissed the gypsy.

The punch from Mickey was hard and unexpected, Tom fell backward from the blow and tumbled to the dirt and brown leaves behind the stump.

Mickey came to his feet fast and hurried to where Tom had fallen. As he moved close, Tom shuffled backward expecting more violence. Sitting among the detritus of the forest with his hands behind him he was unable to retreat faster than the gypsy's approach.

""Khul! I'm sorry" the gypsy cried out. Mickey dropped to his knees beside Tom and reached out to lightly touch Tom's chin where his fist had impacted. There was no mark and with little flesh over the bone it was likely there would be no bruise. "So sorry, it was a reflex."

Wide-eyed and shocked Tom was frozen to the spot. He let the youth squat beside him but he couldn't take his fearful expression from the face of the man who had punched him. Unsure how to react to the apologies that tumbled from Mickey he remained immobile as the gypsy knelt with one knee beside him and his other at his back.

Mickey's examination of where his blow had landed softened and his manipulation of the youth's head slowly became a caress. Mickey leant in and unprompted, he gently placed his lips to Tom's and kissed him. "I'm sorry" he reiterated.

Tom didn't know what to say. Mickey pulled back and sat on his heels, his eyes showed a new nervousness as he waited for the youth to react. Time froze for the pair as they sat, clothes touching but each unsure of what to do. The gypsy was like a bad puppy waiting for a punishment; Tom was startled and confused.

Swallowing back his upset, Tom stretched his palm to Mickey's cheek and held his hand against the tanned skin. Raising his own hand, the young gypsy placed it over Tom's as though he feared without the reinforcement of the contact, Tom may withdraw his own hand.

A tear trickled from Mickey's eye and over his cheekbone. It touched Tom and ran slowly down his finger to nestle against his thumb. The two youths moved toward each other once more, consciously, they closed on each other to kiss again.

The laughter of children ripped the moment from them and Mickey pulled away. His hands dropped to the dirt and he span in a circle to come standing in a swift motion and his eyes locked on the direction of the sound. Glimpsing the primary colours of skirts through the trees he knew immediately the laughter had come from Ruby and Dinah.

Angry with himself as much at the two girls, his ire quickly turned to fear as the potential repercussions filtered into his thinking. Quickly Mickey grabbed Tom's hand and pulled him to his feet. "Come wit' me, make no sound."

Still holding Tom's hand, Mickey pulled the youth deeper into the woods. The young villager had spent a lot of time in the woods and fields when he was growing up but he struggled to keep pace with the sure-footed gypsy as they hastened at least two hundred yards further into the forest.

Finally Mickey stopped. Tugging Tom against a tree, he pushed the gorgio against the trunk of an oak and held him still with one hand. Fingers widespread against the boy's chest, he stared past the tree in the direction they had just left and said nothing.

"Who was it?" Tom asked in a whisper but Mickey simply shook his head and quietly shushed him. Tom had barely heard the laughter and the more he tied to remember the moment, the further it slipped from him. Initially he hadn't given the incident much thought beyond it being an interruption of his kiss with Mickey but now, with his back to the tree and having nothing to do but imagine, he started to worry.

If whoever it had been spoke of it Tom realised the foretold pain of his future could be much closer than he had imagined. The youngster began to imagine the police being called, a public court case and a subsequent jail sentence. Despite Mickey's urging for quiet, Tom began to cry in earnest. He no longer felt the pain of the punch of he had received, now he wept from fear and shame.

Mickey tore his eyes from the trees where he had been watching to see if the two girls would return and glared hard at Tom. "Stop it!" Despite only being in contact with the boy with his fingertips he managed to shove the youngster hard against the tree.

"We're going to go to prison!" Tom wailed.

Mickey stared intently at Tom and he frowned. "Prison? Amria!" Mickey shook his head. "Don't be worrying for prison; my da learns of this, the Familia will see me muller'd. Dead. You understand that?"

The gypsy's words sobered Tom up instantly and suddenly a terror grew in him. "What?"

Mickey didn't reply but turned his eyes back to the trees. His hand moved from the chest of the young man and while he kept his gaze locked in the direction of the camp he shifted his arm upward so as to rest his palm against Tom's neck. Gently he caressed the soft skin, his fingers lightly touched behind the teenager's ear.

Still worried at their combined fates, Tom let the gypsy's soothing hand ease some of the tension from him. With nothing to do but try to hold in his fears and suppress the sobs that were still trying to escape him, the boy closed his eyes and focussed solely on Mickey's touch.

Chapter Sixteen

The young Ruby stood her ground as Rosa's first punch landed but ducked the second. There was no denying the woman's strength and aim but even at thirteen the child was alert enough to avoid most blows thrown her way. It was fortunate enough they had found her apart from the crowd of women the older girl had just left but the noise Rosa made was enough to draw some of the children away from their chores to see what was occurring.

Biting her tongue as a small gathering grew around her, Rosa managed to calm herself enough to start to rationalise. When she was asked what was happening she had the wit to chase the youngsters from her but as Ruby and Dinah made to retreat, she grabbed the youngest girl's arm.

"Kek you two!" Roughly hauling the twelve year old toward the trees she turned to glare at Ruby. "An' tu!" Hesitant to argue, the thirteen year old followed behind already regretting having spoken.

Rosa had ceased her accusations of the girls lying and though she struggled to believe them, she knew they gained nothing by lying of what they claimed to have seen. Half pulling, half dragging the youngest girl, Rosa found a secluded spot and threw the youngster to the ground. She kept her tone low and growled at Ruby to sit beside Dinah.

"I'm sorry Rosa" Ruby said, glaring back at the older girl. "We saw what we saw an' I ain't saying I didn't just to be making tu right."

Clenching her hand back into a fist the oldest gypsy wanted to hurt the girls again. As stubborn as Ruby always was, one thing she wasn't was a liar and however angry Rosa got with her, if the girl said she'd seen Mickey kiss the gadjo, then that was what she saw. Though she had lashed out at both girls it had only been because Mickey hadn't been there. Right now she wanted to hurt Mickey and the boy with him but she had to be practical first.

"Iffen tu seen what you say, then I do no more to tu iffen tu never be repeating." Rosa watched on as the two girls turned to each other. Dinah was clearly intimidated by the older girl but she still looked to Ruby before she was prepared to say anything more.

With a frown, Ruby asked if Rosa was telling her to lie.

Realising reason would only work if the girls were prepared to be reasonable, Rosa fell back to tried and tested methods. She squatted down low so her head was on the same level as the young teenager and faster than Ruby could react to, she lunged forward, her hand going straight to Ruby's throat. She gripped the delicate neck of the gypsy child and squeezed.

At first, Ruby simply stared back defiantly but as the seconds ticked by, her face began to darken. The tanned flesh took on a reddish cast and the girl brought her own hands up, her fingers scrabbling ineffectively at the grip the young woman had on her. Dinah sat and looked on, close to tears.

Staring intently into the girl's eyes, Rosa held her grip firm. Ruby's eyelids fluttered and her eyes began to roll back as the world grew unfocussed around her, her hands dropped uselessly to her sides and then Rosa released her grip and pushed the girl hard so she fell gasping on the grass.

Moving to a standing position, Rosa moved forward to where the girl lay coughing, her hand was rubbing her throat and she was trying hard to suck oxygen back into her lungs. Rosa dropped to one knee and gripped the chin of the still gasping girl.

"Tu saw nothing, say different... tu'll wake up dead." She shook the girl hard to ensure she had her attention. "You getting me?"

Red eyed and fearful, Ruby nodded and when prompted by Rosa she said "I see nuffin. Nuffin."

Still gripping the girl, she paused to ensure there was nothing additional to be said and when the girl looked away from her glare,

Rosa let go of Ruby and turned her attention to Dinah. Rooted to the spot, Dinah simply shook her head and in a wavering voice she said she hadn't seen anything either.

Satisfied with the result she had gained but upset at how she had achieved it, Rosa nodded and stood up again. She turned her full attention to the youngest girl and in a softer voice she asked "The thing tu never saw... where?"

Swallowing hard, Dinah pointed into the woods behind them waited for a reaction. Still angry and a little ashamed, Rosa nodded gently and glanced at both girls again. Ruby had risen to a seated position again and it seemed she'd be fine. A look of understanding passed between the two oldest gypsies and as much as the violence and force should have distanced them, the silent exchange bound the girls tighter. They were Familia, they were gypsies; Rosa had done what she had to do and Ruby respected her for it. She hoped when she was older she would have the strength of mind and body to do the same.

Rosa walked in Dinah's direction and then continued past her to move further into the wood in the direction she had been pointed. Her nails drew blood in her palm as she squeezed her hands tight into fists again.

Mickey pressed himself against Tom trying to minimise his

profile when he saw Rosa walk into the little clearing they had so recently vacated. Her cursing came through the trees clearly and the gypsy could feel the tension in the gorgio's body.

The girl halted by the stump and stared at the ground, Mickey knew she was making a reasoned assessment of the scuffed footprints in the dirt and would be able to tell where Tom had fallen after he'd been struck. Nothing would indicate what had passed but it was clear from her tone she knew.

The gypsy was both relieved and doubly worried Ruby and Dinah had sought out his fiancé rather than having told anyone else. The woman would say nothing of what the two children had told and that was a blessing but equally, for Rosa to have been told meant a price was going to be extracted from Mickey when they did meet up again.

The young man withdrew from peering around the tree and he bowed his head to rest his forehead on Tom's shoulder. The teenage local boy placed his hand on Mickey's back, part to support him and in part to reassure himself he wasn't alone.

Mickey could feel Tom's heart beating against his chest, rapid and strong the drum beat echoed his own. Both pairs of lungs drew air fast and released it slowly, Mickey could feel his friend's breath against his ear and he closed his eyes to try to shift his focus from the distraction to strain to hear what Rosa was muttering beneath her breath.

It would have been sensible to have faced her and denied everything. There was no reason for her to believe children over his word and yet, the fact he had hidden from her said more than any assurance he could give. What mattered now was that Rosa didn't find them.

Unable to retreat any further without drawing attention to himself, Mickey was trapped as surely as a rabbit in a snare. The trouble that would arise if he and Tom were discovered was greater than anything the youth had ever faced before and yet, despite himself, Mickey felt a thrill run through him.

Rosa's curses grew in volume again as she tried and failed to identify where Mickey had gone. Her ability to read trail was good but it wasn't something the women were trained in. A man would have seen the disturbance in the leaves that trailed further into the shadows and a dozen feet from the dead-fall, he would have spotted the broken twigs where heavy, booted feet had carelessly hurried from the tree stump.

With his hand still resting on Tom's neck, his fingertips reading his pulse as the boy's heart pumped blood around his body, Mickey smiled. Something of the danger he was in spurred him to life and with Tom's hand grasping at the thin linen of his shirt, Mickey could feel his blood rising. Though the situation should have killed his ardour, the gypsy found his passion increased and his arousal was apparent with his crotch pressed against Tom's leg where he had forced him against the tree and out of sight.

Turning his head a fraction Mickey raised his head from the gadjo's shoulder and delicately kissed his neck beside his ear. He felt Tom tense but with a hand braced behind him and his right hand at the neck of the boy, the young gypsy drew back and holding Tom still, he moved his lips to meet with Tom's and after a split-second hesitation, Tom began to kiss him back.

In the clearing by the tree stump, Rosa was silently fuming. She knew she was less hurt than angry. It wasn't that Mickey had kissed the chav from the village but the fact he had been seen. There was going to be hell to pay when she caught up with her promised. How could he? Did he not understand what he was doing?

The Rom Baro had to be the epitome of Romania behaviour; the title could be earned by any but it was rare for it to leave a family. Father to son through generations but it didn't have to be that way; if the Familia knew of this day, Mickey would never be allowed to lead the camp and Rosa would never gain the position she deserved at his side. Her children in turn would never be who they should.

Rosa spat on the ground and cursed again. Her thoughts ran a little deeper and she thought beyond the structure of the camp hierarchy. If word got out, leading the camp was going to be the least of the young man's worries. Jacky Ray wouldn't tolerate a she'chrone son.

Rosa began to chew at her nail, her anger faded and she began to calculate her next actions. Mickey wasn't going to be a problem; she could manipulate him, if need be, she could threaten to cancel their vows and tell everybody why. Mickey would come around to her thinking and he'd be a proper man as she would make him. The boy was the issue; Rosa took her time working out how to deal with the boy.

Unaware of Rosa's scheming, Tom and Mickey were locked together in a clinch. With their shirts undone, flesh was pressed against flesh and hands roamed. Caution added to their fervour as silently, they explored who they were.

Chapter Seventeen

Mary Quatrell noticed the teeth mark in the crook of her son's neck almost immediately but she chose to say nothing. It was apparent the bite was no sign of violence but of passion and when she turned her back on him, she grinned to herself. She'd known Thomas was quiet and reclusive but this was the first time she'd had any indication of him having a girlfriend and she wasn't going to say anything to him that may cause a change in his behaviour.

It was still early in the afternoon when Tom had returned home and he had tried so hard to act normally he was convinced he was overdoing it. The youth was exhilarated at the events of the morning and though he knew Mickey was alarmed at their having been seen, the stresses had faded from Tom as he'd walked home.

There had been a momentary flicker of fear as he'd crossed the road just prior to the Half Moon public house and found constable Matthews stood in the shadows directly in his path. The unpaved walkway beside the newly tarmacked road wasn't the easiest to navigate and Tom had his eyes down carefully watching where he placed his feet when the policeman had spoken. Just the shock of his voice had caused the boy to jump but when he'd raised his eyes and seen the dark blue uniform and the domed helmet he'd suddenly become tongue-tied.

"You're the Quatrell boy aren't you?" Matthews had asked and after swallowing hard and nodding, Tom had eventually managed to squeak that he was. "Thought so, something of your father about you lad."

The officer had smiled and Tom had automatically smiled back. Precious few people in the small town had known his father as although they'd moved to Midhurst years before war had broken out, they kept to themselves. Tom couldn't remember any other home aside from a vague recollection of a garden with a swing and a blue bedroom that had a closet door that creaked open at erratic times throughout the night.

"You knew my father?"

Constable Matthews beamed. "His team from the Bricklayer's played our lot in thirty-nine." The policeman cocked his head to one side as he relived the moment. "I was drawn against your Dad, he took the first game one throw outside of a nine darter. I pulled the second back when his finish was ruined by bouncing off the wire." Matthews unclipped the strap that secured his helmet and scratched at his grey and black beard. "Lost the last game trying to get treble nineteen, tops. Hit a single then went for double fourteen and bull." The man laughed aloud. "Got the double with my second try. Your dad stepped up to the oche... treble seventeen, double fifteen. Not the way I'd have gone but it worked for him."

"I didn't know he played darts." Tom raised his eyebrows. He knew his dad had a board in the shed but he thought it was just somewhere he went to smoke his pipe.

The policeman turned and the two of them began to slowly walk toward the junction where Tom would head up the hill to home. Knowing it would appear furtive but unable to help himself, Tom kept glancing askew at the tall, slightly overweight policeman beside him as the man wheeled his pushbike beside him.

Gripping the handlebars with one hand, Matthews kept his gaze ahead. "Shame about your dad, Salerno wasn't it?" Tom nodded but the policeman wasn't looking at him. "I was at Tarento. No resistance really; pretty much gave up as soon as we made the town."

Keeping quiet, Tom found his mind conjuring the map he still had of Italy. He hadn't heard of the town the officer mentioned but he knew everything there was to know about Salerno. It had been his need to know more that had introduced him to the town's library.

"Anyway, what would your father make of you getting in to fights do you think?" Matthews didn't even pause in his stride as he finally got to business.

Nervously, the boy beside him wondered about the change in tack the policeman had suddenly taken. He said nothing but lowered his eyes to his feet, carefully matching pace with the older man.

The bearded man stopped walking and removed his helmet altogether, retied the strap and hung it from his handlebars. "That was you this morning in Cussies Row wasn't it?"

Was it only this morning? Tom halted with the policeman and raising his gaze, he met the blue eyes of the constable. He hesitated a moment and then nodded. He knew he was likely in trouble even though he'd been the one who had been hurt but he was relieved the policeman knew nothing of his last few hours.

With a deep sigh, the policeman started forward again, pushing the bike a dozen more paces before he spoke again. "Nothing official but... you might want to watch yourself around the Trent boys. Their parents aren't happy but I'd be more inclined to think the boys will try to even the score. You get my drift?"

"Yes" Tom said. "Thank you."

Matthews stopped his bike and threw a leg over the saddle and positioned his pedals, one foot resting on the ground, the other ready to push away. He smiled at the boy and winked before pedalling off.

Tom watched him go and shivered. Taking a deep breath, he ran his hand over his temple and swallowed to try and stimulate saliva in his dry mouth. Just fighting, that was all the policeman had wanted to talk about. As reality bit hard, Tom felt his legs turn to jelly and he had to sit against the bank beside the road as his trembling muscles refused to hold him up. Leaning forward he put his head in both hands and tried to even out his breathing.

Still tense and nervous, the youth started to laugh for no reason he could think of.

Sitting now in the kitchen with his mother, Tom chopped carrots to go with the sausages his mother had bought at the butchers. Three saucepans competed for space on the rayburn and the kettle had been pushed back against the flue. Tom tried to keep his concentration on the short knife in his hand but his mind was wandering.

Tomorrow was Sunday and it was one of the few days Mary didn't work. Typically they would prepare the roast in the morning, then head to church for the Sunday service before coming home to eat together. It had always been something Tom had looked forward to but sitting in the kitchen with the sun streaming down outside the window his thoughts were firmly locked to the recent past.

Staring out of the kitchen window Tom watched the rays of sunlight as they danced across the leaves of the beech trees opposite. The dappled pattern of shadows cast on the darker trunk were reminiscent of the flickering pools of light he'd watched on the damp earth as he'd stared over Mickey's shoulder. The sun had been filtered through the canopy of branches and small, penny sized patches of sunshine had danced across the twigs and natural detritus of the forest.

The sparkling outside was hypnotic and Tom could almost feel the gypsy's hands on his body as he lost himself in the sway of branches.

"Tom! Carrots!" His mother smirked to herself as her son snapped back to reality from whatever daydream he had been lost in.

Colouring at his embarrassment, Tom dropped his eyes back to the chopping board and resumed cutting quarter inch rounds from the already peeled vegetables. Grinning to himself, he covertly cast a look to his mother and was relieved to find she had turned back to the small worktop beside the draining board where she was separating the string of sausages as she unwrapped them from the greaseproof paper.

Try as he might, Tom couldn't think of a way to get out of their tradition of going to church together. Once in a while he had managed to cry off when he had not been well but even if he feigned illness in the morning, it wouldn't permit him the time he needed to walk to the gypsy camp and return before his mother made it back from church. The afternoon and evening would be his own but as he would be due back to work the following day, he was loath to waste any time that he could spend with Mickey.

Letting a long frustrated sigh escape, the youth constantly rethought ways to escape his Sunday obligations. He was so caught up in his own imagination he didn't notice his mother had been coughing for a few minutes until she tumbled to the floor taking the sausages with her in her fall.

Without any consideration for anything but his mother, Tom jumped to his feet, his chair falling behind him with a crash. He dropped the knife he was holding and as it clattered to the tiled floor, he trod on the blade as he rapidly dragged himself around the table as fast as he could. Squatting over his mother, he was relieved to see she was conscious and alert.

Holding a hand to her chest, her other hand was gripped tight to the handle of the cupboard under the sink. She coughed hard and released her handhold on the cupboard and placed it on the cold tiles to support herself.

"Are you okay Mum?" Tom asked, placing a supportive hand behind her as their combined efforts raised her to a sitting position. Mary smiled weakly and nodded, muttering about being a little short of breath.

Helping his mother to her feet, he sat her in the chair opposite his own and rescued the sausages. Mary Quatrell was clearly pale and though Tom wasn't able to hear the sound, Mary could feel her own breath rattling in her chest as she breathed in. Trying to force a gentle cough to clear her throat set her hacking cough up again and when she managed to calm herself, she sufficed with shallow breaths to avoid a repeat performance.

Tom couldn't help but worry but he wasn't practical and had no knowledge of any use. His mother was the nurse, he didn't know the first thing about looking after somebody. It was that self-knowledge that had him accept her assurances she was okay. When asked, he picked her packet of Players from the window sill and set them beside her in the ashtray.

Clasping the hand that held the lit cigarette with her other hand managed to hide the trembling from her son and Mary sucked gently and briefly at the filtered tip so as to not induce a fresh bout of coughing. Letting the smoke trickle from her mouth, she again reassured Tom she was fine.

Not knowing any different, Tom accepted his mother's assurance and turned his attention back to the cooking. He finished cutting the string of sausages and lay six on a tray to slip into the oven. At a brief word from his mother, he reduced the number to five but wondered if she was genuinely not so hungry or if she was trying to reduce the household bills.

The sausages went into the oven and Tom scooped the carrots into one of the waiting saucepans. The potatoes were already boiling and the peas had been shelled ready. Satisfied tea would be ready in half an hour, Tom managed to persuade his mother to go into the living room and have a rest while he cleared up and set the table for the two of them.

Alone in the kitchen again, Tom worried less about his mother. She'd always seemed strong when he'd been a child but now she seemed to be tired and drawn so much of the time. Try as he might, he couldn't find the time she had changed from being the robust mother who could do everything to the woman who was out of breath simply walking down the stairs. There was no doubt she was resilient though. Mary Quatrell always bounced back.

Tom dug into his trouser pocket and pulled out his baccy pouch and unzipped it. Opening it out in the light he found the two roll-ups he'd pre-made had been crushed and he clamped his lips together as he realised how they came to be damaged. His eyes sparkled and he stifled a giggle as he broke the remnant of paper from the home-made cigarette and re-rolled the tobacco in a new paper. Running his tongue across the glued edge he stuck the paper to itself and clamped it between his teeth before lighting it with the lighter his mother has left on the table.

With his elbows on the table he sucked the toxins into his body and tried and failed to blow a smoke ring. He leant back in the chair, the cigarette between the fingers of his right hand resting on the lip of the table and his left hand resting on his thigh as he stretched his legs out under the table.

Closing his eyes, Tom gently caressed his thigh through his trousers and his breathing deepened. Cautiously he opened his eyes and ensured he was alone in the room, then slid his hand into his pocket and slowly let his fingertips push their way under the elastic of his underwear. With a very gentle and slow touch, he simulated the touch he had experienced earlier but it wasn't the same and he sighed deeply and brought his hand back to the table.

Tom leant forward once more and with both hands before him, he passed the cigarette between the fingers of his opposing hands. Staring ahead with no thought, he brought the roll-up back to his mouth and drew deeply on it. A strand of tobacco caught his lip and he freed it with his fingers and dropped it in the ashtray.

"What to do" he muttered to himself. Tom exhaled deeply and wondered anew if there was a way he could make Sunday all his own. He grinned and interlaced his fingers, carefully flicking ash toward the ashtray and missing. He lowered his face to the tabletop and blew the small mound of burnt tobacco to the floor.

He'd have to wait for tomorrow to arrive to decide what he could do but he remembered there was no reason to stay in on a Saturday evening. His mother would listen to the radio as happily on her own as with him sat there reading. It wouldn't get dark until after nine and he could have the washing up done by six. Tom's grin widened and he stubbed his cigarette out in the ashtray and silently urged the rayburn to cook a little quicker.

Chapter Eighteen

Mickey had avoided returning to the camp for over an hour but eventually he accepted he couldn't stay among the trees indefinitely. Circling the camp to the west he took the long route, passing the outlying vardos and coming back into camp from the bottom of the river.

His family's caravan was close to the bank of the river and he passed the benders that were clustered around the central vardo of his uncle, weaved through the blanket covered struts of ash and made his way to his father's van. The gloss black of the ford prefect reflected sunlight into Mickey's eyes and he squinted as he made his way around the rear of the vehicle and came to a dead stop.

Sat on the painted steps of the family vardo was Rosa, his mother was reclining on a wicker weaved chair beside her. The gypsy's heart beat thumped loud and hard, fear tore into him. The possibility of Rosa telling anyone seemed slim at the time but seeing her sat guarding his only retreat and with his daj as company he worried he'd made a bad assumption.

Lilly Ray and Rosa both glanced up and in his direction at the same time and caught sight of the young man. Mickey couldn't read anything from either woman's expression. Despite the age difference, even an outsider could see the two had a shared bloodline; their facial features meant they could pass as mother and daughter but the relationship was more tangled than that. Rosa was his mother's, mother's, niece's daughter.

With a slight indication of her head, Lilly summoned her son to her side and though he dreaded the meeting, Mickey did not dare ignore her. With wide eyes locked on Rosa's neutral expression, he fearfully stepped toward them affecting a nonchalant, casual swagger he didn't feel. A few yards distant, he recognised the face his daj wore. Mickey was in trouble.

"Mickey Ray, what is this my ghel tells?" The thirty-four year old woman was frowning and the young gypsy was hesitant to make any comment. "Says you two gonna wed in Stow. That right?"

Dread ran from Mickey as relief flooded him. He looked to Rosa who maintained an impassive look that reeked of disdain. The young woman looked directly at him and he knew they were going to have a long talk in the not too distant future. Mickey knew he wasn't going to say much, it would be Rosa doing all the talking.

Releasing a pent-up breath, the gypsy nodded. "Arvah, shee

vortimo" he admitted. "Still things to talk of but arvah, Rosa be my bori then, iffen she be willing."

Rosa blinked slowly and conceded a small curt nod that passed unseen by Mickey's daj. Despite having said the words in front of his mother, the gypsy was still plagued with doubt. Marrying Rosa was the right thing to do for her and his Familia but it was a future he feared and worried over. Sometimes he wished he was more his father's son and not troubled by the longings he felt. Rosa would make the most wonderful wife and she had ever been his best friend. It was a good match, sensible and a strong union that would bind their respective families tighter together at the top of the kumpania.

There would be no need to fake affection for the girl but Mickey wasn't confidant he could convince her he felt anything more than friendship. There was going to come a time when the night would call on him to make a son. How could he father a child when she did nothing to stir him? The days held no great fear for him as he had spent every day playing out the great lie but the night had always been his own.

"Khushti" Lilly said. "Shee been a longo drom."

Rosa nodded "Arvah!" Gathering her skirts, the girl rose from the red, yellow and green steps and moved forward to Mickey's mother. She lowered her head and took the woman's hand in her own, touching it to her forehead as a mark of respect, then turned to her son. "Me and tu Mickey, we best be avree. We need words."

Lilly Ray's eyes flickered between her son and prospective daughter in law. She identified the tension but knew of no cause. Shifting her gaze to scour her immediate surroundings, her head snapped up to lock on Rosa's face "Kaj shee Stefan?"

Mickey quickly scanned the area and realised the ever-present Stevo was absent. Thinking back, he hadn't seen the youth all day. Had he been at the river in the morning, Rosa wouldn't have been able to try to seduce him and yet he hadn't seen the protector of his promised's honour for the entire day. His brow furrowed and he looked to Rosa for an explanation but she ignored him and spoke to his mother.

"Kak Victor wanted him for a budjo i' the foros" the girl explained. "He ain't needed, we only go to talk me daj."

Lilly didn't worry overly for the girl's virtue and she beamed when Rosa addressed her as 'mother'. Maybe they would talk, maybe they would do more than talk. Stow was not so far away that a babe conceived now would be questioned if it were born a little early. The Familia had commented how big a baby Mickey had been when he had been born two moons early but none had said anything to her face. The woman met the young girl's gaze and though her mouth gave no hint to her assumption, her eyes sparkled as she bowed her head and sent them on their way.

Mickey had initially trailed behind Rosa with reluctance. A reckoning was coming his way and he knew it. The girl dropped back a pace and grasped her husband to be's hand, interlacing her fingers with his. Though she didn't drag the hesitant youth along, she led the way firmly toward the woodland and traipsed her way into the forest.

It was apparent the girl sought privacy and Mickey wondered if he had read the situation correctly. At first he had been convinced he was going to have to explain what Ruby had seen but now he wondered if his thinking might be flawed. They didn't need to trek so far from camp for her to rage at him and with his hand held firmly in hers, he considered it a possibility she planned more than talking. Neither option appealed to him.

Halting in the forest, Mickey realised they were in the same clearing he had been with Tom. With his blood running cold, he still felt hot and flushed. Rosa released his hand and turned on him, pushing him backward so his ankles struck the tree stump where he had sat earlier and he fell backward. With his hands behind him to stop his tumble, Mickey landed hard on the split and damp wood and he braced himself for whatever came next.

Rosa had managed to contain her ire had but the rage in her had been simmering for many hours. "Tu bi-lacho beng" she barked. "Tu an' dat gorgio khul chiavala!" She bent down to scream at him, pushing her face right before his eyes. "Tu kek lashav? Tu want his kabaro kek me mindj?" She swung her hand and slapped his cheek with all the force she could muster.

The blow turned his head but he turned back swiftly. Mickey neither spoke nor made any move to defend himself. Glaring at Rosa, he put his palms to the wooden stump beneath himself and as he clenched his hands to fists, his nails dug into the soft wood.

Frustrated at Mickey's failure to react, Rosa hit him again. She didn't slap him the second time, she bunched a fist and punched his nose with all the strength she could muster. "Say something you khul" she screamed as his nose split and blood splattered his cheek. Infuriated at his silence, she opened her palm and slapped him across the cheek again and again.

Mickey took the blows as they rained down on him. As much as the punch and slaps hurt, he knew he deserved them and as much as he wanted to retaliate, he held back. The open palmed assaults stung and tears formed in the corners of his eyes but he still stayed stationary and silent.

"What is it tu want? What does that gadjo do for tu that me can't?" Rosa knew she had lost any moral high ground she'd had. She staggered back from him and crossed her arms tight across her bosom to bottle in her rage. "I'd do anything for tu Mickey, anything."

Bowing her head, her long hair spilled over her face. Mickey wiped his eyes with his sleeve and touched his fingers to his face. They came away bloodied and he thought Rosa had managed to break his nose. Eighteen bouts against the best fighters the Irish and Romany gypsies could muster and she'd managed what none of them could. Despite his pain and worry, she made him proud.

"I've never meant to pain you" Mickey whispered. "All I've said I've meant. It's just..." The gypsy stopped talking. How could he ever explain? He couldn't sum up who he was and what he felt in a few sentences. He wiped the blood from his fingertips onto his trousers and leant forward, folding his arms across his chest in a mimicry of her posture. He leaned his elbows on his knees and stared at the dirt at his feet. "Arvah, I kissed him" Mickey admitted. "Maybe I did more, maybe I didn't. That don't be changing us."

Rosa's anger resurfaced and her head snapped up as she flicked her hair back behind her. Tear tracks stained her face and Mickey felt her anguish. She moved toward the young man and though he didn't move to defend himself, he tensed, ready for more violence.

Her hand reached out slowly and she ran her fingers through his tangled hair. Her breathing was slow and deep as she tried to regulate her mood. Her fingers closed into a fist once more, she grasped his hair in a bunch, pulling it where she gripped it so tight. A minute passed and she forced her hand open again, gently she stroked his locks flat again and raised her wet face to the canopy of leaves above her.

"Mickey, Mickey, Mickey..." she muttered. She put her other hand to his head and pulled him against her stomach where she held him tight. Hesitantly, he raised his hands and wrapped them around her, gripping his own wrists behind her. He turned his head, resting his ear to her skirts as he stared unseeing to the side and into the trees.

Rosa was lost. She had no idea what she could say to make everything as it should be. She'd known for a decade they would wed and always be together and yet, she didn't know how to make him see the world as she did. A tremble shook her frame and it took a moment for her to realise it hadn't come from her own body. Staring down at the top of Mickey's head, Rosa realised he was crying.

"Dosta Mickey" she said quietly. "Opre!" Moving back out of his reach, Rosa made the youth release his hands from behind her back and waited for him to stand up. Rubbing his face of tears whilst carefully avoiding his injured nose, Mickey rose to his feet.

Finding it hard to meet his fiancé's eyes, the young man continued to stare at the ground. Both gypsies were confused but only Rosa was angry and that had been tempered by Mickey's crying.

"What d'we do Mickey?" Rosa said very quietly. She let him approach her and as he came to a stop just before her. Pulling a square of linen from a potchee in her skirts, she wet it with her tongue and delicately dabbed at the blood he had smeared across his face. Calmly and slowly, she continued, "First tu says we'll wed when you have a vardo an' a grast to pull it" she wet the cloth again. "Then you push me away when I come to you."

Mickey raised his face to hers and she saw there was nothing in his expression that thought her words unfair. "Tu tells me we'll wed at Stow fair, then I get told tu been seen kissing a gorgio chav." Rosa pressed hard enough against the cut where she had split the cartilage with her fist to gain a groan from the gypsy. Eye to eye, neither spoke of the discomfort he felt. "Now you say to your daj we be marrying in Stow a'er all."

The youth opened his mouth to comment but confusion held him in thrall. He closed his mouth and looked away from her stare again.

"What's it be Mickey?" Rosa stopped trying to clean the blood away. Most of his face was cleaned but blood still trickled from his left nostril, his tongue slipped out to taste the coppery tasting seep. He turned and spat and the girl watched as he returned to the tree stump and sat himself back down. With a sigh and a grimace, he eventually looked up at the young woman who still waited for a response.

Mickey shook his head softly and shrugged. "Been knowing we'd be together a long time" he said. "Ain't a woman I'd rather be with than you Rosa but... it ain't all the time I want to be with a woman."

There was a silence in the forest as Rosa waited for Mickey to continue and he struggled to say more than he already had. Both knew the little he had said was enough to cut a rift between kith and kin so wide it'd never heal if they had heard his words.

The gypsy wrung his hands together as though he could rub away who he was. Turning his palms over, he placed one on each knee and the knuckles whitened as he consciously forced himself to not make fists of his hands.

"Not rightly knowing what to do" he whispered. Rosa strained to hear him and moved closer to him and knelt in the dirt in front of him and placed one of her hands on his. Mickey reached out and caressed the side of her neck, his hand raised a fraction and he brushed her cheek with his thumb as his fingertips brushed her earlobe. "We's Romany. I ain't carrying much in options. Amria Rosa! What to do? Tu tell I!"

Putting her anger away, Rosa felt the pain of the young man and for a brief time, she returned to being nothing more than his friend. She thought what she would tell another if they had told him as much and she knew what her advice would be to them. It wasn't hard to know what she would tell them.

"Mickey Ray" she said. "Tu got no option. You keep from this gorgio boy, tu make me yours an' tu says nothing more. Not ever."

Mickey acknowledged her words and told her he knew it was what he should do but added that he couldn't promise to be the rom she needed or deserved.

"Got no choice has tu?" Rosa climbed back to her feet. "Tu knowing what your da will do he ever learns."

In a swift motion, Mickey jumped to his feet and slapped Rosa in the face hard enough to cause her to fall on her side. "You threaten me?"

Putting her hand to her own face where the imprint of his hand was turning from a pale imprint to a red four-fingered mark, Rosa glared at the youth standing over her. She called him an idiot as she shifted to her knees, then stood upright to stand toe to toe with him.

"Tu dinilo!" Rosa yelled. "Won't be from me! Just saying, your da learns of it, you're done." She prodded a finger against his chest and slowly, the fire in the youngster died as he came to understand what the young woman meant. "Tu go being a ghel for a chava, tu make sure none see; 'twas Ruby and Dinah this time and I done for them. *I* done for them! Me! Not for me, you'd be muller'd, slit belly to gizzard and all to know."

Rosa was panting at the rapid diatribe she'd directed at the gypsy and her eyes were wild. Mickey hadn't understood her words to begin with but he'd had no idea she had done more to keep his secret than he himself had. Staggering backward as though struck, the realisation of his indiscretion struck home.

"Get from my sight Mickey Ray" Rosa snarled. "I can't be doing wit' tu now. Get gone and think what tu be wanting." The woman turned to head back toward the camp and hesitated, she retraced her steps to come face to face with Mickey once more and added "You want a boy, then you ain't Romany no more. Your life will be with them. You decide you want to be gypsy still, your future's wi' me. Think on that!"

The confused youth stood stunned as Rosa span on the spot and stormed back toward the camp. Still standing, Mickey watched her leave and wondered if everything was as simple as she painted it.

Chapter Nineteen

Still in the blackest mood of her life, Rosa snapped and barked at any child who got in her way as she stomped aimlessly through the camp. The girl in the multi-coloured skirts had criss-crossed the area half a dozen times, each time a destination had presented itself, she dismissed it. There was precious little privacy to be had aside from beneath a blanketed bender or wooded vardo and those that were a welcome to her would hold questions she had no will to answer.

Laughter had sounded to the side of her and she'd glared in the direction of the sound. Allen had been hurriedly pulled out of her way by an exceptionally pale Dinah and Rosa felt a pang of guilt at how she had terrorised her and Ruby. Justifying her actions with the knowledge she was looking out for Mickey eased her conscience a little but thinking of him only reopened the tear in her heart all the more.

Barely a dozen steps past the retreating children she

encountered Stefan who had grinned and asked her if she'd missed him. "Feck orf Stevo!" The harsh bite from her caused the sixteen year old to swallow hard and hurry out of her way. Rosa in a temper was rare and in itself it was enough warning for the boy to take the hint.

Rosa fumed silently as she continued her angry walk and her mood soured further still when she caught a glimpse of Stefan still dogging her steps. There was nothing to be done to be rid of him. Uncle Victor must have returned and set the boy to watch for her virtue again. She let out a snort as she thought much may have been solved if they had set a watch on Mickey instead.

As she skirted a fire-pit outside an improvised tent, Rosa realised she had again come to the edge of the camp. Tired of trampling the same ground, she briefly considered heading for the road and seeing where it took her. Glancing to the tarmac strip at the edge of the flattened meadow, the girl recognised a vardo where she knew she would be welcome.

Her grandmother's caravan was always the best decorated. The primary colours were freshly painted and the designs on the wood were perfectly shaped. Her puri-daj wanted for nothing, the men of the kumpania did all she asked and oft times, they did more than she requested.

Sniffing the air, Rosa grinned briefly then crossed to the

wooden steps that led up the door. As always, the top half of the door stood open. Peering into the vardo from outside, nothing could be seen but darkness and shadow but her father's mother was always inside. Reaching her arm over the top of the lower door she unbolted it, stepped inside and closed and bolted the door behind her.

Once inside, Rosa could see May Easton lying back in the chair that doubled as a bed for the old woman. The bed itself had been taken out long before Rosa had been born. The space it occupied was too valuable to waste on sleeping. Frowning at her life, the young woman stepped softly past her elderly relative and picked up a clay jug from one of the shelves above the window.

Where the bed once had been were a row of wooden barrels, their tops balanced precariously at varying angles. Lifting the closest, Rosa dipped the clay container into the foaming liquid and drew out a jug full. She drank down half of the contents, paused for a breath, then downed the remainder

"That one ain't ready for another week."

Rosa looked to her grandmother and hesitated a moment before ignoring the motionless old woman and filling the jug again from the same barrel. She watched her puri-daj this time and when she spoke again, nothing moved but her lips.

"Suit y'self" she said. "I'll be telling your daj I warned tu."

The girl sat in a small space between two of the barrels behind the old woman and drank her second jug a little slower. There wasn't a lot of room in the vardo with all the brewing and bottling equipment but Rosa had claimed the little gap she was in as her own when she was six. It had been her bolt-hole when she'd been in trouble and though it never stopped her father taking his belt to her, it had always afforded her enough time for beer to take the sting out of the beating.

Over the years, it had become her sanctuary but as she drank from the clay jug, she realised it must have been at least three years since she had needed to hide. Evidently she wasn't the only person to realise this as her grandmother took that moment to ask what troubled her. Rosa replied there was nothing wrong and drank some more.

The wicker chair of the gypsies' brewer creaked and cracked as the woman pulled herself upright with the arms and twisted in the seat to look at her granddaughter sat at the back of her caravan. Rosa managed to hold the gaze of the elderly gypsy and the pair of them said nothing as they stared at each other. Seconds ticked by then slowly, as though all had been resolved, the grandmother caused her chair to protest as she returned to her previous position and closed her eyes again.

Rosa's puri-daj returned to her near comatose state and muttered "Is that so?"

Rosa waited but the woman said nothing more and to all appearances, she seemed to be fast asleep again. Upending the jug, she drained the last of the brew. It was a strong concoction and even with her familiarity with her grandmother's beer she was already started to feel a little light headed.

She scrabbled to her feet with a little difficulty and procured a third jug full, slipping slowly down the barrel back to her favourite resting spot. She stared into the foam at the head of the deep jug and realised it contained at least a third more than one of the bottles usually did. Poking her finger into the froth Rosa stirred the brown-topped, cream bubbles. Removing her finger she licked it clean then wiped it on her blouse before taking another large swig then sighing deeply.

"It's Mickey."

There was no reaction from May and Rosa sighed again. Cradling the clay jug the young woman stared at the chipped, brown glaze of the rim, then raising it in both hands, she tipped it to her mouth and over a half dozen seconds, she drank down the last of the alcohol. She coughed as the last drop when down and burped quietly. Relaxing her neck muscles, her head fell backward and cracked against the metal ring of the barrel behind her. The jolt kept her awake and she rubbed at her eyes as she tried to stand the jug on the wooden floor.

"Mickey is..." Rosa couldn't find the words she wanted. "He's..."

"Just spit it out ghel" the older woman said. "Ain't nothing I ain't've been hearing afore."

Rosa laughed and gently shifted her position so she could comfortably lean her head against the barrels without gaining a concussion. "Not so sure Nana May."

The dried wood of her chair protested as the gypsy woman rose out of it. Standing in front of her undeniable favourite grandchild, she looked the youngster over. "He got tu with chavi?"

Rosa's laughter rang out loud but slowly dissolved as her smile turned into a frown and the merry sound of her mirth caught in her throat. She looked up at her grandmother and sniffed, her eyes watered and she tried to blink the tears away. Rosa sniffed harder and wiped at her eyes with the palms of her hands. Screwing her face up, her lip trembled and a wrenching sob burst from her.

As the old woman dropped to her knees with surprising agility, she wrapped both arms around the girl as she began to wail. Drawing a ragged breath in, Rosa grasped at the shawl covered shoulders of the woman and clawed at the material as she cried hard.

Saying nothing, the woman gently rocked the child as all the pain of the last few days took its toll. Rosa managed to release her steel grip on her grandmother and tried to disentangle herself. Even sitting, the young woman was finding it hard to stop the room from swimming and she didn't object as the elder woman managed to sit against her still and pull Rosa onto the bottom of her skirt and wrap both arms gently around her.

"I don't know what to do Nana. He ain't seeded me." Rosa's tears hadn't gone away but aside from the sniffing, she was mostly in control of her hurt. "Mickey don't... he..." she swallowed hard and closed her eyes. "Oh Nana, he don't want a wife... he wants a husband."

The old woman's face lost its compassion for a moment as she absorbed the words. Her sharp mind read a hundred sentences from the one her grandchild uttered but she pushed everything away and focused on the girl in her arms. "You still want to be wed?"

Rosa only hesitated a moment before she nodded vigorously and her tears returned with a vengeance. Her body shook with the strength of the sob that tore through her and she began to rock back and forth, a low keening wail sounding in her throat.

"Tu be stopping that now!" Rosa's puri-daj snapped. "The women in our family ain't ones to go narky at things that can't be fixed."

With a snort, the young girl managed to bring herself a little tighter under control. How Mickey could be fixed was beyond Rosa's comprehension but the reprimand was so unexpected it came across as an order.

May Easton leant herself back until she was resting against wood and drew the girl back with her. Gently stroking her hair as she had done when Rosa was little and she'd been whipped with her da's leather belt, she spoke evenly and quietly. Rosa had to stop her own noise in order to hear the words that were whispered to her.

Rosa's grandmother asked if anybody else knew and nodded approvingly when it was explained how Ruby and Dinah had been effectively silenced. Several questions were asked and answered as the full story was told to the woman.

Taking in a long deep breath and letting it out just as slowly, the old woman paused before saying "Ain't the first to be that way, won't be the last." Rosa felt the arms that enfolded her slowly draw away and she had to sit up as the woman rose to her feet. "Nothing we can't deal with my girl. Light me my pipe an' dry those tears."

Rosa managed to get to her feet by rolling forward and pushing onto her knees where she could reach forward and grip the curved back of the wicker chair and she hauled herself upright. The room swam and her knuckles showed the effort of remaining vertical as her hands tightened on the frame of the ancient chair. She blew out a breath and sucked air in to clear her head.

In the small space at the front of the vardo the girl and the woman almost danced as positions were shifted. Her grandmother sank back into the padded seat and pulled her shawl tighter around her as Rosa shuffled forward to the row of small boxes that sat squarely on the shelf above the door.

Gripping the bottom half of the door the young gypsy kept her balance as she rose onto her tiptoes and drew down the box that held the thin, white clay pipe and tobacco. Pulling a mass of threaded strands from the paper wrap, she tamped down a wad of baccy into the small bowl and held the stem of the pipe between her lips. The match flared with a slow orange flare and briefly, the smell of fermenting was disguised by the sulphur of the match.

Rosa puffed and inhaled the first wisps of smoke as she sucked the fire into the brown, dried leaf; a second puff confirmed the tobacco had caught and she drew deeply of the rich tasting smoke. Opening her mouth, the girl held the smoke, a stray strand spiralled from the corner of her lips and curled up to the arched roof of the caravan.

Stretching to the top of the door the girl returned the tobacco and matches, then moved back across the small space to her grandmother. She took the long stem from her lips and passed the pipe over.

Beneath the headscarf the old woman wore, her eyes were sharp and clear. Just on the other side of seventy, the woman had no infirmity but she was content to have others do things for her. There was no pretence, it was a matter of honour. Even before she had taken over the brewing of the camp's beer she had the respect of the camp. Mother of eight children, the aged woman remembered the birth of three quarters of the Familia and aside from Sara, she was one of the oldest gypsies in the community. The respect afforded her came in a large part to her age but many among the gypsies were careful to not cross the woman; beer wasn't the only tonic she made.

"Sit at my feet youngster" she said. "I warned you that ale weren't ready!"

Gingerly and with her stomach threatening to rebel, Rosa lowered herself to the floor and looked up to her grandmother. Though still tearful, the girl was curious at what remedy the woman had in mind. Nothing of substance had been promised but Rosa felt a confidence beginning to return now she had spilt her pain out.

Staring up through the fog of smoke that hovered around the woman in the still air, Rosa chewed at her lip. "What you mean, 'he ain't the first'?"

"What tu think I mean? Seems me rocka be plain." May stared down into her granddaughter's eyes. "More 'an one been dihkin' t' shav presha baro kar-shera prey a chiavala's khul!"

Rosa sat open mouthed at the words her grandmother uttered. Her shock was less to do with what she had said as to her choice of terms.

"Close your mouth ghel, tu'll catch flies."

Wide-eyed, Rosa found a new respect for the old woman. She paused, then asked in a plaintive whine what she could do. Grinning, the woman winked at the youngster.

"First we get tu with child, then we get tu wed." Drawing deeply on her pipe, she waited for the inevitable question.

It took a moment for Rosa to muster the courage to point out the flaw in her plan but as soon as she replied, she knew she'd been tricked into speaking by her grandmother's still widening grin.

Cackling quietly to herself, May Easton elaborated. "Tu listen well my ghel, a rom is a rom and the day one can best a chavi of me blood is the end of I." Leaning forward in her chair she rested an elbow on the arm of the chair and lowered her voice in case listening ears should pass her door. "Got an ale that'll make 'e perky. Feed him just one, then blow out the light and raise those skirts of yorn. Tu bend like a dog an' he'll not be thinking tu's a girl. He'll rut like a rabbit."

"Maw Nana! May be a dozen times afore his seed takes though." Dismally, Rosa sat back on her heels. Her puri-daj's idea had merit, Mickey might be fooled a few times but she knew he would get wise in time. Frustrated, the girl felt her sadness starting to return.

"Dinilo girl. Tu don't need months." Surprised at the naivety of the young, the older woman shook her head in disappointment, then spoke again to explain. "Take him once, next night, tell he tu carrying his chiavala. Men don't be knowing no more. They ain't as wise as they be thinking. Tu can do this iffen tu's my blood at all! His honour be seeing to the rest. Tu can be in his bed as rom and bori in days an' then tu got ways to make what was said into what is."

It seemed unlikely at first hearing but the more Rosa thought her grandmother's words through, the more she began to see it could work. There was a flaw in it all though.

"I can't be getting alone Nana. Stevo watches me." With a new respect for the old woman, Rosa's intuition told her there would be a solution to the guardian of her virtue but she hadn't expected the answer she got.

The brewer's eyes hardened and an angry look crossed her face as she scowled. "I be seeing to the boy. Leaves him to me. Now get gone from me, your Nana needs rest."

May Easton leant back in her chair and closed her eyes, Rosa wondered if she had genuinely fallen asleep so quickly. It was hard to tell as the woman adopted the same pose and position most of the time. Still slightly under the influence of the drink, the girl managed to climb to her feet and had unbolted the door when behind her, her puri-daj spoke again.

"Come back at dusk, I'll have a bottle ready for your rom."

Chapter Twenty

With the washing up done and his mother resting in her easy chair in the living room, Tom loitered in the kitchen. It was unusual for the boy to go out on a Saturday evening and he was running excuses through his mind that he could use to escape the house. Nothing he thought of sounded credible and though he had kept his activities secret, he feared he was too transparent to fool anybody least of all his mother.

The washing basket between the sink and the rayburn caught his eye and he gave some thought to making a start on the laundry to save his mother tackling the extra chore. The actual washing wouldn't take longer than half an hour but putting it through the mangle in the garden would take much longer. Tom decided against it but chose to clear away the cutlery and crockery so as to make the washing easier when his mother made a start on it.

Taking the last plate from the draining board he dried it and put it away, then sat at the table. Extracting his tobacco pouch from his pocket he unfolded the leather purse and poked into the tobacco for his papers and came out with a packet that held a single paper and he smirked to himself. He rolled a cigarette and put it between his teeth without lighting it.

Pushing the wooden chair backward, Tom rose and moved to the door to the living room. He leant against the door frame in what he thought was a nonchalant pose and struck a match to light his cigarette. Through the first flame of smoke, he called to his mother who opened her eyes from the light doze she had slipped into.

"I'm just going to head into town, I'm out of papers. Did you want anything?" He waited for a response and Mary smiled in her cushioned seat.

Twisting in her seat the woman shook her head and said she was fine for now. Tom nodded and left the room again and his mother's smile became a grin. All the shops would be closed and the only place Tom would get papers was going to be the pub. Mary wasn't as naïve as she let her son think. She hadn't forgotten the passionate teeth-marks visible at the base of the boy's neck but if he wanted to pretend he didn't have a girlfriend, she wasn't going to call him on it.

Closing the door behind him, Tom nodded to his neighbour mowing his lawn and tracked to the end of the path and at the end of the garden, he started the long trek down the hill.

At the bottom of the hill where the track joined the main road to

Petersfield, Tom's grin slipped as he began to examine the practicality of finding Mickey among the expansive camp of the gypsies. If he'd known he would be returning so soon he could have arranged to meet the youth somewhere but the thought hadn't occurred to him.

Tom had never fallen easily into friendships and he was alert to the fact he had only known the gypsy since the preceding afternoon. Letting his memory entertain him, he found his thoughts revolving around their last meeting and he blushed furiously. It was illegal, it was immoral and it was completely alien to him but it had felt right. Sense told him he should stay away from the gypsy camp but he felt a need to be with the young gypsy that he couldn't explain.

Though his childhood hadn't been strict and his visits to church were restricted to Sunday service and a rare family event, Tom couldn't equate his feelings with anything he had experienced before. His heart told him it was love but his upbringing told him love was between a man and a woman.

Tom paused at the junction, a contented smile on his face and wondered if it really mattered. Too many years had passed without friendship for him to worry what feelings meant. Mickey was a pleasure to be around and he seemed to think the same.

Continuing along the Petersfield road and turning down the track to the bridge, the youth knew he couldn't bypass the camp. The approach from the road would take him directly to the site and the only way he could circle the camp would be to head to the left; that would leave the river between himself and his objective.

Resigned but not unduly concerned, Tom continued along the road. He may have not received a warm welcome from other gypsies but he'd not encountered the hostility he had been expecting. If his reason for visiting were generally known, he knew the attitudes of the Romany may change but he wasn't going to tell and it seemed a certainty Mickey would say nothing either.

The camp came into view and once more, Tom marvelled at the intense concentrations of bold colours. There seemed to be a delight in the community to make even the most basic item something of beauty. Aside from Miss Corbett at the library, Tom hadn't heard anybody speak of the gypsies with anything other than loathing.

They smell, they're dirty, they're thieves and tricksters. Tom knew different. The children were dirty it was true but it was an honest dirt that he'd seen mother's clean away in moments. If anything, the gypsies seemed cleaner than most of the people he knew and the woodsmen he worked with smelt worse than anybody he'd encountered in the camp.

Whether they were the thieves and conmen the locals believed Tom couldn't comment but he'd had Mickey in his home and the boy hadn't taken anything except the beer he'd been given. The town was dismissive of the gypsies and yet, when they needed some copper pot patched, they turned to them, when they wanted a fortune told, they sought them out. It transpired most homes had positive contact with the Romanies and yet they shunned and disparaged them at every turn. It was small wonder Mickey's father hadn't trusted him with a coin when he'd had need of oil.

Walking off of the road and onto the flattened grass of the meadow, Tom tried to be discrete and circle the camp by following the course of the river. Through a gap between tents and wagons, he caught sight of a small group of young children playing a game in the dirt he couldn't identify.

While he stood and watched, two men stopped beside the children and as one sat in the dirt with them to join their game, the other swooped in and caught up a giggling boy of three or four years old and threw him into the air, catching him as gravity took hold and hugging him close.

The lilting, unintelligible words of his speech came to Tom and he smiled at the clear delight the man was sharing with the youngsters. Envy stabbed at the youth as he watched the fun they were sharing and he thought back to his own childhood.

Martin Quatrell had loved his son and Tom knew that now as much as he had then. There was a huge contrast in the way that love had been shown though. He had been hugged if pained and he didn't doubt the affection his father had for him but Tom had no instances of the unconditional expression of love he could see with the family he was spying on. The gypsies didn't care who watched and gave no thought to what others thought; family was everything to them.

The sadness of his own childhood was balanced by Tom's witnessing of how a childhood could be and he knew he was smiling as he watched the adults roll in the dirt with their children as if there was nothing more important than their happiness. Tom lived in the real world, the gypsies lived in Narnia; he envied them.

Continuing forward and alternating his gaze from his feet to the trees that stood ahead of him where they hung over the river, Tom made a casual, carefree approach. He was heading toward the point of the river where he had been led by the young gypsies earlier. There was no assumption on his part that he would find Mickey there but it seemed sufficiently distant to the camp to not seem an intrusion.

At the bush he'd been pulled through by the teenage girl, Tom stopped and stared. There was no sound beyond it except for the sound of the flowing water as it rushed by just out of sight. Probability told him even if there was anybody sat on the bank behind the bush, it was unlikely to be Mickey. Hoping none the less, Tom reached forward and grasped a large branch of the bush and pulled it to the side and stepped through.

The bank was deserted and though he felt a little disappointed, the boy still kept smiling. He lowered his head and chuckled quietly as he realised he had been smiling a lot recently. The weekdays of frowning and fear seemed a world away. There was a comfortable familiarity with his surroundings and he knew much of it was due to the memories associated with the places he visited.

Releasing the branch of the green leafed bush, he swore as the supple limb sprang back to its former position and smacked him in the face. Laughing to himself at the idiocy of his own action he put a hand to his cheek and was reassured when it came away without any trace of blood.

Moving to stare back at the camp he spotted the young teenager who had led him to the same spot earlier. Ruby was a dozen yards further along the river bank and he scoured his memory for her name as he walked toward her.

"Hey there!" Tom called softly.

Ruby had been kneeling on the grass plucking wild daisies and hadn't seen Tom but when he spoke to her, she looked up and her eyes went wide. She stood up and turned to face him, then she slowly stepped backward away from him.

Tom held his hands out to his side to appear as harmless as he could. "Remember me?"

The girl backed away a little further, then shaking her head while holding his gaze, she turned and ran back to the gypsy camp leaving a confused Tom behind. The girl had seemed terrified and the youth couldn't understand the total change in her attitude.

Caught between wanting to pursue the teenager to find out what he must have done and fearing what her reason could be, Tom simply stood rooted to the spot as he watched the red and yellow of her clothes appear and disappear as she weaved between caravans and tents.

Losing sight of Ruby, the young man frowned and began to cautiously follow the path of the river behind the camp. Careful to avoid being seen but taking extra care not to seem as though he was sneaking, Tom passed another hundred yards before he encountered anybody else.

Approaching a bend in the waterway, the sound of laughter came to Tom, splashing accompanied the sounds of joy and summoning his courage, the outsider rounded the line of trees to see what was occurring. The river widened where the land flattened out and a small cluster of gypsies where gathered at the edge of the water.

Children were being grabbed by adults as they ran out of the river and the three men barring the way to dry land would hoist the youngsters to their shoulders, hold them firmly, then rush forward and throw the escaping children far out into the river where they would splash furiously before swimming back to the bank to try and get past the men again.

As one of the youngsters splashed out of the river he stopped dead in his tracks when he caught sight of Tom. The child pointed at him and when he spoke to the adults, Tom caught the word 'Gorgio' but none of the rest of his words. All eyes turned to him and his smile faded as he sensed the hostility of the crowd. Even the children still in the water stared in his direction and Tom was tempted to turn away and retreat but one of the men spoke directly to him.

"Tu dihkin' a Mickey? Tooti Mickey's didikai?" The man was huge. He was likely only five years Tom's senior but he towered over the youth as he stepped closer. Bare chested and with biceps that made the woodsmen he worked with seem puny, Tom swallowed and unconsciously took a step backward.

The youth's grasp of language took a moment to engage and he finally registered a few words. "Looking for Mickey?" Tom echoed. "Yes, arvah. Mickey!"

The man beamed and beckoning Tom forward, he switched his attention back to the children and yelled something at them that Tom couldn't decipher and they resumed their play. Still wary, Tom approached the man.

The hulking giant threw an arm around Tom and steered him toward the edge of the water. Thinking he'd misjudged the situation,

Tom was convinced he was about to be thrown in the river with the children but as he felt his toes grow wet where his shoes let in the water, the man turned him again and faced him further along the river.

The man pointed down the gentle incline. "Atch arey baro rukh y ga adre wavver. Arvah?"

Frowning, Tom shook his head. The only word he'd understood had been when the man had asked him if he understood. The man laughed deep and loud and keeping his arm around the boy, he shook him hard as though they were sharing a great joke. Pointing again, he tried again in stilted, halting English. "Big tree. Arvah?" Tom nodded. The man swung his arm to his left, "Ga in wood. Arvah?"

Almost certain, Tom checked his understanding. "Turn left at the big tree and go in the wood? Mickey's there?"

The gypsy grinned and nodded, he released his meaty arm from the youth's shoulders and slapped him so hard on the back Tom fell forward and barely managed to stop himself from landing face first in the river. Laughing hard, the man said something to the other men with him and they laughed too. Unsure if he was the amusement or if he was part of the joke, Tom couldn't help but chuckle with them.

Steadying himself and traipsing out of the water, he started in the direction the bare chested man had indicated and then turned back to face him. He wanted to thank the man in his own tongue but he realised he'd never heard a gypsy thank anybody for anything.

Tom let his amusement drop from his face and as sincerely as he could, he inclined his head the way he'd seen Mickey do and held the gaze of the man until he nodded back. Satisfied he had acted in a way that caused no offence, the boy put his back to the gypsies and walked in the direction he had been given. Part of him wondered if he was being sent on a wild goose-chase for the entertainment of the gypsies but with no other information, he figured he had nothing to lose and went looking for the big tree.

Chapter Twenty-one

Mickey was perched on the same tree stump that had seen both passion and rage in the same day. A fire had been crafted in front of him and a skinned rabbit was turning on an improvised spit. Under normal circumstances he would feel guilty at being so unsocial but he justified his isolation with the assurance he wasn't good company today.

Rubbing his thumb across his lower lip he realised he had his thumb nail between his teeth and he hurriedly snatched his hand away and shivered. He rubbed his face with his hands and tried to shake away his distraction. Introspection wasn't something the youth often indulged in but few days had been as conflicted as this one.

Putting his hand in the small of his back he unclipped the sheath he had fastened to his belt and pulled his knife free. The blade was going to be needed for the rabbit but he took the sharp steel and began to pare his fingernails. He scraped the dirt from his cuticles where he had chased down and caught his tea, then he started to dig the black soil from under the nails. Once they looked reasonably clean, he began to trim the nails themselves.

Each splinter of nail he cut he threw into the flame of the fire before him. It was a habit deeply ingrained in the young gypsy. Nothing of the body was to be discarded, he didn't know the origin of the superstition but he was Romany, he didn't need to know, he just needed to follow tradition. Maybe he had an enemy who could work a spell with a clipping of his hair or nail and maybe he hadn't. It seemed an unnecessary risk to assume none would work magic against him simply because he was careless.

Turning his hands over, Mickey examined his trimmed nails and satisfied he hadn't missed any, he took his knife, upended it and thrust it hard into the wood of the tree stump on which he was sat. He leant forward and inspected the rabbit. Fat was dripping from the meat onto the flaming wood beneath it and he knew it was close to being cooked.

Hands were suddenly clamped over the gypsy's eyes and Mickey responded instinctively. Grabbing the wrists of the hands on his face, he ducked low and pulled his assailant over his shoulder. As his attacker thudded hard into the compacted dirt beside the fire, Mickey tugged his knife free and made to launch himself at the form anticipating where the person would make his stand.

In a defensive crouch, Mickey's brow furrowed as the body by the fire failed to rise as expected. His frown vanished in an instant as Tom groaned and remained immobile. Trying hard not to laugh, Mickey apologised. "Din't know it were tu!"

"Trust me, it won't happen again!" Tom slowly rolled to his stomach away from the fire. He groaned again and moving to a kneeling position, he put his hand behind himself and rubbed as much of his back as he could reach. "You gypsies really need to relax more!"

Mickey returned to his perch on the stump as Tom shifted to sit cross legged beside the fire. Tom was smiling, proud at his teasing comment. The gypsy had a sad detached air about him and Tom had a feeling he'd spoken out of turn.

"Had a cousin, few years back" Mickey began. "Were in woods not far out from Oxford. He was sat alone much like this, minding his own." The gypsy sighed and glanced up at the tree canopy above him. "Two days he were gone. Turned up on the road outside camp." Mickey slid forward off of the splintered wood and shuffled closer to the fire, he lifted the spit from the wooden support he had fashioned. "A beating wouldn't have been too bad." Avoiding eye contact, Mickey picked a sliver of meat from the rabbit and stared into the flames of the fire. "They cut him bad and left him to die. If not for the finding of him afore dawn, he'd not have lived."

Tom sat in horrified silence, his mouth was open and he could feel the hurt in the voice of the young gypsy opposite him.

Mickey raised his face and caught Tom's eyes, holding his gaze. He said nothing more, nothing more needed saying. He held the spit out to his friend and released it when Tom took the heavy stick from him. The boy stared at the rabbit and despite the pleasant aroma, he'd lost his appetite.

"I'm sorry!"

"Why? Weren't tu?" Mickey replied in a flat voice taking the rabbit back when it became apparent the youth had no interest in the food.

Sitting quietly and beginning to understand why the gypsies were so unwelcoming of outsiders, Tom knew he couldn't take Mickey to task for having reacted how he had. He'd thought it amusing to creep up on the gypsy but now he realised how stupid he'd been. "I'm still sorry none the less."

Wriggling where he sat, the young gypsy managed to reposition himself so he could sit on the ground and lean back against the stump that had been his seat. With an elbow behind him and the rabbit held firm on the spit, he brought the meat to his face and chewed at his hastily prepared meal. The fat from the rabbit dripped down his chin as he bit into it and while he chewed, he wiped his face with his sleeve.

"Wouldn't have thrown had I know it were tu." Mickey said.

"Tu knows that?"

The youth nodded impassively recognising the hint of an apology as being the best the gypsy would ever manage.

A few more strands of flesh were pulled from the spit whilst Mickey continued to watch his friend sit in an uneasy silence. The pair of them exchanged glances that slowly evolved from a terse distance to a shared amusement at the circumstance they found themselves in. Wordlessly the pair changed gear and the frowns gave way to evasive smiles and subdued chuckles. Neither was angry with the other and each was able to identify the uncomfortable silence as being of their own making and the longer they avoided speaking, the more amused they became.

Tom was casting glances around the clearing while biting his lower lip to prevent the smile he could feel from becoming apparent. Consciously he avoided looking in Mickey's direction but when he did occasionally let his eyes wander toward him, he noted the gypsy boy was acting in exactly the same manner.

Clambering awkwardly to his feet with his hands still occupied with the roasted fare of his tea, Mickey walked to the edge of the clearing and slid the carcass from the stick he'd been using to cook the meat on. Hefting the bundle of meat covered bone in one hand, he tossed it a dozen feet into the denser part of the forest where it vanished into a bramble patch. He tossed the greasy stick after it and turned back to the fire. Tom's curious eyes finally caught his own and he said "For the foxes."

Uprooting the two forked posts he'd used as a support for the spit, Mickey threw them after the carcass and turned his attention to the fire. The flames had burnt down low but the wood was still red with the heat and he knew better than to leave it alight. Unbuttoning his fly, the gypsy made to put the fire out by urinating on it but he was too aware of Tom's eyes on him. "Can't go with tu watching!"

Tom began to laugh, then hurriedly clamped his own hand over his mouth. Still staring at the gypsy and his inability to put the fire out, Tom couldn't help himself. "Shouldn't you be pointing that downward?"

Spluttering partly in embarrassment and partly with shared humour, Mickey raised his face skyward and tried to clear his mind. When Tom asked if he needed a hand he looked directly at the boy and considered a dozen different replies but eventually he simply gave up, redressed himself and with rare restraint, said nothing as he tried to kick dirt over the fire instead.

The ground was too compacted for the gypsy to smother the fire with earth and he surrendered to the fact he couldn't extinguish the small pyre. Shaking his head, he returned to the stump and sat down once more.

"I don't believe it!" Tom said, a grin plastered across his face.

"Is the gypsy actually blushing?"

Mickey clasped his hands to his face, the harder he tried not to let his embarrassment show, the more his cheeks flushed. Even with his weathered and tanned skin, it was apparent the youth was colouring. "Feck orf! Tu's not funny!"

Tom shifted back to his knees and shuffled toward the tree stump and the gypsy. He reached out and took Mickey's hands in his own and gently lowered them to reveal his shy grin and red cheeks. He put his own hands over Mickey's cheeks and held his face so the youth had no choice but to gaze back at the eyes of his tormentor.

"Tu's happy now?" Mickey asked, still trying to keep the humour in the situation.

Tom stared deep into the gypsy's dark eyes and for a moment he said nothing. The boy had always been timid around others, boldness wasn't for him, he wasn't the type to initiate conversation but around Mickey he felt more comfortable than with anybody else he knew. The grin on his face dropped away and he cocked his head to one side. "Arvah Mickey" he said mimicking the tone he'd heard the Romanies use. "I'm as happy as I've been."

The gypsy blinked and he grew as serious as the gorgio before him. Tom leant forward and kissed Mickey; initially the young man responded in kind but then, he pulled away from him and turned his head away. "Can't be doing this" he whispered. "Tu an' I, we got no future. Can't be doing this!"

Tom kept his hands on the youth's face and Mickey did nothing to pull further away. The gypsy's words hurt but he understood him, he understood much better than he wished. "What if we have?" His voice was scarcely a breath on the wind and it prompted the gypsy's head to snap back up and looked at the youth with a puzzled expression. "What if we made our own future Mickey? What if we just ran away, just you and me?"

"Tu ain't understanding." Mickey took Tom's hands from his face and lowered them. Gripping his wrists tight he kept the youth from touching him, he eased his grip and gently began to caress his palms with the tips of his fingers. Under his breath the gypsy quietly muttered for the youth's ears alone "Dordi Tom, mira mora, mira rinkeni rom." He took a deep breath in and let it out slowly as he shook his head, his eyes staring down where he held the boy's hands in his own.

"I don't know what you're saying" Tom said, a moistness coming to his eyes at the feel of the words on his soul. "We can do this, we can make it work. I know it's not just me, I *know* it. Tell me you don't feel for me like I feel for you?"

The gypsy chose not to translate the Romany words he'd uttered. It was enough for him to have said them and had he been overheard, they would have been enough to damn him to the community he called his family. Releasing Tom's hands he managed to turn away from the youth and rubbed at his own eyes. His distress at the situation was every bit as painful as Tom's but he understood the world better than the youngster who had grown up sheltered from the harshness of reality.

"Ain't so easy Tom, ain't simply what tu want and what me wants." Mickey stood and paced slowly around the fire as he tried to explain. "Could tu leave your daj? Your ma? Could tu?" The gypsy shook his head. "What she wi'out tu?" Again he shook his head. "What of me? Never mind the gavvers, never mind what's law. What of being hunted by mine? Familia wouldn't just let us go. Better dead than..." Mickey left the sentence unfinished.

"We could live like this!" Tom gestured to the clearing the fire still burning between the two of them. "You know how to live wild, you could teach me."

A pleading tone had entered Tom's voice and Mickey began to imagine the picture the youth was trying to paint as he continued to talk of living as he'd read of in stories. Tom elaborated and the gypsy smiled as he saw the improvised tent they could build, more bivouac than anything more substantial but he could envisage the pair of them entwined together as night fell. Hunted meats and scavenged vegetables for their fare and travelling at dusk and dawn to keep ahead of any that hunted them. It was an appealing fiction but

Mickey knew more than his friend. There would be winters when food was scarce and the cold could not be banished with a simple fire. An injury could lay one of them so low they would need the wisdom of the women that Mickey hadn't learnt. Sickness could take Mickey for a fortnight and without his skills, the pair of them would starve before he got well. There was a temptation though, even knowing all that could be risked, the thought of being himself for once nearly swayed the gypsy and with his eyes on the man before him, Tom knew it was what Mickey wanted.

"We could make it together Mickey, you and me, we could make our own future."

The final words were whispered in his ear and Mickey opened his eyes from the shared daydream to find Tom stood directly before him. The two young men were close enough that the buttons of their shirt touched. Raising his hand, Mickey ran his fingers through the hair of the boy before him and despite knowing the fantasy they had just created could be nothing more than that, Mickey couldn't bear to shatter the moment. Leaning his head forward, he kissed Tom who had been waiting for just that. Passionately they embraced and though the gypsy knew he was encouraging the lie, he needed the youth this one time. Later he would break his heart but he would do it with the memory of a moment that would always stay with them.

Chapter Twenty-two

Tom was grinning when he'd left Mickey sleeping in the wood and as he skirted the gypsy camp following the river back the way he'd come, he was still grinning. Mickey hadn't said no to his idea of the two of them running away together and the youth was imagining the fun they would have making camps of their own, just the two of them.

It'd be like the Boy's Brigade he'd been a part of for two brief months some years earlier. The war hadn't been over more than a year and he'd joined just as he'd completed his eleven-plus but before he'd gained his results. He hadn't exactly made any friends but there were a few boys there he'd got along well enough with to make the summer camp they'd shared an enjoyable experience. Remembering the time now, Tom realised it was the last time he could actually remember being truly happy.

It was the first time he had met Paul Smith and the pair of them had enough in common that the differences they had were of little consequence. Put together in the same tent, they'd smuggled stolen chocolate from the camp store into their tent and had eaten so much they'd felt sick for hours but neither of them regretted it.

Thinking back, Tom started to wonder if he had more in common with the twelve year old than he'd originally thought. It had been the older boy who had suggested they both cuddle together for warmth under the same blanket and though nothing had happened, Tom only now remembered that Paul hadn't been able to keep still and he'd made a lot of quiet noises as he'd fidgeted and explained his pyjamas were uncomfortable.

Tom stopped dead in his tracks as he the recollection of the older boy stripping naked under the blankets suddenly came back to him. Frozen to the spot, the youth finally realised the truth of that night and he couldn't believe it had taken seven years to gather what Paul had been doing.

Wondering if he'd had the knowledge then that he had now would have changed anything, Tom began to wonder what had happened to the boy. They'd lost touch as soon as Tom had left the Brigade. The friendship was based on the fact they were both only children and had both lost their fathers but the only other thing Tom could recall was that Paul came from a village that was quite a few miles from Midhurst.

Maybe if he hadn't been accepted into grammar school, Tom

would have kept going to the Boy's Brigade but he hadn't been able to keep it going with the homework he'd been given. It wasn't the only reason he'd left, he could be honest about that now. His mother didn't know but even in the Brigade his education was beginning to set him apart from the others and with the exception of Paul, nobody treated him the same.

Tom hadn't thought of Paul Smith for a very long time but he wished only good things for the boy. He'd scarcely given him a thought over the years but now he felt the loss more than he could rationalise.

Shaking the past away with a chuckle and a smile, Tom started back on the track the gypsy's had worn alongside the river and suddenly halted again as he spotted a figure under the shadow of an overhanging branch. Whoever it was stood completely motionless and he had to peer hard to be sure there really was somebody there. It was gradually growing dark and Tom figured the time must be close to nine o'clock. He was going to have to get a move on if he planned to be home before night had properly set in.

"Hello?" Tom called as he ducked his head to peer at the figure ahead of him. "Who's that?"

From the darkness under the heavy bough, Rosa stepped out on to the track and slowly walked toward the gadjo. "Where's Mickey?"

Tom breathed a sigh of relief. "You made me jump" he said. It's

Rosie isn't it?"

The girl slowed her approach and asked again where Mickey was.

"He's in the wood back there" Tom said, indicating behind with a nod of his head. "He's asleep." There was something about the woman that unnerved the young man but he couldn't determine what it was. Halting himself, he waited for her to come to him.

Even with the dullness of twilight Tom should have noticed the scowl on the young woman's face but after such a positive day he didn't entertain the idea a gypsy could mean him ill. "Name ain't Rosie, it's Rosa" the gypsy girl said. "An' Mickey's mine not yorn!"

She punched Tom hard in the stomach and as he doubled over, she raised her knee hard and fast to smash against his descending face. Just as the first blow had doubled him over, the second straightened him back up just in time for her to throw another closed fist into his face.

Tom's hands rushed to his face as pain burst across his vision. Rosa swept a foot behind the youth's ankles and pushed him so he fell on his back. She launched herself and landed astride him, sat on his lap with a hand pressing him down on his chest, her weight heavy on him as she leaned forward.

Staring up into the shadowed face above him, all Tom could see was a wild tangle of long hair as it hung down toward him and the silhouette of the figure that held him pinned to the earth. With her knees across his elbows, he couldn't move but he bucked uselessly a few times before he felt something sharp at his throat.

Gripping the hilt of the six inch blade in her right hand, her left still pushing down on his chest, Rosa raised the knife from under his chin. Twisting the steel in the fading light, she turned it so the gadjo gained a clear view of the metal. At the sight of the knife, Tom froze in his feeble attempt at shifting the woman from him.

Once more the blade was moved to contact with the boy's throat, held lengthways he could feel the sharp edge and felt it sting as he involuntarily swallowed.

Rosa shifted further forward, her weight pressing on his groin as she crossed an arm and leant herself low across the body of the outsider. Bringing her lips close to his, she retained her hold on the leather wrapped hilt and whispered to Tom. "He's my rom and tu ain't going to claim him. Tu understands me?"

Unable to nod for fear of the knife at his throat and too scared to speak, Tom simply stared upward.

"Stay avree from my Mickey or I chin tu. I cut tu, make tu dead." Rosa raised the blade from the boy's neck and expecting him to make some kind of defence, she wrapped her fingers tighter around the handle to form a hard fist and punched him once more in the face.

Though still conscious, Tom was too dazed to acknowledge the girl had climbed from him and vanished back among the trees. Sitting up on the dusty track, the youth put a hand in the dirt behind him to steady himself and felt the injuries the gypsy woman had caused. There was a bare scratch beneath his chin where the knife had cut him that bled less than he managed himself each morning with his razor and though tender, his cheek seemed unmarked. Touching his nose brought a rush of discomfort and the youth hissed through his teeth.

Gaining his feet, the young man staggered a little as he found his balance and he slowly and warily continued down the path he had been walking. Once out of the shadows of the trees he looked down. In the dim and disappearing light he could see the top of his shirt was darker than the cotton beneath it. Touching the fabric he felt the damp material and bringing his fingers to his face, he observed the tell-tale shimmer of blood.

Tom rubbed at his top lip to wipe away what blood he could, then over the next few paces his fingertips returned touched and retouched the bottom of his nose to determine if it still bled. Holding his fingers in front of his eyes he thought the black looking liquid was still flowing but he couldn't be sure.

The sound of a violin came from the centre of the gypsy camp and the youth turned at the unexpected melody that rang out sharply in rapid, staccato pulses before the notation lengthened and a tune began to sing through the tents and vardos. In other circumstances Tom would have wished to get closer to the music but for now, he was grateful for the entertainment that pulled the last of the Romanies from the bank of the river ahead of him into the camp.

Steering toward the vacated water, Tom stripped his shirt from his body and kneeling at the water's edge, he made the best attempt he could at rinsing the shirt clean. With the cotton saturated he brought the wet cloth to his face and wiped his cheeks and mouth, then delicately dabbed at his painful nose.

There was going to be no hiding the beating he had taken from his mother but he tried the best he could to lessen what must have looked terrifying. Satisfied he had done the best he could with his face, Tom returned his attention to the shirt. It was growing too dark to be certain but he thought he had washed the worst of the blood away. Once more he scrubbed the material against itself in the running river, then drawing it out again, he wrung as much water from the fabric as he could and pulled the cold cotton over his head and re-buttoned the shirt.

Returning to the path the youth walked the remaining distance to the road and turned right toward the bridge. A slight breeze was blowing and though it would speed the drying of the thin material, it chilled his body where the damp clothing clung to him.

Periodically testing his nose both to ensure the blood had stopped flowing and to check for a break, Tom was satisfied he had done all he could to hide the worst of the injuries he had suffered. His stomach hurt from the first blow Rosa had inflicted on him but though it hurt more than his face, it was not a worry to him. Considering loitering on the edge of the wood so as to ensure his mother turned in before he came home, Tom realised it wasn't going to work so easily. Mary Quatrell would stay awake until her son came home regardless of what time it may be.

Tom made his way up the hill to his home and hesitated at the gate into the small front garden. A faint flickering light shone out from the kitchen window but its glow was muted enough he was able to determine it was the light from the living room as the paraffin lamp burnt down low.

As quietly as he could, the youth raised the door catch and slipped into the kitchen. The radio in the living room was muttering in the otherwise silent house and Tom used the minimal light that shone through the door to examine his appearance. The shirt was not as clean as he had hoped and it was immediately apparent the stripes that ran down the material were blood.

Tom tiptoed across the room to the sink in the hope of washing his face in case he had missed any tell-tale marks but he did think it redundant when his shirt told the story so clearly. Reaching his hand to the tap he managed to stop himself in time. The pipework in the house was ancient and as soon as he turned the tap, the clattering of the tank and subsequent roaring of water running through the house would announce his presence as thoroughly as a fanfare.

Giving thought to his situation the youth looked for the dishcloth thinking to let it serve as a flannel but remembered he had dropped it in the laundry basket after he had finished washing up. Peering around the sink, he spotted the laundry basket still full and frowned. It was unlike his mother to not have done the washing but Tom felt his luck begin to change as he spotted his work shirt sitting on top of the pile. Shrugging himself out of his bloodstained shirt he tucked it beneath the mass of clothing and drew his work shirt on instead.

From his reflection in the window he couldn't be sure but he felt he might survive a cursory inspection. Bracing himself, he moved to the living room door and peered in on his mother.

Laughing quietly to himself, Tom couldn't believe his devious efforts had been wasted. His mother was sat in her chair just as he'd left her. Her head was leant to one side and a magazine was sitting partly open on her slippered feet where it had slid from her lap when she had fallen asleep.

Debating with himself as to whether to wake her or to leave her comfortable in her chair, Tom took the selfish decision to let her sleep where she was. It was possible by morning his injuries wouldn't be apparent as they seemed at the moment. Smiling to himself, he turned the oversized bakelite radio off and turned the control on the lamp down until the flame extinguished itself. In almost complete darkness, Tom crept from the living room to the kitchen and quietly made his way up the stairs to his bedroom.

Chapter Twenty-three

Mickey could feel a body pressed tightly against his back when he woke and he rolled over to wrap an arm around Tom and hugged the form tightly. He opened his eyes and was shocked to find Rosa's eyes gazing into his own. He swallowed and forced a smile on his face to hide his surprise.

"Want to wake to tu everyday Mickey" Rosa whispered. "Don't rightly care if it be under a vardo, a bender, canvas or just patrin like now." She snuggled close to the young man and her arm snuck beneath his and she held him as tight as he had first held her.

"Time will see what time sees Rosa."

Glaring at the gypsy's evasion, the girl lowered her head and pressed her forehead against his chest so he didn't see the anger and wistful sadness in her eyes. She stroked her fingers along his shirt, feeling the muscle that protected his ribs. The feel of him caused her mixed emotions to falter and before she knew it, she felt content again. Part of her still wished to rant at him and to tell all she knew of the gadjo and their time together but she wasn't willing to spoil the moment.

It was a complicated situation the pair of them found themselves in but Rosa was sure of herself. Once she was married to Mickey she knew she could make him happy. There was nobody else for her and she knew, much as he didn't, she was the only one for him too. When they were wed he'd come to see that. What could a man offer him that she couldn't?

The young man rolled backward and Rosa reluctantly released her hold on him. Settling on his back and staring up at the leafed canopy above him, he tucked his hand under his head and tried to ignore the girl's hands as she traced patterns across his chest through his shirt.

The young gypsy's thoughts were tied to Tom. His mind wasn't on the touch and feel of each other but on the preceding conversation. The fantasy the boy had spoken of had more appeal to him with the rising of the sun than it had the evening before. There were serious risks involved in the two of them running away, not least the very real possibility of every gypsy hunting them. The more the gypsy gave thought to the idea, the more the romanticism appealed to him.

Mickey sighed deeply and Rosa felt his chest rise and deflate dramatically. "So tu thinking?"

Wondering how much he could or should admit to his promised, the youth sighed again and opened his mouth to speak, then clamped his lips together again.

"Rocka Mickey, tell me."

Closing his eyes, Mickey lifted his hand to his own chest and took hold of Rosa's pushing his fingers between hers to hold her hand under his own. "Wanting tu for to be happy Rosa. Want it bad but... not sure it being me that can do that for tu." Waiting on a reaction, the youth expected either tears or rage but neither happened. Without moving, she quietly told him it wasn't for him to tell her what would make her happy.

Gypsy men had a reputation for being hard and unaccommodating. They were singular in thought and deed and life was lived in black and white. It was the image of every gypsy whether they were Romany or Irish and the reputation was merited. Gypsy lives were hard, from cradle to grave they fought for all they got and weakness wasn't something any was willing to show. It wasn't always so where Mickey was concerned and Rosa knew it better than any.

As good a show as Mickey made of being the perfect Romany, it was moments like this that the girl loved and hated. Rosa knew the world saw the boxer, the unrelenting warrior, the rock in the stream. Occasionally, only when they were alone, Rosa got to see the soft side of her man and even after years of these glimpses, she couldn't decide if they boded well or ill.

Part of the young woman wanted him to stay the perpetual Rom Baro, the certain successor of his father and yet, when she caught him in the rare moments when he let the façade slide, she knew she was privileged to see the real Mickey.

Rosa was tempted to tell her fiancé she could satisfy his wants without him needing to turn to a gorgio chava but she feared what she saw as honesty would be a match to dry kindling. She couldn't tell him as clearly as her puri-daj had told her, she only needed to kill the lights and raise her skirts and he could pretend she was whoever he wished her to be. The night before it had seemed such a solution and yet now, sober in the daylight, she didn't feel willing to be so dishonourable.

"I'd be happy by making tu happy Mickey. I *would* make tu happy." The gypsy winced as she heard the pleading in her own voice. She didn't want to beg but if it would have worked to meet her ends, she would have been willing to beg for him.

The man sighed again and squeezed her hand. "I knows Rosa, I knows." He spoke slowly and gently, it was clear it wasn't all he was thinking but he wouldn't be drawn beyond the little he said.

Raising herself onto her elbow, Rosa peered down at him and let her eyes roam over his face. It was rare to see him without bruises or cuts from his fighting bouts and she couldn't help but stroke his cheek. Mickey didn't look at her but kept staring upward, looking for patterns in the clouds through the dense leaves, seeking out some divine guidance in the cumulus that drifted in the summer breeze, the edges of the clouds lit gold by the rising sun.

He wanted to say something that might set the girl at her ease but he was so uncertain of what the future held. Over and over again he kept seeing the lightning card of his tarot reading. A secret revealed Sara had said. Was this that moment? Was this as far as his secret was going to be told? If more were to learn of his nature it would make running away with Tom his only option. Closing his eyes, he let Rosa continue to caress his face and when she moved and started stroking his hair, he relaxed and his breathing deepened.

Rosa continued stroking Mickey's hair until he fell back to sleep beside her. She took her hand away and sat up, cross legged beside him, she took a handkerchief from one of her pockets and wiped her eyes. It was clear from his changing moods the youth had no certainty about what he wanted from life and she felt sorry for him while also keeping an element of anger about herself.

The boy from the local village wasn't going to be a threat to her now, she'd made sure of that. There was no great pride in hurting the chava but she had done what she must and that knowledge gave her the assurance she needed that it had been the right thing to do. Still she wondered about the next time. The next village or the one after, there'd always be a risk another boy would try to steal Mickey from her unless she acted.

"Maw ghel" she hissed to herself, careful not to wake her man beside her. "Tu is Romany. Be Romany!"

Steeling herself for what she accepted she had to do, Rosa rose quietly and stood looking down on her promised as he continued to sleep. "I's doin' this for us Mickey" she said quietly. Clenching the handkerchief in her hand she balled a fist around the linen square. She turned back to the track that led away from the clearing that had seen so much activity over the past day and walked back toward the gypsy camp and the vardo of her puri-daj.

Chapter Twenty-four

The sound of the cheap steel hammer against the tin bell of his alarm clock woke Tom just after six o'clock and he knocked it to the floor as he fumbled for it from under his blankets. Still beneath the covers his bare arm reached under the bed and after a little aimless flailing, he caught hold of the clock and drew it under the sheets where he silenced the clatter by pushing the pin into the metal body.

There was a pause of inactivity before the youth finally threw back the covers and stood the alarm clock back on the bedside cabinet he'd knocked it from and swung his legs to the ground. Standing in just his pyjama bottoms, Tom stretched and grimaced as his stomach wall protested at the yellow bruise that pulled tight with his motion.

With a groan, the boy clasped a hand to the aching pain and the memory of his encounter with Rosa came back to him. Tentatively he put his fingers to the bridge of his nose and he gently pinched the cartilage between his thumb and finger, slowly moving down the length to the tip of his nose. It felt tender but seemed no more crooked than it had previously and he was surprised and reassured it didn't appear to be broken.

Starting with his hands on his cheeks he examined his face for injury as he crossed the room to the small mirror that sat behind the curtain on the windowsill. Parting the curtains with an extravagant swish that pulled again at his bruised muscles, he blinked in the bright sunlight that shone into the back bedroom of the house.

The mirror revealed dried blood under his nose that he suspected had bled again while he slept and one eye had a tinge to it that suggested it may turn black in time. It was surprising how little sign there was of the punishment he had received but he was relieved he wouldn't have to explain to his mother a broken nose, two black eyes and cuts to his face.

There was still going to be some explaining to do though as his mother had expected him to back much swifter than he had been. Putting the mirror back on the windowsill Tom tried to get an excuse ready to explain how it had taken three hours to walk to town to buy some rolling papers. Nothing came to mind.

With his bedroom door open Tom had expected to hear the tell-tale sounds of his mother washing clothes or sweeping the kitchen but the house sounded empty. Had his six o'clock alarm not gone off he may have thought it was later in the day than it was and that his mother could be pulling carrots from the vegetable patch; any earlier and he may have hazarded the unlikely guess that she was still asleep.

At the foot of the stairs he could see nothing had changed in the kitchen from the night before and was both puzzled and amused at the possibility he had managed to wake up first. Crossing to the living room door he peered into the living room and allowed himself a slight chuckle. He leant against the door frame and smiled, looking at his mother still sat in the chair exactly as he'd left her the previous night. Shaking his head softly to himself he tried and failed to lose his grin as he reached for his mother's hand to gently wake her.

Mary Quatrell's skin was limp and cold to the touch. Stone cold. Tom's cheerful smile dropped away and he called his mother's name as he gripped her hand more firmly. Reaching to her shoulder, he shook her, then called her name again, louder. Breathing hard Tom back pedalled in to the centre of the room and turned a full circle as confusion took a firm hold of him. He snatched at the curtains and in yanking them open, he exerted more effort than intended and ripped the left hand pole from its support leaving the drapes to hang at a crazy, skewed angle.

Light shone into the living room and onto the cold grey face of Tom's mother. Her eyes were open and unseeing and the muscles of Tom's jaw locked tight as he tried to keep control of himself in the worst of circumstances. Tears fell unchecked, they ran from his eyes, across his cheeks and tumbled from his jaw to spot the carpet where he stood firmly rooted.

With a long sniff he gazed to the ceiling and blinked hard before turning his attention back to the still form in the chair in front of him. He leapt forward and dropped to his knees at her feet, he clutched at her lifeless hand and cried her name again.

"Mum!" He wept, "Mum, wake up. Please."

Knowing it was futile, he continued to call her, he pleaded with her, blowing out his cheeks, he held his breathing in check then let it out again in an explosion of air. "Mum!" He wailed. Tom buried his head against his mother's breast as he continued to clasp her hand. Shaking her body with the tremors that passed through his own, he eventually pulled away and hid his own face in his hands and rocked on his heels. "I'm sorry, I'm so sorry" he cried.

Tom didn't know how long had passed, nor did he really care. There was no recollection of Percy Johnson arriving, he remembered nothing of being prised from the corpse of his mother by the elderly neighbour, neither was he aware of the doctor and Constable Matthews walking past him through the kitchen and returning a few moments later. The cup of tea that stood on the table in front of him had been cold for an hour. Tom had stared ahead at nothing, an echo of his mother's actions in the other room.

"She's got a brother" he muttered.

The policeman turned to the boy at the table and waved the other two men into silence. The question had just been asked of Mr Johnson if there was any family he knew of and as he'd shook his head, Tom had suddenly come to life.

Constable Matthews pulled the remaining chair out from under the kitchen table and dragged it across the tiled floor to rest it beside the shell-shocked boy. Lowering his bulk onto the wooden seat, the man indicated with a nod of his head for the doctor and the neighbour to step outside.

"A brother you say?" Matthews asked.

Tom nodded and lowered his eyes to the cup in front of him. His lips narrowed at the blue, willow pattern design. This is her cup. The youth trembled as he tried to contain a fresh outpouring of grief but he failed and a sob escaped him, his face screwing up at the hurt inside. "I'm sorry" he sputtered, briefly regaining his composure then ripping back into uncontrolled sobs, he gabbled an apology again before halting himself and turning his head away from the policeman. Dragging his bare arm across his eyes slowly, Tom grimaced and sucked air through his teeth as he fought to come to terms with his grief.

Ordinarily the policeman had little time for men in tears but he completely understood how the death of his mother had devastated the boy and though he wasn't good with compassion, he knew when to keep his mouth shut. Matthews nodded his sympathy and began to speak softly and without haste. "Your Mother been tired a lot lately? Coughing?"

Sniffing again, Tom nodded. Somehow the action of being questioned distracted him from his grief. "She works a lot; worked a lot" he corrected himself. "And she's had a cold, had it for weeks." The boy wiped his face again and tried to smile but it was a sickly imitation and he gave up on it immediately.

Putting both hands on the table in front of him, the youth placed a hand either side of the tea cup and cautiously slid it toward himself. "She wasn't ill though. She was fine last night." Tom lifted the cup and considered drinking the tea but the Japanese pattern caught his attention and he found himself staring at the blue bridge painted on the porcelain. He put the cup back down and sighed. "She was asleep in the chair when I came home."

Constable Matthews asked Tom what time that had been and the boy had told it was about ten o'clock. He bit his lip and wondered how much he should tell the boy. Doctor Beavis was of the opinion the woman had been dead since early evening which would have meant, the young lad had said goodnight to a corpse. Matthews knew he had no purpose in the house. The doctor had found a handkerchief that was stained with phlegm and blood clutched in her closed hand.

Although it wasn't a certainty that it was tuberculosis, the boys telling of her having been tired, out of breath and coughing for some time was enough to suggest it was likely an accurate diagnosis. It certainly wasn't a police matter.

"This brother" the policeman said, returning to the original topic rather than exploring the health of the boy's mother. "He'd be your uncle?"

Tom nodded, "I guess so. I don't think I've ever met him though."

Matthews asked if Tom knew where he lived but the boy wasn't able to provide any information other than the fact he existed. His name was either Robert or Rupert but even on that insignificant detail Tom wasn't certain.

Doctor Beavis stepped back into the house through the open kitchen door and beckoned to the policeman. Matthews excused himself and left the table to talk with the doctor; Tom wasn't trying to listen but he caught enough words to know a funeral director was on his way. Idly he wondered how things had been arranged so swiftly but he wasn't to know Mr Johnson actually had a telephone in his house.

"Have you got anywhere to stay Thomas?" Matthews asked.

Tom thought for a moment before replying that he'd stay where he was and he was then asked if any rent was due on the property.

Shaking his head the boy smiled as he realised the mustard yellow window frames identified his house as being part of the Cowdray estate. "Due at the end of the month" he said, then began to think about the practicalities of paying his way without his mother's income. Closing his eyes a moment, he opened them and consciously decided not to think about money for the time being.

"I'll be okay" he managed to say. He still hurt and he knew the pain wasn't going to go away any time soon but worrying would be no help to anybody.

Matthews stepped back to the table and held his hand out to the youth and they shook. "You might want to think about having a friend stay for a day or two" the big man said. "You're going to think you're doing fine for a while but trust me, nights are the hardest." The policeman walked to the door and almost as an afterthought, he told the youth to let him know if he needed anything. Leaving the door open, the constable stepped outside and Tom watched his helmet pass the window as he cycled down the garden path.

"The doctor's just left" a voice said from the doorway and looking up, Tom saw Mr Johnson standing silhouetted against the summer sunlight. "You're welcome to come round to mine until... well..." The man's speech dried up as he accepted the impossibility of finding a neutral way to describe removing the body of the dead woman from the living room. "Come round when you want Tom.

Okay?"

Tom nodded gratefully though he had no intention of taking the man up on his offer. He watched his neighbour walk past the window and cut through a gap in the boundary hedge between the properties, then he got up and closed the kitchen door.

Leaning against the door, oblivious to the latch pressing into his back, the youth scanned the kitchen from right to left and his eyes came to rest on the door to the living room. One of his visitors had closed it and Tom realised he'd never knowingly seen it closed before. It didn't seem right. He crossed the tiles and turned the handle to release the catch, then slowly pushed it open.

His mother and the chair she sat in were covered with a white sheet. Walking back into the room, Tom stopped beside the chair and considered uncovering his mother. It didn't seem right for her to have a sheet draped over her like a piece of forgotten furniture in an abandoned house. He chose to leave her covered but he couldn't have explained why.

Parts of Tom's mind were tormenting him. Guilt probed into his soul as he recalled numerous occasions recently when he had wanted a little more freedom than he had. Without direction, his thoughts turned to Mickey and he considered how free he had truly become. There was nobody to suspect why he was home late, nobody to make excuses to for wanting to leave the house unexpectedly, nobody to pressure him to go to church when he wanted to go elsewhere. Tom felt the tears return and he sighed; he wished there was somebody to stop him. Somebody to say no, somebody to take him places he didn't want to go.

Turning his back on his mother, Tom walked to the unmade fire and rested his fingertips on the mantle. Ignoring the lock of hair of his father, he turned his attention to the photograph. "Look after her Dad."

Thinking he was in control of himself, Tom was taken unaware by the cry that escaped him. He coughed out a sequence of racking choking sobs that stole his breath. As he knees gave out under him, he hit the floor and doubled over. Crying so hard as to be soundless, the only noise in the room was the intermittent gulp of air as Tom's body snatched breath where it was able.

Chapter Twenty-five

Mickey had been sitting with his back against the trunk of the tall oak tree with his legs astride a branch for over an hour and he was willing to admit, it wasn't as comfortable as he'd found it when he was ten. From his vantage point he could look down on a large portion of the camp to his left but his view to the right was obscured by more forestry.

Sleep had finally run away from him an hour before dawn and he'd been at a loss as to how to kill the time before Tom visited again. Waking to find Rosa had left him had left mixed feelings in his mind and he still wasn't sure what he should do with his future. The idea of leaving his extended family to run away with Tom was a daydream he kept revisiting but it was likely nothing more than a daydream.

It wasn't simply the harsh reality of a life in the wild through every season. Even the knowledge his family would send people to track him and drag him home wasn't the fear it should have been.

Mickey kept imagining how much suffering he would bring to those he loved.

The young man shuffled and swung one leg over the branch to sit more comfortably. Without the bole of the tree behind him he found his perch to be more precarious than he had anticipated. Glancing down through the branches beneath him he let a slow breath out and wondered how he had enjoyed the height and the risk when he had been younger. Deciding a lower branch would still permit him to watch the road for Tom's approach without surrendering his hiding place, he clambered awkwardly down first one limb, then another.

Where the branches grew denser the lower he moved, Mickey acknowledged his view was too obscured. With more relief than he was comfortable admitting, he swung from one branch to another, descending with each acrobatic swing. Setting his feet back on firm ground the youth pouted and with his eyebrows tight across his face he glared back up the oak. It was either the fault of the tree or changes in himself that made the memory of tree-climbing so disillusioning and as much as he wanted to blame the tree, he knew the truth.

"Feck it!" Mickey growled and surreptitiously skirted the undefined border of the wood toward the road to the town. It wasn't his intention to walk far, maybe just out of sight of his family where he could gain a little peace and think hard on what he really wanted from his troubled life.

The bridge over the River Rother was as good a place as he could think of to wait in the hope Tom was going to come looking for him. The young gorgio was going to expect a response and Mickey still didn't have an answer. Maybe the youngster had more of an understanding of what living rough entailed but Mickey didn't think so. Eighteen he may be but Tom lived in the fiction of the stories he read and knew so little of the real world.

Both youngsters may be of an age but there was an immense difference between them. Mickey had been an adult since he was thirteen and Tom still hadn't matured. The gypsy grinned as he mentally amended his thinking, some of the youth was sufficiently mature.

Alert to the movements around him, the young man halted as a deer skittered from a field onto the tarmac ahead of him and the youth froze as he watched. Deer was a treat he gained once in a while but he didn't think of this young doe as food. Halting in the centre of the road she turned her eyes to Mickey and he knew she would identify his silhouette as a threat and he fully expected her to dash away.

Struck by the beauty of the wild animal in front of him, Mickey held his breath as the naïve young creature ignored her instincts and slowly trotted toward him. Without a sound he waited for the doe to steer away from him and flee into the trees on the side of the road. The deer lowered her head as she approached and came so close he could have reached out and stroked her head.

The tap of her hooves slowed, then she halted and lowering her nose, she sniffed at his shoes for a moment before raising her neck and thumping her head gently into his stomach.

In his entire life Mickey had never encountered a wild animal so fearless. The doe turned away and trotted slowly away back to the field she had emerged from and left the gypsy alone again. Releasing the breath he had been holding in, Mickey rubbed a hand across his brow. Despite the cool start to the day, a sheen of sweat had formed and his fingers came away damp.

It was an omen, that much was apparent to the Romany but he had no knowledge if it boded well or ill. If this was the sign he'd wished for to determine what path his future should take, it didn't help.

Still with his eyes on the gap in the fence where the animal had appeared, the youth took a few more steps and sat on the grey stone wall of the bridge and marvelled at the bizarre nature of the event.

Maybe a lone young deer represented himself and it was a reassurance that survival was possible without family. Maybe the deer was Tom and the youth was at the gypsy's mercy. Mickey sighed as he tried to find meaning to what he was sure was a portent. The prevailing thought he had was that the deer had been so vulnerable and he identified with that far too closely. Chewing his lip he knew whatever the sign had been intended to convey, it had failed.

As unsure as he'd been before, the boy was more unnerved by the deer than reassured. The strange occurrence highlighted the importance of the decision he faced. Whatever future he chose would see people hurt. Staying with his family would hurt the least people but it would mean living his lie for the remainder of his life; he wasn't even sure it was the right thing to do for the sake of Rosa despite her assurance it was what she wanted.

Waiting on the bridge for Tom he began to doubt he was being wise in even that small action. Was he leading the youth down a path neither of them should be treading? If he put his mind to it, he could easily avoid the gadjo and the kumpania would be away from the area before the end of the week.

The work the local landholder had provided them with was a fraction of what they had come to expect. With the pheasant season scarcely more than a month away there where places they should be looking to head to. There was precious little to keep the camp where it was.

Knowing it wasn't sensible, Mickey took himself off the wall and turned to look up the incline toward the main road. He hesitated a moment, then stepped forward, heading toward the junction that would lead him to Tom's house.

Mickey loitered under a stand of beech trees fifty yards short of the house where Tom lived. It was apparent to him that if anybody passed they'd have assumed he was planning to rob one of the houses that sat behind the privet hedges opposite. It was the lot of the gypsies. There was an element of truth that crime rose in an area while gypsies camped nearby but Mickey was never aware of it being anyone he knew. Besides, there was such a defined sense of 'enemy', even the youth couldn't feel sympathy for people entombed in brick houses who valued possessions above family.

Trying to shake the intimidating feeling he encountered when he approached a permanent home, Mickey forced himself to walk toward the end house of the block of four. Thrusting his hands in his pockets to hide his trembling hands the youth puzzled at how he could face a tough and violent man in a fight but the manicured lawns and planted flowers of a garden made his blood run cold.

Fumbling with the gate catch, the gypsy managed to step into the grassed space split by a path of broken stone that led to the door of Tom's house. A man was stood in the bordering garden watching Mickey intently but the gypsy ignored him. On reaching the yellow door the young man struggled and considered what he would say if it was Tom's mother who answered his knock.

Having tapped the door and turned his back on it to stare at the swaying leaves opposite, Mickey eventually heard the catch click upward and he spun on his heel to face whoever had opened the door.

"Khul Tom" he growled, "Tu dihkin' dush!"

Alarmed at the state of his friend, Mickey lost his fear of the house and without giving thought to anybody else being in the building, he followed Tom into the kitchen when he backed away from the door.

Tom didn't speak at all but sank into the wooden chair as Mickey lifted the youth's head by tipping his chin upward. Familiar with the early signs of a fight, the gypsy knew from the swelling of the boy's nose and the dried blood beneath it that he'd taken a blow to the face. Even if he hadn't noted that, he would have been able to tell from the hint of blue forming at the soft tissue around the eyes.

"Amria! Kon did this? Who were it?" Mickey was filled with an undirected rage.

Calm but troubled, the white faced youth stared at the wooden grain of the table. He could have explained it was Rosa that had caused his injury, he could have made a story up. The truth was, he didn't give his appearance any thought. Maybe he could have used his injuries to try to win Mickey's support for the idea to run away. Shaking his head softly, Tom started to speak but his voice was a faint, unintelligible croak. Coughing to clear his throat, he again shook his head, then drank a mouthful of the cold tea from the cup in front of him and raised his bruised face to the gypsy.

"My mother's dead." The words were cold and impersonal. Detached from the emotions that had ripped him apart three hours before, Tom was quietly proud at his restraint and his ability to communicate clearly. It didn't last, he could feel the well of his tears filling again and he bowed his head back to the table.

Stunned at the words, Mickey was lost for something to say for a heartbeat, then he asked "What did tu do?"

The boy raised his eyes back to the gypsy, momentarily failing to comprehend the question. Then despite his hurt, he closed his eyes and grinned, shaking his head as an inappropriate laugh crept from him. "No!" His chuckle weakened and deteriorated into a fresh sob. Pushing his fingers hard against his eyes to suppress the teardrops he managed to smile again.

"This..." he gestured at his face, "this is something else." The boy blinked repeatedly, he had thought he was all cried out but despite learning there was more within him, he managed to contain his tears. "She's not been well... I didn't know. This morning..." Tom exhaled rapidly and gave up.

"I thought..." Mickey was annoyed with himself. Though he didn't want to give voice to his fear Tom had physically fought with his mother he'd already said enough to imply it and he felt both foolish and embarrassed. "Sorry!"

Leaning back in his chair, a hint of a smile still haunting his face, Tom gently waved his hand dismissively. In other circumstances he would have laughed hard and knew the gypsy would have soon followed suit. The loss of his mother pained him and he knew it would do so for a long time still to come but he was numb to it all at the moment. The grief was like a tide that washed in and overwhelmed him one moment, then it slid away and a false belief of having accepted it came in the lull of his emotions.

The young gypsy sat at the table and leaning forward, he took Tom's hands in his own as he stretched across the wood to reach him. Neither youth spoke; there was nothing to be said. The two boys were silent but each consciously ran conversations through their minds. Mickey measured the words he felt he should say against those he wanted to convey and Tom considered sharing his own guilt about his mother's death. Rationally, Tom knew he had done nothing to contribute to the tragedy but a small voice kept surfacing to remind him of the freedom he had wished for suddenly being a reality.

Mickey broke the silence first. "What now?"

Unsure what the gypsy meant, Tom hesitated to ask if he was referring to their relationship or if he was meaning something more practical. The youth shrugged his shoulders and pulled his hands from Mickey's grip. Mickey released him and looked on as the boy stood up and crossed the kitchen to the living room door. Standing in the doorway with his back to the kitchen, Tom stared at the small room before him, his eyes focussed sadly on his mother's chair.

Mickey's hand on his shoulder caused him to jump and he glanced to the man beside him who had snapped him from his reverie. "Have you thought anymore about what I was saying last night?"

Nodding, Mickey looked into the room with the youth. He tilted his head to lean it against Tom's and he shifted his hand on his shoulder to encircle the boy's waist. "Ain't sure on it Tom. Really ain't sure." He gave the youth a one armed hug meant to soften his words. "Ain't sure this be the time neither."

Tom walked away from the teenager into the living room. Coming to a stop behind the high-backed chair of his mother he picked strands of loose hair from the white square of cloth that rested at head height and carelessly dropped them to the carpet.

"Might be the best time to talk about to be honest" the boy said as he changed his actions to lightly scrape a nail across the material of the seat. "I can't afford to keep this place on my wages. Either I move or... or I find somebody to share the rent with me."

It was more than a hint. Mickey fell quiet again, his breathing was soft and shallow as he absorbed the full weight of what the youngster was implying.

Tom kept his gaze lowered, his eyes focussed on the trivial detail of the weave of the fabric he idly scratched at. The youth didn't see the young man shudder at the idea. It wasn't simply the thought of relinquishing his freedom to travel, Tom was asking the gypsy to break with tradition and belief he had lived with his entire life. Brick and stone was a greater prison than any bars could make and the knowledge of maybe not just one spirit being tied to the house but two was enough to send Mickey from the room.

Concerned he had spoken with too much haste, Tom slowly moved to follow his friend to the kitchen but as he looked through the living room door he couldn't see him. It wasn't until he stepped fully into the kitchen he saw him sat on the step with the front door open. The eighteen year old sat between Tom's world and his own.

"Have you got a cigarette?" Mickey asked.

In a bowl on the windowsill Tom found his tobacco pouch and was about to open it when he realised he never had got around to renewing his papers. Beside the bowl was the ashtray his mother habitually used and sat inside it were her packet of Players. Pausing long enough to scratch an imagined itch at the back of his head, the boy made a decision and picked the packet up and drew two filter tipped cigarettes out and moved to sit himself down beside Mickey.

It was a tight squeeze for them both to sit side by side in the doorway but neither of them complained. Tom lit his own cigarette, then held the match for Mickey to light his too. Mickey wrapped his hand around Tom's and held it steady as he drew the flame through the tobacco until satisfied it was lit. Releasing the boy's hand he turned his face back to the garden and stared at the organised rows of plants and blew a stream of smoke toward them that dissipated a scant few feet from his mouth.

"Ain't an answer but... don't be reckonin' I's could be living here." Mickey said eventually. "For all I'd like to be wit' tu, I couldn't share a house with the dead. Not for nothing." The youth continued to elaborate, trying to explain the fear any house instilled in him, the feel of being caged and not being among nature. When he ventured back to explain in a small way how his people considered the dead, he made it clear his mind was made up.

"You mean they get rid of everything?" Tom asked, still trying to grasp that the Romany were more superstitious than he had ever imagined.

Mickey explained again about the death of a gypsy, everything that belonged to the deceased was either sold to gadjos, or burnt. It was considered bibaxt, bad luck for anything to be kept. "Yes" he admitted, "the bibaxt may go to them as buy but, they's looking to profit from t' dead. Why should we's be worryin' for they? They makes their choices."

Tom screwed his face up "Even the caravans?"

The gypsy grinned and rolled the cigarette between his fingers. "A vardo is different. I'nt something that's owned. Leastways, ain't owned by one; family own a wagon. Might be as the bed is burned but don't often happen much that the vardo gets lit." Mickey paused thoughtfully. "Sometimes though, like with Sara. When time comes as she be a mulla, odds be she'll be set in her bed an' 'er vardo be burned."

Choosing to ignore the idea that the gypsies would burn one of their caravans with the occupant still inside, dead or not, he pointed out the tarot reader lived in a tent.

The gypsy laughed. "She don't live in that. That's just where she does her reading!" He shook his head in amusement. "Kek, she's a big Romany, a baro romina. Day comes as she dies, there be a great pomana; singing, dancing. Come the end, she'll get a mighty pyre an' a send off the likes the gypsies ain't seen in a long while."

Tom was both horrified and envious. It sounded both barbaric and beautiful and he couldn't decide if perhaps they had the right of things after all. Tom drew a final drag on his cigarette and leaning forward, he stubbed the butt out on the step and glanced at what remained of the smoke Mickey was savouring. He felt a pang of guilt in that he'd inadvertently caused Mickey to go against his own beliefs in giving him a cigarette from the dead but he certainly wasn't going to mention it.

Silence fell between the two youths again. Mickey was well aware he still hadn't answered Tom's implied question fairly. The youngster had intimated he wanted Mickey to move into the house with him and he'd managed to explain in a way Tom could accept that he wouldn't be doing that but he hadn't elaborated about the idea of running away together.

Time was running out for the gypsy to decide but he was no surer today than he had been yesterday. For Tom everything that had tied him in one place was gone from him but it did nothing to help Mickey; all the day had brought was added pressure. Yesterday if he had said he was staying with the Familia, Tom still had a home and a family to retreat to; knowing Tom no longer had that option would make a refusal so much harder.

The truth was Mickey did want to leave with Tom but whatever choice he was to make would destroy somebody he loved.

Chapter Twenty-six

The long walk back to the meadow where the kumpania were camped had Mickey constantly considering his choices. He'd spent all the morning and part of the afternoon with Tom though most of the time had been spent in the back garden. The gypsy could spend short periods of time inside the walls of the house but he grew tense and irritable.

The rear of the house wasn't as well kept as the front garden but as it wasn't overlooked by the neighbour, there was a privacy that allowed Mickey to comfort Tom whenever his emotions overwhelmed him. Neither thought they would be condemned for the innocent arms that enfolded and supported the youngster but they didn't wish to attract any attention to themselves.

Tom had cycled through moments of silent introversion into sporadic enthusiasm for his idea of running away together and crossing over to distraught pain and anguish for his mother's death. It seemed he had accepted the guilt he felt was unfounded and though the feeling remained with him, he kept it to himself.

Mickey managed to cook the roast for Tom his mother had planned but being unfamiliar with a rayburn and having to keep retreating outdoors periodically, it wasn't the greatest of successes. The beef was still red in the middle despite the outside being almost charred and the vegetables had barely managed to retain their shape after the thorough boiling they underwent.

As awful as the dinner was, the two youths enjoyed themselves. There were moments it was clear Tom was lost in the memories of his mother's Sunday roasts but in the main, the hours passed with laughter, inane and irrational amusement.

When Mickey had announced he should return to his camp, Tom had managed to maintain a calm attitude despite the discomfort he felt at being alone in the house. Urging the gypsy to think hard about the voiced idea to live rough, just the two of them, Tom watched the youth walk to the end of the path, turn down the road and disappear from view.

Turning back to the house and stepping inside the door, Tom cast an eye over the kitchen and the chaos they had brought with a simple meal. His smile slipped slowly away as his thoughts turned back to his mother. The boy had always been passionate about his solitude, relishing the time he had to himself when his mother had been working. He'd always considered himself to be somebody who thrived when alone but the house felt wrong. Could Mickey be right about the spirits of the dead? It wasn't that he felt his mother's presence any more than he felt his father's but the house didn't seem to know Mary Quatrell wouldn't be returning. In every room, on every surface something of hers caught his eye and it seemed she would call out from the living room to him at any moment.

Moving to the living room, the youngster straightened the curtain pole he had almost wrecked when he had drawn the curtains open. Turning to face the room he became aware for the first time how his mother's chair dominated the small space. The positioning was such there was nowhere he could stand and not feel it was facing him, staring at him.

Whatever Mickey decided, Tom knew he couldn't stay in the house. There was still a few weeks rent paid up and even if he didn't find the funds to pay the following month, he wouldn't be chased for it immediately. Rationally he made the decision not to even try to raise the money for the next month of rent. With Mickey or without him he was going to flee his memories, good and bad, he'd leave them behind. The money he didn't pay on rent would help keep him for a short time.

Mentally preparing a list, Tom tried to assess what he would need to take for a life on the road. Some of the practical items he imagined he would need could be found in the house, other useful tools could be taken from his work. He already knew the lock to the tool shed could easily be broken. He was going to need more knowledge than he had and was frustrated that the library didn't open on a Sunday. Confident there would be something in the reference section that could identify plants that were safe to eat, he promised himself he would visit tomorrow before the whole town knew of his mother's death and the false sympathy overwhelmed him.

The youngster closed his eyes. He shouldn't be able to think so sensibly, he shouldn't have been able to laugh with Mickey. What was wrong with him? Tom sat in his own chair and stared at the other chair as if his mother still sat there. Tempted to speak out loud, Tom managed to keep his thoughts to himself as he wondered why he wasn't still distraught and emotional.

He'd tried to ask Mickey the same question but the gypsy had been no help. Aside from the fact the two boys had wildly differing understandings of what death meant, the dark haired youth had told Tom he would grieve in different ways at different times. As much as Tom loathed the wretched, pain-filled moments that sadness brought him, he wished he could be normal and weep as he first had.

Shaking his head at himself, he rose from the chair, trooped through the kitchen and headed upstairs. Though it was early afternoon, Tom lay on his bed and closed his eyes expecting to stay awake with his thoughts but the full stomach and drained emotions claimed him and he was asleep in minutes.

It was a little after three by the time Mickey found himself at his father's vardo. There was no sign of his da and the youth was relieved. He'd been neglecting his training and his next fight was due in ten days somewhere in Hampshire.

Knowing he should either go on a run to aid his stamina or haul some wood in the forest to keep his muscles toned the young man found himself reluctant to tackle anything so energetic. It was partly due to the amount of beef he had eaten and partly his preoccupation with Tom. He found it hard to understand how death could rule the gadjos as completely as he saw it ruling Tom. The upset he could understand but nothing could change what had already come to pass. The gypsy way was to drink and celebrate the life of the dead and to move on.

Thinking about Tom's wish for them to flee their current existence, Mickey found the idea more appealing as time wore on. Are you happy? Tom had asked and Mickey had been stuck for an answer. There were moments in his life the gypsy had been happy but as a generality, he guessed the answer should have been no.

Mickey had been a wayward child even by Romany standards but he'd been happy then. Simpler days when Rosa was content to sit with him and throw stones into the sea. Laughing with her as he had raced her to the edge of a wood with Stevo and Jack trailing behind. It was curious how much of his childhood happiness involved Rosa. He frowned as he also realised how much of his current unhappiness involved her too.

None of the gypsy's sadness was the fault of the girl. She had been his best friend for as long as he could remember. Even the disapproval of the women in the camp at how much time the two of them spent together had done nothing to keep them apart. If he was going to marry anyone, Rosa was the only person it could be.

Turning away from his family's caravan Mickey headed deliberately back to the clearing he had all but claimed as his own. He couldn't face anyone while he was lost in his thoughts. Tom wanted to know what the gypsy wanted from his life and for the first time, Mickey had no idea. Two possible futures, two completely opposing chances at life.

If he didn't run away with Tom he knew what his life would bring. He'd be married before the year was out, his first child would be born the following summer and by the following winter, Rosa would be swelling with a second. Life could be worse. A decade or two beyond that he knew the camp would be as good as his. He didn't want the responsibility that went with being the Rom Baro but he knew the pride Rosa would draw from it.

Poor Rosa. Her wishes were so simple and honest. All the girl wanted was all any gypsy girl wanted and had she chosen to raise her skirts to any other in camp, she would have her dream and yet... she sought only him. Could he refuse her such a simple thing? Would it crush him to live the life he had always thought he was destined for?

Reaching the seclusion of the clearing in the forest the youth initially sat on the stump, then shifted to lay on the ground resting just his head against the split, aged wood. "I keeps living my lie and hurts none but myself an' Tom... or I lives as I wish an' destroy me family an' bring danger to me an' Tom." The gypsy growled and rose to his feet in a rush. He strode to the closest tree and bunched his hand into a fist as he prepared to take his fury out on the bark of the silver birch.

Slowly Mickey tried to calm himself. His breathing evened and he unclenched his hand. He knew he needed a fight; something to spend his aggression on. The youth wasn't naturally violent but his upbringing had focussed on body over mind. If you were wronged, you righted it with strength. It worked fine when the wrong you felt was caused by another but it was useless when you were your own enemy.

When all his troubles were thrown into one pot, they boiled down to two seemingly simple choices; Tom or Rosa. It wasn't so hard to create a justification for making a choice except, as soon as he selected one option, the other rose above it. If anything, the struggle he fought was made harder with the knowledge that Rosa knew his secret; she knew his secret and still she wanted to wed him.

There was no way to make everything work out. Should he choose to side with family and tradition, only Tom would suffer but Tom was the person who least wished to see hurt.

Chapter Twenty-seven

The young woman closed the door behind her as she made her way down the steps of the vardo. The two bottles clutched to her breast clinked together as she hopped from the last step to the ground. Looking around with a furtive glance, Rosa skirted the side of the caravan and out of sight of the four Romany sat playing dice in the space between two tents.

Stefan paid his debt to his cousin and passed the dice back to the man on his right and clambered to his feet to head after his charge. Rosa had managed to lose the youngster three times in as many days and the sixteen year old felt the welts from his uncle's leather belt. She wasn't going to shake him off again.

Behind the caravan Stefan found Rosa sat on the grass beside a shoddily made bender. Halting his step as he realised he had nowhere to put himself where the girl wouldn't see him, the youth began to slowly backtrack before she spotted him.

"Feck's sake Stevo!" Rosa said. "I's seein' tu. Tu's gonna follow me, might as well set yourself down aside me an' watch from here."

Flushing with embarrassment the boy chewed the soft flesh inside his cheek as he considered her suggestion. It wasn't as if she didn't know he was supposed to follow her everywhere. There was a sense in the fact that if he was sat beside her, she wouldn't be able to slip away unnoticed.

Cautiously the youth moved a step closer and lowered himself down to sit next to Rosa. He closed his eyes as he inhaled the smell of her. Stefan didn't know the scent the girl wore so often was made by her puri-daj from rose petals, nor did he realise the perfume was all the stronger having only just been applied. The odour wouldn't last as long as something bought from a shop but it was cheap, pleasant and a perfect accompaniment to her name.

"I hope da didn't go too hard on you."

Stefan glowered briefly at the memory of the beating he'd received. "Nothing so bad" the boy lied. Aside from the fact a gypsy didn't complain, he certainly didn't want Rosa to think he couldn't take a beating without crying about it after.

Rosa put her hand down beside her and lifted one of the bottles that sat on the grass beside her and passed it to Stefan. "Maybe this'n bein' a fair chop." Holding the bottle by the neck she watched as Stefan grinned and took the offered bottle.

Pulling a small folding penknife from his pocket, Stefan angled the blade against the silver cap and prised it free. A small amount of froth bubbled up and over his fingers. Bringing the bottle hurriedly to his lips, he sucked away the head from the lip and swapping hands, he licked his fingers clear of the sticky ale.

Inclining his head in appreciation, he tipped the bottle at his mouth and drank down the first two inches to leave the liquid within settling at the base of the neck.

"Khushti, as always." The youngster drew his knees up and eyed Rosa's ankles peering out from the bottom of her skirt. She was barefoot as always and a light coating of dust covered her feet. More for the sake of conversation than any true interest the boy asked where Mickey was.

Rosa shrugged. Mickey was in the forest and though she believed she knew where she could find him, she had no intention of telling Stefan. It mattered that her unwilling chaperone had no suspicion of where she might be found in the not too distant future.

The ground they were sitting on was on the tip of a rise that led down to the stream. The incline wasn't sufficient for the second bottle that sat beside the girl to roll away but it was enough to afford a clear view of the edge of the water. Without exchanging any words, Rosa watched the mother's from the camp bathing their youngest children as Stefan watched her watching. She couldn't deny she was envious as she saw Maria raise her toddler into the air and splash him down into the shallows. Maria was a year younger than one of her sisters and though the girl had married Rosa's brother to keep her honour, Rosa knew they made a strong family.

Maria, her babe and her Rom all slept in the vardo of Rosa's parents. Rosa didn't begrudge her and her brother the place under the wooden roof as she and her two sisters had to sleep under the canvas of a tent beside the caravan. It was part of the reason she had initially been content to wait for Mickey. Becoming wedded to Mickey would have her expected to sleep on the second bed beside Jacky Ray and his wife. There was nothing unusual in such sleeping arrangements but she was as eager to wait for Mickey to buy his own wagon as he himself was.

The sixteen year old with the beer in his hand coughed to clear his throat. "Fine looking girl your brother's wife."

"A fine looking, married woman Stevo" the young woman responded. "An' you shouldn't be looking." Glancing askew at her father's, brother's son, she kept her expression neutral, keeping the amusement from her face as the boy averted his eyes and looked down at his ankles. "Thought it would be you who she got bound to in honesty."

Rosa grew curious as she saw Stefan blush but she chose not to push the boy on the subject. She remembered well enough how the youngster was ever eager to be among the girls these last three years.

There was no denying he had the look the girls all welcomed and rumour told he had no reason for shame when time came as he would entertain a girl on her back.

For Stefan's part, he didn't know anything with certainty but he was not so naïve as to not have counted the moons between his time with Maria and the birth of the chiavala. The truth of the matter and the issue that riled the boy so often was Stefan wasn't the catch the girls were always seeking. It was the fault of none but himself and as much as he wanted to lay the blame for his low standing on Mickey, it was all his own doing.

There was no gypsy in the camp who didn't know the young lad had a weakness for his cousin. In itself there would have been no issue except Rosa didn't return his affection. When Jacky Ray had called on his uncle, Rosa's da, Stefan had been on the steps of the vardo and he heard them arranging the wedding. Maybe he should have known it was coming but it pained him. Mickey had been a hero and a friend to him for a decade and to hear he was to steal Rosa from him soured their relationship beyond mending.

The training Mickey had arranged for Stefan after he'd overheard both parents discussing the darro for Rosa had gone badly. The younger youth hadn't listened to Mickey's instruction, instead he had simply lashed out with all the strength he had. Forced to defend himself more than planned, Stefan had suffered more than a beating, he had been humiliated and it was the last time he had agreed to train with Mickey. Their relationship had soured instantly and though it was nobody's fault but his own, the boy had never forgiven Mickey.

Sitting beside Rosa now, all the feelings he had for her bubbled to the surface and even knowing it was foolish, he put his hand on her knee and turned to try and kiss her. His hand sliding up her thigh to pull her skirt higher up her leg. "Was never Maria that had my attention" he whispered.

Rosa slapped the youngster hard across the face. Stefan shrugged the blow off and slapped her back knocking her to the grass. Clambering over her, he pushed the girl on to her back and gripped her wrists in his hands, pressing them down beside her head as he leant over her to place the kiss he'd failed at before.

Staring up into Stefan's face, Rosa let her body go limp for a second, permitting the boy to position himself so his legs were astride hers, then she acted. Her knee came up with all the strength she had and Stefan fell to the side as she shoved him away. Rolling in the dirt, clutching his testicles through his trousers, Stefan was barely aware of Rosa getting to her feet and moving away with the last bottle clutched in her hand.

The young woman retreated back into the camp a little shaken by Stefan's actions. There was no surprise that the boy felt strongly for her, she'd always known he'd wanted her but she hadn't thought for a moment he would try anything without her permission. It was ironic she had mentally dismissed him as a potential husband because he was too timid. His attempt to force himself on her had been laughable from Rosa's perspective as she could easily fend him off but she found it curious he had even made the attempt.

Once out of sight of the youth and before she was sighted by any other gypsy, Rosa smoothed her skirt down and checked her appearance in the reflection of a window in the caravan she was beside. Content there was no indication of anything improper having happened she stepped around the vardo and back into the dirt circle where gypsies of various ages were all tackling small tasks of repair and maintenance to their own wagons.

Men tackled the larger issues such as greasing wheel bearings and in some instances, replacing wooden spokes. One vardo had two men holding the caravan off the ground as a third man was aligning the wheel against the hub in order to replace it. The younger family members were engaged in simpler activities from refreshing the paint where the woodwork may have become chipped to plucking feathers from pheasants caught by teenagers in the woods of a nearby private estate.

Rosa hunkered down low beside twins, a boy and a girl about four years of age. They had a paint pot between them and a brush each. Although it was clear from the amount of paint they were each wearing that they were enjoying themselves, they were making a fair job of colouring the red part of a design on a detached door that lay on the ground between them.

Without saying anything to the children, the older girl reached for a third paintbrush and joined in. Where the youngsters concentrated on the centre of the painting, Rosa carefully established the outline that would contain their limited ability. As she brushed the gloss paint over the faded image, the woman kept glancing up to see when Stevo would appear and where he would go.

Ten minutes passed before Stefan walked around the corner of the vardo following the same route Rosa had taken. None the worse for the damage Rosa had caused, the youth was walking a little slower than usual but otherwise seemed fine. Rosa was relieved as she had nothing against the boy.

Keeping her head low, the girl kept a wary eye out and hoped Stefan wouldn't notice her but as he emerged fully from around the caravan, Rosa was curiously puzzled to see he was towing a laughing Ruby behind him. The young teenager was clearly not under any duress as she swung his hand in hers and kept sidling close to him in order to run her hands over his chest.

For his part, Stefan was oblivious to anything except the attention Ruby was paying him and Rosa noted the hungry look in his eyes every time he looked at the younger girl. Once in the midst of the gypsies, the boy's steps slowed even more but Ruby took the lead and led him from the small circle and away toward the far side of the camp.

A little disconcerted at how easily the youth charged with watching for her virtue had been side-lined, Rosa set down the paintbrush and rose to her feet to follow the pair as they vanished from sight. Some unusual behaviour had been anticipated after he had drunk her puri-daj's special concoction but this wasn't quite what Rosa had expected.

The camp consisted of ten vardos and maybe two dozen benders and tents. Rosa thought she had caught a glimpse of Ruby's yellow shirt twenty yards away through a narrow view between two tents. She picked up her pace to catch the two youngster's up, not so hurried as to overtake them but with just enough pace to keep them in sight.

Reaching the far edge of the camp the young woman realised she had lost them and she frowned. Wandering a little aimlessly for ten minutes she eventually caught sight of Dinah and Allan huddled beside one of the improvised benders and crossed the grassed expanse that separated them.

Dinah glanced up as Rosa came within a few feet of them and punching Allan playfully on the shoulder, the two children sniggered to themselves and ran from where they had been squatting and dashed away toward the centre of the camp.

Reaching the spot the two youngsters had been Rosa was puzzled why they had run away but then she smirked as realisation came to her. She could hear what had amused the pair and she stood listening herself to the grunted moans of pleasure that sounded from the other side of the blankets of the bender.

Ruby had always been strong willed and she had managed to snare herself a man at last. Rosa didn't judge the girl, in many respects she was envious of the girl. At least she had achieved with Stefan what Rosa had so far failed to do with Mickey.

Satisfied Stefan was going to be occupied for a while, Rosa turned her attention to the next part of her grandmother's plan. Maybe Stefan had been taken out of action differently to how Rosa had expected but the result was the same. Turning to the forest, Rosa gripped the remaining bottle tightly in her hand with a mix of eagerness and trepidation, she started walking the path along the river bank that would ultimately take her to Mickey.

Chapter Twenty-eight

Rosa found Mickey in a funk in the clearing where she had been certain she would find him. There was no way to tell what had put him in such a sour mood short of asking him outright. As much as she wanted to know, she had a suspicion she wouldn't welcome knowing the answer even if he were willing to provide it.

Taking a deep breath, the young woman swaggered out from behind the densely packed coppice of willow and attempted to appear confident and bold despite how hard her heart was pounding. Having spent a night and most of the day considering what she intended, she still had reservations. It wasn't exactly trickery but she found it hard to justify her plan as honourable.

"Mande camo-mescro" she whispered to herself as she stepped into the clearing where Mickey eventually caught sight of her. Rosa yearned for the day she could declare her love to him in a bold voice that he may hear but for now, she settled for speaking the words in secret.

"Sastimos Mickey" Rosa said as she invaded his space and wrapped her skirt modestly around her legs to sit demurely on the cast leaves of winter that crunched beneath her. "You been hiding away?"

Slow to reply, Mickey looked pensive and thoughtful. He sighed and nodded eventually. There was no intention of inflaming her mood by making mention of Tom but part of him wanted to share the young boy's grief that she might better understand the black mood that hovered over him. "Not been in the mood for com'ny" he managed to admit, careful not to elaborate.

Tucking her feet beneath her and leaning on her hand, Rosa scratched at a mosquito bite she found on her ankle. "For what's worth, what it may mean for tu, me's sorry iffen I be making busnis for tu."

"You ain't made busnis for me, me pain ain't being down to tu" Mickey responded. "Makes it for meself good enough." Raising himself from his spot leaning against the trunk of a fallen tree, the gypsy walked toward the stump he had been often using as a seat and continued toward Rosa. Settling himself cross-legged before her he smiled weakly at the girl. "I's the one is sorry. Don't rightly know me own mind o' late and that ain't being fair on tu. Knows that, dealing with."

Sometimes the young man knew the right thing to say to Rosa

and she winced at the honesty of his words. Suddenly her intentions seemed unjust and she gave serious thought to what she was planning. Much as the woman wanted Mickey to speed the day they were wed she felt guilt at the contrived idea her puri-daj had helped set loose.

Considering leaving him to his own thoughts, Rosa's indecision was taken from her when the youth spotted the bottle that lay between her skirt and the hand she rested on the ground. "Brought that for I?"

It would have been no effort to say the beer was for her da or for somebody else entirely but with the briefest hesitation, Rosa nodded and sitting upright, she passed the gold capped bottle to Mickey wordlessly.

With the tip of his sheath knife, the gypsy carefully levered at each individual crimp of the lid. Little by little he loosened the cap. Rosa watched him, a lump in her throat. The longer he took to open the bottle the more tempted she became to find a way to take it from him and yet, she said and did nothing but watch as in due course, he stabbed his blade in the earth and gripping the glass bottle in one hand and the cap in his other, Mickey twisted the cap, pulling it free in one smooth motion.

Mickey flipped the cap to Rosa who caught it with one hand then toyed with it in her lap, rolling it between her fingers. She stared at the evidence of her guilt as she listened to Mickey gulping down the tainted ale.

"Iffen I weren't here" Mickey began. He scratched at the neck of the bottle in his hands, staring at the neck to avoid making eye contact with his promised. "Iffen I weren't here, what'd tu be adoing?"

Rosa's brow furrowed, confused at the question. "How d'ya mean?"

Mickey roughly ran his hand over his face as though trying to wipe away cobwebs. He frowned as hard as Rosa did and tried again. "Tu an' me, if we wa'nt to be wed, iffen something took me away, what would tu be doing?"

The girl stared at Mickey from under her tight knit brow and her mouth turned down as she sensed where Mickey was trying to take the conversation. "Something takes tu from me Mickey Ray, I'd be findin' that something an' making it give tu back!"

The gypsy nodded non-committal as though it was the answer he'd expected. He managed to explain what he'd said wasn't quite what he meant but he couldn't word his thoughts any clearer. Raising the bottle to his lips he drank the remaining half of the contents and sat the empty bottle in the gap between his knees. "Never mind" he said. "Just wool-gathering." The gypsy looked to the girl opposite him and he grinned.

Smiling back at him, Rosa felt a reassurance in his smile that contradicted his words and she forgave him for worrying her. She didn't tell him he was forgiven, she kept any such lassitude to herself. "Sometimes Mickey Ray, tu's as dinilo as hen-house o' foxes!"

"Arvah, ain't that kosko!" Mickey nodded. Blinking slowly, he rubbed his face again and lowered himself to the ground, unfolding his knees to lie down on the ground facing Rosa. "Never been meaning to do wrong by tu Rosa. Be remembering that" he muttered.

Rosa felt a little anguished as she thought she could as easily say the same. Watching Mickey watching her, the gypsy girl felt her heart go out to him. It wasn't simply his good looks and his dark eyes that attracted her, even the muscled arms and torso that strained his shirt was not what she found most appealing. His position as son of the Rom Baro was incidental. What separated him from every other man she could have chosen was his gentle nature.

Mickey Ray always acted from kindness even when the need was for strength and force, he could apply it fairly and that was what Rosa found so appealing. For as long as she could remember knowing him, she couldn't ever remember a moment of spite. Harking back to the days they had played together when they were scarce old enough to be left to their own devices he had been the fairest spirited person she knew.

The first memory she had of Mickey was when they would have been four years old or close to. Uncle Victor had somehow come by toffee apples and she remembered she and Mickey had one each. Somebody had jolted her arm and hers had fallen from her hand into the dirt. Even the recollection caused her eyes to tear up.

Treats were rare at any time and candy and sweets were the rarest of all. Luxuries such as that only came from the villages and towns and as it took coin to obtain them, such wastefulness wasn't the gypsy way. She remembered bursting into tears as she stared at the spoiled apple lying in the dirt and the swarm of ants that crawled over it. Just one bite had been taken from the toffee apple, just enough for Rosa to appreciate what she had lost.

Mickey had put his arm around her just like an adult would have comforted a child, then he had passed his apple to her, ensuring she had a firm hold on the stick.

Rosa shook her head to bring herself back to the present. She sniffed and wiped her eyes with the back of her hand, a little ashamed at tears coming to her from the memory. Staring up into the canopy above, she took a deep breath and blinked away the last sign of her upset. She switched her gaze back to Mickey expecting him to tease her for crying for no reason and saw he had rolled onto his back and lay sprawled out on the ground. She chuckled and called to him asking if she was boring him.

"Mst wor" Mickey muttered unintelligibly.

First of all Rosa giggled at the gypsy's nonsense, then in a moment her face fell and she worried at her promised's continued mutterings. Giving no thought to her clothes, the girl walked forward on her knees to Mickey and she sat beside him, her knees against his ribs.

Mickey's eyes were unfocussed and though still awake, his face was vacant of expression. She called softly to him and again he muttered something indecipherable.

"Feck!" Rosa spat. "Kek! Tu shan boshing!" She swore to herself some more as she gently slapped Mickey's face to try to bring him around from his drugged condition. Growling to herself Rosa put her hands to her head and squeezed her temples between her fists. She shook her head and sat back on her heels. "Oh Nana!" She shook her head in frustration.

It was possible it was Rosa's mistake but the more she tried to remember, the surer she was it had been her puri-daj who had erred. Looking back, she may have realised sooner if she'd been thinking to look for the obvious signs.

Now she understood why Stefan had grown so amorous and tried to force himself on her. She'd given the wrong bottles to the wrong men! With Stefan getting the silver capped ale Rosa had turned him into a rutting beast. The cries of Ruby's passion echoed in her ears as she fumbled with the gold cap in her fingers. Mickey had been given a soporific in his beer that had been intended to keep Stefan from watching out for honour.

Rosa stood up and swore some more as she paced the clearing, kicking the piles of dead leaves that had gathered wherever the wind blew them. Returning to Mickey she sat down beside him again and rested her hand on his chest. Though it was apparent he couldn't concentrate on anything Rosa realised he wasn't actually asleep and she whispered to him how she felt for the first time. Her fingers danced over his shirt buttons slowly descending until she reached the point where his shirt was tucked into his trousers and she smiled as a possibility began to take form.

Shifting herself a little lower down his body, Rosa began to gently caress the front of Mickey's trousers and she smiled a little more as she noticed the fabric grow a little tighter. Increasing the pressure she applied with her hands she was rewarded by feeling him stiffen at her touch.

Rosa bit her lip and glanced around the clearing to ensure there was nobody anywhere near. Satisfied they were alone she put both of her hands to his belt buckle and unlooped the leather from the metal fastening. Pulling the end of the belt free she shifted her attention to the buttons of his fly and had them undone in short order. Pulling his trousers down to his knees wasn't easy but she eventually managed it and then she was able to fasten her hand around him, carefully squeezing and stroking him until he responded as much as needed.

Once more Rosa looked around the open space before she stood up and raised her skirts to her waist, bunching the material in front of her stomach so none of the fabric would get in her way. She placed a foot either side of Mickey's hips and slowly lowered herself toward him, her free hand reaching for him to guide his way.

Chapter Twenty-nine

Tom had been sitting alone in the house trying to kill time until he had arranged to meet up with Mickey. They hadn't set any time to meet; time didn't seem to have the same importance to the gypsy as the rest of the world. Mickey's day appeared to be split into four distinct time zones. The day began early, halted briefly at noon, ran into the afternoon and then slipped quietly into the evening.

Pinning the young man down to anything more precise was pointless. The youth gauged the hour of the day by the position of the sun and arranging a specific time for something was liable to leave the other person waiting.

Exiting the house, Tom began to slowly stroll in the direction of the main road. The past few days had been hectic with excitement and sadness and the young man was so engrossed in his own thoughts he wasn't aware of his surroundings as he usually was.

A stone struck his arm and as the impact slowly registered, a second stone passed in front of him.

"Puff!" A high pitched voice called out from behind the bush to Tom's right.

In the past Tom would have shrunk from the name calling and any violence targeted his way. He didn't know if it was his contact with the gypsy or if it was the grief of having lost his mother but the boy was no longer willing to be cowed. Bending down to the road he picked up the stone that had struck him and with more luck than judgement, he threw it back into the bushes where he was rewarded with a shriek of pain.

"Come on!" Tom yelled. "Come on, come out, let's settle this!"

With little hesitation, the two older Trent boys walked through the rhododendron bush that had provided scant cover and paused at the roadside. Behind the two youths of Tom's age were three younger boys who were reluctant to emerge. With a glare from Mark Trent they reluctantly shuffled out from under the dense, wide-leafed foliage. The West twins were maybe twelve years old and Dick West must have been fifteen.

Andrew Trent sneered at the younger three as they looked embarrassed at having held back. One of the twins was bleeding from his temple and it took the support of his brother to keep him on his feet. Mark turned his attention back to Tom. "Okay faggot, you want to settle this?"

It wasn't the education that Mickey had given him that

emboldened Tom but events over that last few days had conspired to make him angry enough to retaliate. Some words of advice from the gypsy had sunk in and it was time to try the words out. First and foremost was Mickey's assertion it was better to lose than not to fight.

He ran through the rules Mickey had espoused. 'Don't fight fair, they won't. Don't jab, swing, if you jab you'll pull your punches. Take the meanest first, the others will stand back. Expect pain.'

As Mark Trent swaggered toward Tom the youth made himself appear small to bring the cocky teenager closer. When he was close enough Tom withdrew a half step brining his right leg behind his left and watched Trent grin at his apparent retreat. Tom lunged forward and swung his foot as hard as he could, his heavy work boot impacting between the taller youth's legs.

Trent let out a yell and dropped to his knees where Tom smashed his kneecap into his face and knocked him sprawling on the tarmac. Whirling to face Andrew Trent he swung a closed fist into the side of the brother's head. The youth swayed at the impact and Tom swept his leg from underneath him causing him to drop to the ground beside his brother. 'When they're down, keep them down' Mickey had said. Tom kicked the prone figure in the stomach. Mark was on his hands on knees attempting to clamber to his feet.

Ignoring the three younger potential assailants, Tom grasped a clump of Mark Trent's hair and yanked back hard to raise the bully's face to meet his own as he bent low over him. "Come for me again and I'll kill you" he rasped, it didn't carry the weight of threat Mickey would have managed but it was enough of an impression that the young man swallowed nervously. Tom twisted his hair to pull the youth's head to the side and he punched his face and watched him drop back to the road.

Tom felt exhilarated. They hadn't laid a single blow on him and he had downed two antagonists who should have beaten him to a pulp. He unclenched his hand and strands of hair from the older Trent boy dropped through his fingers, he brushed the last strands away and walked between the two groaning men to the trio staring wide eyed at him.

Tom halted a few paces from them and glared at them. "Feck orf" he snapped in his best Romany dialect. The twins and their brother glanced briefly behind Tom at their injured cousins and without a word even among themselves they turned and fled down the road. Unable to help himself, Tom grinned and bit back a laugh.

With a glance behind him he watched as the two brothers rose to their feet, circled him warily and headed down the road after the younger boys. Mickey had been right, not that Tom had doubted him. Had they been of a mind, the two Trent boys could easily have come at him together and he would have lost the victory he had just earned. The gypsy had said Tom only needed to beat them once. They wanted to keep him down and when he showed they couldn't, they'd either stop or they'd come at him harder the next time.

If they came back for him again they'd be disappointed. Tom didn't plan to be around Midhurst for much longer whatever answer Mickey gave him. Inspecting his split knuckles and flexing his fingers to ease the discomfort his punches had caused Tom started back along the road to find his gypsy and learn what their futures held.

Sara had been right he mused as he meandered down the road. She'd promised him a pained future and he could see now she must have meant the death of his mother. Part of the youth was relieved the pain had eased but a second part of him felt immense guilt that he thought he had come to terms with it so quickly. Had it really only been that morning he had found her dead in her chair?

Before he knew it Tom was at the main road. His cheeks were wet where he had been crying and yet he had no recollection of weeping. Time had eluded him, the last three hundred yards of the walk down the hill seemed to have not happened. There was no recollection of passing the fire damaged tree, no memory of the blocked ditch that trickled water across the road for ten yards, even the bush that had been the usual haunt of aggressors had been passed without notice.

Wiping his face in both hands Tom puzzled at how he could traverse the distance he had within knowing it. Briefly he considered the idea that his euphoria at having finally tackled the bullies had caused his lapse of attention but deep down he knew it hadn't been that. Deep down he knew it had been the resurgence of his grief that had dulled his observations.

The young man smiled to learn he still suffered. He had no desire to feel the loss of his mother but it was reassuring to know he hadn't lost his humanity.

Crossing the main road Tom headed down Brambling Lane and moved into the wood before the bridge so as to avoid the gypsy camp completely. It put him on the wrong side of the river but there was a point he could swing across toward the clearing where he always met with Mickey. There was a tree that angled over the Rother and it had low branches that had afforded him a way of crossing the water without getting any more than his feet wet.

Tom felt immortal. The fight with the Trents and the Wests had been liberating and despite the loss he'd experienced at the day's start it seemed as though things were starting to go his way.

Moving through the forest the young man found the tree he had been seeking further along the bank than he remembered. Staring at the branch that hung from the beech tree he tried to remember the last time he had used it to cross the water. It didn't look as strong as his memory said it was. The more he thought on it, the surer he became that he'd not attempted the trick he was contemplating since before he'd completed his eleven plus. Glancing along the river bank in both directions he could see clearly there was no other option aside from backtracking and taking the bridge.

With a hesitant breath, Tom moved to the very lip of the bank, he hastily stepped back as the edge crumbled underfoot dropping soil into the flowing river. He gazed up at the trailing branch and reassured himself that although his weight was greater now than the last time he'd made the leap to the low limbs, he was also taller and could reach higher to grasp the stronger part of the branch.

Stepping back a further three steps to permit a small run up, Tom dashed toward the river and leapt up and out, his hands grasping frantically at the branch in front of him. Catching the limb with both hands he tried to swing himself forward. It wasn't going to work. The beech was flexible enough to permit him to gain some momentum and strong enough to bear his weight but where he had caught the limb higher to compensate for his weight, the transit of the branch wasn't sufficient to allow him to move any further than midway across the river.

Suspended above the middle of the river Tom had to give serious consideration to simply letting go but he knew the water beneath him may not be flowing very fast but it was deep enough in the centre to create an issue for a non-swimmer. Tom was a non-swimmer; letting go wasn't an option.

With his fingers aching the young man accepted he only had one remaining choice and slowly and with great care he pulled himself hand over hand up the smooth bark of the beech tree until he was close to its trunk. So close to the bole of the tree, the branch had no spring to it and Tom had to swing his body. After a few attempts he managed to wrap his legs around the trunk sufficiently to hold himself in position. It took substantial effort and he had to climb the wrong way along the tree but he managed to eventually clamber from the underside to the top of the tree.

Standing on the trunk of the canted tree Tom slowly walked down the slick surface of the beech until he was almost at the base. He leapt the last few feet and landed on the opposite bank with a huge amount of relief and vowed to never try that again.

Taking his bearings he weaved through the wood toward where he expected to find Mickey. He was early and he knew it but there was nothing else for him to do. He also liked the idea of beating Mickey to the clearing and seeing his face when he found him there. The gypsy had said he would let Tom know his final decision in the evening and even by Mickey's erratic understanding of time, Tom was early.

Moving through the wood with an optimistic smile on his face,

Tom slowed when he heard sounds coming from ahead of him. Hesitant at the unexpected presence of people in what he considered Mickey's clearing, the youth crept cautiously from tree to tree.

With only twenty yards left to cover, Tom caught a glimpse of the people in the clearing and his blood turned cold as his heart all but stopped beating.

At first it was only Rosa he saw; she was straddled across somebody on the ground and was wriggling back and forth. Then he saw who she was sat upon and he staggered backward. Mickey was making quiet noises but Rosa wasn't as restrained. Tom could hear her speaking in Romany to the gypsy beneath her and though Tom had no understanding of what she said, her fervent, passionate tone told him all he needed to know. Her skirts were gathered around her waist and her bare thighs were against Mickey's waist and from the rise and fall of her body, Tom knew what they were doing.

Turning from the scene, the youth fled back into the wood until he reached the river once more. He collapsed to the ground and struggled to breathe. Rolling onto his back he stared upward unseeing and wept. The sound was a whisper but his body contorted as it shook with the attempts he made to contain his anguish.

Chapter Thirty

When Mickey finally awoke he was alone. He didn't remember falling asleep and he only has a hazy memory of coming into the woods at all. Sitting up he found his throat was dry and his head was pounding. Glancing around he saw nothing to hand to drink but an empty unlabelled bottle sat a few paces from him that he could only assume had come from Rosa's grandmother.

Rosa had been there. It wasn't simply the bottle, the gypsy boy had a recollection of her face. Trying to remember, Mickey was certain of nothing. Rosa had given him the beer, he was almost certain of that but as he managed to reach out to grasp a fragment of recollection, it drifted away from him. There had a been a dream while he slept, it wasn't definitive but some of his mind recalled Tom's hands on his body, then Tom morphed into Rosa, then back to Tom again.

Moving unsteadily Mickey gained his feet and swayed as though still drunk. Casting his eyes about his surroundings he scoured the leaves and tufts of grass looking for the rest of the bottles he must have drunk. The home brew was potent but it usually took four or five bottles for the gypsy to feel the way he did.

Something was wrong with his clothes, he straightened out the hang of his shirt and realising he was untucked he made to dress himself properly. It was only when he pulled his shirt tail up he noticed his belt was undone and his buttons were done up unevenly.

Tom must have arrived while Mickey was deep in his cups, he rubbed at his temple in the hope of shifting the haze that fogged his thinking. Undoing the buttons so as to do them up again in the correct order he felt a mild discomfort in his trousers and he lowered them briefly to find his underwear had been tugged down to his thighs.

Spreading his knees apart to keep his trousers from falling to his ankles he pulled the waistband of his underwear up and shook his head at the distorted memory of Tom taking hold of him. Again the dream shifted and it was Rosa he saw again. The youth frowned, his head hurt already and the disjointed merging of memory and dream felt like his head was in a vice being slowly tightened. Tugging himself into his underpants he felt a stickiness and assuming he understood the situation, he looked at his palm anyway.

The blood on his fingertips worried him more than his lack of memory. Nervous and apprehensive he scanned the area for even a hint of somebody else being near. Hurriedly Mickey dressed himself and wiped his fingers on his trousers.

After making a complete circuit of the clearing partly hoping to find sign of somebody and partly hoping he wouldn't, he satisfied himself whoever he had been there with, he was alone now. A little fearful of the presence of blood on his groin he snatched up the empty beer bottle and headed for the river. Water may or may not help clear his head but it would certainly help him to clean himself up.

There was no certainty but blood was all too often an indicator of being in trouble. Usually the blood was on his fists or clothing, he could imagine possibilities that made the situation as it was but he didn't want to dwell too hard on that line of thinking.

Mickey heard the river before he reached it and he was a dozen yards distant when he saw the body. It lay lengthways to him and he only caught a glimpse of the shirt and trousers before he was convinced. It was Tom that lay unmoving ahead of him and Mickey instinctively knew the boy had to be the source of the blood he had woken to. For a moment the gypsy was frozen to the spot, then needing to know, he cautiously, fearfully edged closer.

"Tom?" Mickey whispered, then a little louder "Tom!" In a few strides he was kneeling beside the gadjo and he put his hand on the young man's shoulder to shake him. There was no need.

Thomas woke, turned to see Mickey and then with anger on his face, he hurried out of reach of the gypsy by rolling away. A few feet distant, Tom sat with his legs stretched out before him and his hands behind ready to scuttle further away if need be. The glare he threw at Mickey was filled with hostility and even knowing how mismatched they were, he had an urge to close on the youth and start throwing punches.

Mickey thought he understood and he began to gabble apologies for hurting the young man. Neither youth understood the other was at cross-purposes. Tom was furious with Mickey for leading him on in his hope that they had a future together, Mickey was apologising for an imagined hurt that had left the youth bleeding.

It was only when Mickey insisted on seeing how he had hurt Tom that the youth had grown puzzled. The gypsy assumed it was a gorgio modesty and assured the youth there was no shame in letting him see.

"What the hell are you talking about?" Tom asked, gaining an inkling that all was not as clear cut as it seemed. "I'm not bleeding!"

Mickey's blank reaction stopped the fight before it began. "If you ain't bleeding, where's the blood on I from?"

Tom knew. He knew and he wanted to tell the gypsy to go and ask Rosa but as hurt and angry as he was, he didn't have enough hate in him to throw spite at the boy he would do anything for. "You really don't know?"

Mickey shook his head, utterly bewildered. He started to speak then faltered. Again he tried but he shook his head, growing annoyed with himself his habit of clenching and unclenching his fists returned. Recognising the habit and knowing it was the precursor to rage and violence, he told Tom to wait where he was for a moment.

Ignoring the instruction, the youth stood and followed Mickey toward the river. A little wary of having paid no heed to Mickey ordering him to stay where he was and still aggrieved at the man for what he had seen earlier in the day, Tom kept a safe distance as the gypsy reached the river bank and threw himself into the water.

Spluttering and splashing in the deep water, Mickey dunked his head under the running water a few times and then stood up. The river came up to the fourth button from top of his shirt. Having left the empty beer bottle where he had found Tom he cupped his hands in the river, he brought a few handfuls of water to his mouth and gulped down as much as he was able.

Shaking the excess water from his hair, the youth pushed himself back through the river toward a bemused Tom. He held his hand out for Tom to aid him in getting out of the water. Despite a feeling he was going to be pulled into the water by the gypsy, he took the risk and reached for his hand as requested. Mickey surprised the boy by not tugging him into the river but instead, he did clamber onto the bank and sat with his arms around his knees and thought again what he wanted to ask and how to word it.

"I don't understand this at all Tom" the gypsy whined. "Me head is aching like the Irish pounded it for a fortnight, I got blood on me kar and no real recollection but maybe tu or Rosa riding me." He shook his head, released his hold on his knees and squeezed the back of his head with both hands and pulled his elbows towards his closed eyes. Dropping his hands to his side he frowned. "I ain't knowing what's real an' what's dream but if this blood ain't from tu..."

"It was Rosa that was riding you." Tom spat out. There had been no intent to be aggressive but the youth was hurt too much to be gentle. "I came to talk with you and there you were, flat on your back with her on top of you." The youth moved close enough to stand over Mickey and he let his temper rise. "So don't you make out like you care, don't you dare play dumb and give me your shit about dreaming. I *saw* you! You weren't dreaming, you were lying there and she... she... Damn you Mickey!"

Tom's ire faded as his emotions came back to cut into him. Wounded deeply the boy bit back his retorts, he turned from the gypsy and took three paces from him and leant against a tree. "I thought you felt for me like I did for you" he whispered. "You don't feel for anybody but yourself though do you?"

Mickey sat stunned and tried again to find the reality of what

Tom said he had seen. It wasn't that he disbelieved him, he believed him completely but the gypsy only had fragmented memories to work on. The more he thought through what the youth described the more credible it became. "Rosa's rat!"

"What? What rat?" Tom was completely lost with the direction Mickey was taking the conversation.

The youth laughed and immediately apologised. "Rat. Means blood. Sorry."

As infuriated as he was with Mickey and as much as he needed to stay angry, Tom couldn't help but laugh. Fighting his own amusement failed and the pair of them exchanged glances that made them both start to giggle inappropriately. In due course the laughter faded but it had muted the tension between them even if it hadn't cured it. Quietly Mickey elaborated, trying to stay brief and desperately hoping he could make everything well between them both.

"The blood on me" the youngster said in as gentle and soothing manner as he could manage. "It makes sense. I didn't take Rosa's honour but I guess, from what tu says... I didn't need to take it iffen she just give it away." Sighing heavily Mickey raised his face to Tom's. "I'm guessing you'll not be believing me but I swear to tu, what tu saw... weren't my wish. Don't be knowing rightwise how it came about and baint be able to make no change to it but, thought tu knew... she ain't the one I be lusting for these past few days."

Chewing at his lip, Tom weighed Mickey's words in his mind. Keeping his eyes on the gypsy he could tell at least some of what he'd said was true. Adding what he already knew of Rosa to what Mickey said, Tom could easily imagine the girl going to any lengths to keep the young gypsy as her own. There was enough doubt in his mind to give credibility to the account he had just heard but he wasn't quite ready to let the gypsy off the hook just yet.

"You're saying I'm the one you want?" Tom asked. Mickey paused as he stared back at the youth, once a few heartbeats had passed, he lowered his head and nodded twice without speaking. "You got to say it Mickey. You want me to believe you, I got to hear it."

The gypsy raised his head again. His dark brown eyes focussed intently on the young man before him and he took a deep breath while his fingers tapped nervously against his trouser legs. "It's tu. The one I want being with? I wanna be wi' tu Tom." Mickey took in another breath and closing his eyes, he pursed his lips and blew the breath out slowly.

Tom kept his own council. It should have caused him to rejoice to hear Mickey tell him what he'd been wanting to hear but whether he had exhausted his abused emotions or whether he simply needed more, the young man pushed further than he ever would have dared before. Crossing the few feet between them he squatted down to Mikey's eye level and brought his face to with a foot of the gypsy's.

"Tonight I'm leaving" he said in a tone that brooked little argument. "I'm gathering up a few things I'll be wanting and I'm going to head south. I don't know where, I'll see when I get there." Mickey opened his eyes, crossed his arms and listened as Tom continued. "You said I'm the one you want to be with. If that's so, come with me."

The gypsy was tempted to agree outright. The man before him had grown immeasurably in the last twenty-four hours and suddenly it was as though their positions had been reversed. Tom had the confidence and certainty that had always been Mickey's and the gypsy was the one who was unsure and hesitant.

"Gi me a day an' we go together." Mickey wasn't sure it was the right thing to do but it was apparent if he wanted to keep with Tom as he'd said he did, he had no other choice. "There be things only I got we be needing to take wi' us. Gi me a day an' I meet tu here, not in the morning but on the morning a'ter."

Reluctant to even delay by a day Tom considered Mickey's counter-bid. The gypsy had a better knowledge of anything they may need and though he worried his own commitment might wane with the wait, he acknowledged the gypsy was talking sense and he nodded. They grinned at each other and Mickey assumed control once more, he rose up on his knees and grabbed Tom by the ears.

"Meantime, come here!" Mickey kissed the youth full on the lips and as they separated, Tom blushed crimson.

Chapter Thirty-one

It was growing dark by the time Mickey returned to his family's vardo and rather than endure questions from his father as to why he hadn't been training, Mickey snuck into the bender beside the caravan. Two of his sisters where already lying on their makeshift beds under the blanketed canopy talking quietly when he pushed his way inside. Shrugging off the questions of where he'd been the gypsy pushed his way to the back of the improvised tent, rolled out a blanket on the dirt floor, curled up on it and ignored them.

Resting on his back Mickey closed his eyes and strained to hear the quiet murmurs of his siblings. It wasn't that he had any great interest in what they had to say but they were difficult to ignore and the more he tried to tune out their words, the more he caught phrases that peeked his interest. There was mention of Ruby that was followed by sniggering and though he wasn't certain, it sounded like she had spent most of the afternoon confined with Stefan.

The snippet of news was little more than a curiosity to Mickey but it allowed him to forget his headache as he wondered if Stefan realised the full import of being so close with the younger girl. Ruby was of age and as matches went, Stevo and young teenager could do a lot worse. Rolling onto his side to face away from the girls in the tent the gypsy smiled at the pairing and gently slipped into sleep while his sisters continued to whisper secrets between themselves.

Coming awake to raised voices outside, Mickey still had traces of a hangover he didn't deserve. Conscious enough to identify his father and another man he knew he should be able to recognise but not so alert as to pick out words, the gypsy managed to manoeuvre himself into a sitting position and struggled to catch some small detail of the disagreement.

"Hokkano tute mande tu shall lel a curapen" Mickey's da said and Mickey glanced at the girls who were both sitting up huddled together nervously. Threatening a man with a beating wasn't so rare as to be a cause of concern but the other voice clearly belonged to another Romany and for his father to suggest he was lying was a serious accusation.

The second voice replied in a quieter tone that reflected how dangerous a path Jacky Ray was treading. "Kek hokka, penchava tu jin tatchipen si."

Mickey puzzled over the reply. The man had said his da would know it wasn't a lie. The voices halted and the sound of one pair of feet walking away could be heard through the entrance of the bender. In the quiet that fell, Mickey heard his mother call his father back inside and feet were heard treading up the steps of the vardo and the door was closed against the last hours of the night.

"What tu been an' done?" Jemima asked of Mickey, the whites of her eyes all that was visible on her silhouette.

Shaking his head the gypsy asked his sister what she'd heard. The question wasn't what he'd done, the question was what had been found out. He saw the figure of his sister shrug in the dark. "Just woke. Somebody be looking for tu and they ain't happy." The girl kept her attention on Mickey expecting a reaction but the youth gave no indication of knowing why somebody would be seeking him before dawn. Suspecting it related to Tom the gypsy lay back down with his back to his sister and he silently worried until sleep claimed him again.

Dawn had already been and gone when Mickey woke again. Alone in the bender he stretched and pulled a face as he caught the smell from his clothes. His moment in the river may have washed his spirit but it had done little for his clothing and if anything, he smelt worse than if he hadn't jumped in the water. Pulling his shirt over his head he brought it to his nose and sniffed, quickly pulling it away from his face. There was a hint of stale sweat but over that was the odour of stagnant water that made his stomach churn. Balling the shirt up he threw it into a corner of the bender and crawled on his hands and knees to the fold of blanket that was the way out of the tent.

In the fresh air Mickey stretched, his tanned skin was creased with lines from where he had slept in his clothes and he heard his body crack and pop as he tried to ease some discomfort from his poor night's rest.

Looking down himself the youth accepted his trousers were every bit as tainted as his shirt had been and he walked to the family vardo to change his clothes. At the top of the steps the door was closed tight and remembering the argument in the night, he grew hesitant as he put his foot on the bottom rung. Either trouble waited within or it didn't, he wasn't going to get to avoid everybody for the remainder of the day and he couldn't walk around partly dressed.

Frowning, Mickey climbed the four steps and raised the catch on the door, pushing it open and stepping inside. The vardo was empty and Mickey headed straight to the chest against the side wall and opened the third drawer down. Pulling out fresh clothes he kicked off his boots and stripped naked, redressing in the new clothing. Just as he started to button up his shirt he sensed somebody behind him and span around to see his father framed in the doorway, ducking his head to step inside.

Jacky Ray was an intimidating man but Mickey didn't fear him as he had when he was growing up. It had been years since the man had taken his belt to him and almost as long since he'd raised a fist against his son. If it came to blows Mickey knew he had the strength to win if not the experience.

"Couldn't be waiting three month" his father said, shaking his head sadly. "Tu gone an' done a dinilo thing boy."

Waiting for his da to elaborate Mickey continued to fasten his shirt. There was no rage in his father's voice, he spoke calmly and softly but the gypsy boy knew that Jacky Ray's temper could be woken in a split second.

The older man leant against the small units behind him and crossed his arms. "Been t' pooker wit' Marcus, Rosa's da. Tu ain't got no option left. They ain't repaying none o' the ghel's darro what tu done but guessing he jin they ain't able to put her on another now leastways."

"I ain't done nothing!" Mickey retorted.

"Ain't what Rosa be saying, nor her puri-daj an' I ain't setting meself against that one." There was a fire in Jacky's eyes that didn't brook any argument. His glare at his son didn't have the rage behind it the boy had come to expect but the tone of his voice indicated his displeasure. "Says her honour is shed and it be tu that's the one they pointing the finger at. Tu denying that? Tu telling you ain't spent in her?"

Mickey swallowed and sighed briefly, he knew arguing was futile. How could he tell he didn't rise for her? How could he claim nothing happened when he knew it was so? There was no getting out of it short of lying and even then, his word against hers with all the camp knowing they was promised and Rosa wanting none but him.

"Think silence be saying it all, don't tu?"

Closing his eyes Mickey reluctantly nodded his agreement. When he opened his eyes again his father hadn't moved but a wry smile had grown on his face. "Ain't bein' the first to try before tu buy but surprised at tu. Only kicker is tu don't get your vardo like tu wanting. So tu mess down on the floor here for three moons, ain't so bad. Done it meself when this were tu puri-da's wagon."

Nodding sadly, Mickey could do nothing but agree. There were aspects of being Romany that Mickey despised, not least the refusal to let him be who he was. What he couldn't ignore was the concept of Romany honour. Maybe he had no blame to do with taking Rosa's virginity but if he refused her, he would damage her honour, his family's and his own. His own would hurt but he could live with it, even his family's honour was something that would recover but as suspicious as he was at Rosa's actions, he couldn't shame her.

Trying to keep Tom from his thoughts, Mickey's mind raced back over his father's last words. "What tu mean me not getting me vardo?"

Jacky Ray chuckled. "Oh the vardo will still be found once we at Stow but Marcus ain't happy waiting so long for his ghel. E' be getting a reverend from the church to see thee two wed afore nightfall."

"I'm not marrying Rosa today!" He hadn't intended to raise his voice but he made no apology for shouting. Watching carefully he saw his father's expression darken and the smirk dropped from his face.

Jacky Ray stepped further into the caravan and prodded Mickey's chest with a meaty forefinger. "That be just what tu be doing" the man growled. "Marcus came for tu last night with two barrels to see thee wed. Vicar gets here an' tu gonna be joined wit' her or tu be a mulla 'fore sun goes down."

Mickey understood the threat. Married at gunpoint wasn't a common event but it happened often enough. The more he thought on it the more obvious it became. The youth could only recall two instances of a forced wedding and both had been over dishonoured daughters. When Tom had told him he'd seen Rosa riding him Mickey should have anticipated the outcome.

"Ain't like being tu don't been planning." Jacky stepped back toward the door. "Just be sooner than was reckoned."

As his father was about to leave, Mickey called after him. "Why we getting a vicar? Ain't you wedding us?"

As the Rom Baro of the camp, every wedding Mickey knew of had been conducted by his father. He didn't have any concern who carried it out but he was genuinely puzzled at the change from tradition.

"They don't want me wording this one funny. Marcus ain't sure I ain't had knowledge o' this afore hand." Jacky grinned. "Truth is, wishing I had. Rosa'll be good for tu an' rather have her on our side than his. Anyway, keep close, don't want tu vanishing into those woods, need tu on hand."

Jacky Ray stepped out of the open door into the sunlight and Mickey watched as his father descended the steps and vanished from view. The youth sat on his parent's bed and put his face in his hands. He should have left with Tom when he had the chance.

Chapter Thirty-two

The Reverend Daniel Stewart was uncomfortable in the pine chair that sat in the gypsy caravan but it wasn't his seat that gave him issue. Only twice before had he had dealings with gypsy folk and he's often wondered what the inside of their barrel roofed wagons would be like. Sitting inside one for the first time was both an education and a fright. It may have been invitation that brought the forty year old into the gypsy camp but it was beginning to feel like a prison.

Mrs Michaels who cleaned the vicarage for him would be horrified to learn he had ventured inside a gypsy vardo but she would never have accepted his account of the interior. To say it was spotless was an understatement; the vicarage was spotless, this home of the self-styled gypsy lord was immaculate. The man, Jacky had left him for a moment to find somebody and the vicar had been unable to resist the temptation of making a quick exploration of the caravan.

Daniel poked fingers into crevices and ran his hands underneath shelving but wherever he touched, his skin came away as clean as it had been prior to his investigation. In a way he was disappointed, it may have been uncharitable but he had hoped to find some small indication that the tales of gypsy's being dirty was true.

Returning to his chair and letting his eyes roam across the decorations and upholstery of the gypsy home Reverend Stewart was reluctantly impressed. He'd come to expect horse brasses hanging from the rafters of the curved roof but he chastised himself when he realised they were no mere ornamentation but practical storage of the tack for the horse that would pull the caravan.

There were trinkets dotted around the room that gave an indication of wealth he hadn't expected either but his biggest education came with the surprising amount of space inside the mobile home. The highly polished wooden planks of the floor had deeply ingrained score marks that ran from the bed toward the door and he understood the lower half of the bed was a vast drawer that could be pulled out into the room if the rug were moved out of the way. He had no reason to know the drawer he had identified was in fact a bed that had until recent years had been the sleeping place of Jacky Ray's four children.

The man began to tap his fingers on the arm of the pine chair as the novelty began to wear on him and he wished the gypsy would return to explain what he was needed for. The first gypsy had spoken of a marriage but his dialect had been thick and he knew so few words of English the church man was aware he may well have misunderstood.

Voices sounded outside the door and Daniel Stewart rose to his feet when two youngsters entered and were followed by both the men the vicar had already had dialogue with. At a guess the vicar put the boy as being in his early twenties and the girl he assumed to be a year or so younger though her bold stare allowed him to revise his first thought and he decided she was likely the older of the two.

Mickey and Rosa nodded briefly to the vicar, the gypsy boy only glancing in his direction as both of them continued on into the vardo to sit beside each other on the bed. The girl tangled her fingers into the boy's hand but he soon untangled himself and sat leaning away from her slightly with his hands clasped together in his lap. She was smiling, he was not.

"This be they" Jacky Ray said, pointing a thick finger at both his son and his bride to be. "Want wedding o' them and we's galbi enough t' see tu khushti. Tu an' they get a fig'rin', take t' time tu need but not so long."

Jacky Ray turned to leave the cabin but the reverend halted him by grabbing at the man's arm. The gypsy turned slowly and stared at the delicate hand that had a hold of the cloth around his bicep and he switched his glare from the hand to its owner.

Daniel Stewart didn't need the gypsy to say anything, he hastily withdraw his hand with a gabbled apology and clutched it to his chest as though the touch had burned him. "I'm not sure we are completely understanding each other Mr Ray. Am I correct to believe you were hoping for these two to be joined in matrimony today?"

Remaining facing the vicar, Jacky shifted his eyes to the two on the bed, then returned his stare to the man in the black shirt with the white strip at his neck. "Arvah, aye... yes." He nodded once as if to invite a challenge. "Today!"

"Well I'm very sorry Mr Ray but that simply isn't possible."

"Possible?" Jacky Ray queried. "I've coin enough. This is very possible."

Looking from one face to another around the room seeking a little assistance, the vicar swallowed nervously, his throat unexpectedly dry. "It's not about coin, I mean the money Mr Ray, it's a question of law." As he watched the gypsy, he saw him straighten his posture and the vicar held both his hands up to try to placate the man. "Not just the police I mean, it's Canon law." Daniel Stewart knew he was gabbling but he was desperate to explain before the violence he sensed began to manifest itself. "I'll happily marry these two but... well... it would take two weeks for the bans to be read for a start. If you still want me to, I can marry them a fortnight

Saturday?"

"Don't be needing no bans Mr Vicar, don't be needing none of that churchy stuff." Jacky Ray clapped a heavy hand on the shoulder of Reverend Stewart and he leant in to speak quietly and with conviction. "Me's the usual for this but I's not t' be da an' priest. Tu don't want to be worryin' about law, we got the law for this, just be needin' you to rocka them words. Tu pooker wi' dem, we break bread thee an' me, then we get these uns tied. Arvah? Khushti?"

Slapping his meaty palm down on the vicar's shoulder he forced his other hand into the damp palm of the man and shook his hand. Satisfied he had made a deal with the Reverend Stewart he turned on his heel and exited the vardo leaving Rosa and Mickey alone with the vicar.

Daniel turned in confusion to the bride and groom he stuttered a moment before asking "Is he saying he wants you both married in the camp here? I can't do that! I thought you wanted to marry in the church!"

The boy sat in a sullen silence but the girl smiled sweetly. "Ain't your God everywhere? Omni... what's the word?"

"Omnipresent" the vicar responded, unaware he wasn't helping himself. "Well, yes but..."

"Well if he omnipresent" Rosa resumed. "Then he be watching wherever we be wed. Ain't truly no harder for him to see us iffen we outdoor than in your church, easier I be thinking, no walls to be dihkin' through."

Daniel Stewart sat heavily back into the pine chair and put his head in his hands. Trying to explain, he told the pair in front of him that a marriage in the camp would be outside of church rules. "It has to be on sacred ground, the church has been sanctified to allow weddings, to do it here... I couldn't possibly write out a marriage certificate or file the paperwork!"

Rosa got to her feet ignoring Mickey as the youth brooded over his fate. Stepping forward she lowered herself to her knees and peered into the vicar's face. "Don't be reckoning any in this camp 'cepting maybe a few of the olds ever seen the inside of a church when they were wed. Ain't being no paperwork for weddings all the time Jacky Ray has been Big Man leastways. Reckon not for some time afore that. Tu saying my da an' daj ain't wedded? Same for Mickey's da and his romni? Tu saying God don't recognise that then tu be calling Mickey an' me bastards!"

The vicar caught the tone at the tail end of Rosa's words and he recoiled as though she had struck him. Glancing fearfully across the room he saw the boy was finally paying an interest in the conversation and he didn't like the expression on his face.

"No, I... I... that's not it. Not it at all." The vicar spoke fast and shook his head emphatically. "I can wed you, I mean marry you both but I can't say how legal it would be. Maybe... I guess if there's gypsy law that says you don't need paperwork then that'll be fine." Deflating at his own evasion the vicar hoped he had defused the situation. It may have been cowardice on his own part but he decided he would just go along with what the gypsies wanted. Perhaps they were right and perhaps they weren't, either way he concluded it was between them and God.

Climbing back to her feet using the man's knee to lever herself up, Rosa returned to sit back on the bed. Reaching over she took Mickey's hand from his lap and interlaced his fingers with hers. Mickey deigned to accept the contact and he raised his face and turned to meet hers. She smiled at him and though he had no enthusiasm, he managed to smile back weakly.

"So what tu be needing to know?" Rosa asked the vicar.

Daniel Stewart took a moment to compose himself and he distanced himself from the legality of what was to come. Assuring himself his part may not have the blessing of the church but satisfied he had done all he could to create a legitimate wedding, he took a deep breath and faced the two gypsies.

"Usually one would first establish you weren't marrying under duress, that is to say it isn't being forced on you" The vicar smiled at the girl. "I think it's clear enough to me this is what you want!" He chuckled lightly as he thought back to her impassioned manipulation to have the wedding on her own terms. With a grin he turned to the boy and his grin fell away as the youth glared at him.

Mickey was tempted to stir the fire by mentioning the shotgun of Rosa's da and her own actions to trap him in a marriage he hadn't sought but he thought better of it. In all honesty, he couldn't claim to have not sought the marriage; until three days ago he had known as he had always known he was to marry Rosa and whatever lengths she had made to ensure it were as much his own fault as hers.

Maybe Mickey didn't want the marriage but he couldn't walk away from it as he may have wished. It was possible but the price would be higher than any would wish to pay and not one person would come out of it better. The young gypsy stared back into the eyes of the nervous vicar and after much deliberation, he nodded once and said "It's what we want."

Where Rosa squeezed his hand so hard in delight at hearing Mickey say what he had, it should have hurt but the boy was in pain already.

Chapter Thirty-three

Time was against Mickey as he wandered around the confines of the camp. The restrictions placed on him as to where he could and couldn't go chaffed at him; he wanted to head to his clearing so he could be alone with his thoughts. As it was, everywhere he went he was congratulated and was expected to be cheerful and eager for the ceremony that would take place after the evening meal.

Circling the tented area for the third time he found himself outside Sara's ofisa and he halted his steps, staring at the open entrance to the tented fortune-teller's domain. Running his tongue over his teeth he sucked air noisily through his wet lips and after a momentary hesitation, he stepped forward and pushed his way inside.

"Sastimos Mickey, Sar san?"

Mickey ignored the greeting, if Sara didn't know how he was then she was plying the wrong trade. He drew the chair that faced her out from the table and sat heavily on it, crossing his arms in front of him and leaning his head on his forearms. "The boy I brought tu" he said. "Will you tell me now what tu saw?"

The old woman considered perpetuating her insistence the cards had said nothing more than she had related but as she looked on the youth she realised he knew different. She sighed and leant back in her own chair to shelter in the shadows.

"There be times a telling is a blessing" Sara said. "Weren't so for this friend. I' mother dead so soon?"

Nodding neutrally, Mickey didn't waste his time asking how she knew. He uncrossed his arms and told her Tom had found her the previous morning.

Sara nodded without comment. "More pain, the boy has a dream that ain't to be, can't be saying f' sure but given the secret tu has branded in your heart, I'm thinking this tu know also."

Again Mickey nodded. "Arvah, the boy lived in words an' he dreams in them too. Maybe not such a bad place to be."

"Not for tu though Mickey, not for tu." The old woman leant forward and the candle showed every line and crease on her face. "That's real pain for the boy. Wish it weren't so but 'tis your secret that will pain him more."

"I'm marrying Rosa today."

With a chuckle, Sara began to rock gently in her chair. "Tu think this news? Ha! Don't even be needing my cards to have sight of this Mickey boy!" Again she leant forward, she reached her withered hands to clasp his and grew sombre again. "His final pain. Betrayal. Tu din't be coming to me for this though. Tu be wanting to see what comes arter. I tell tooti this Mickey Ray, arter his pain comes a long life. Tu doing right wi' Rosa much as heart is paining tu. Don't be doing this, tu nor the boy be living beyond winter arter next."

Sara took her hands away and retreated again into her shadows and sat in silence. Mickey sat still for a few moments and then rose without a word. As he turned to leave, he dug a single sixpence out of his pocket and placed it deliberately in the centre of the table.

Back in the sunshine Mickey smiled at Stefan as he walked past and slapped him on the back in way of congratulations. The gypsy watched him go and then turned his thoughts to what Sara had told him. Though he felt both guilt and pain at leaving Tom with his grief and his troubles on his own, he felt reassured by Sara's words.

While Mickey stood in the sunshine and deliberated where to wander next, he saw Dinah skip between tents and into the path that had been worn through the grass toward the centre of the camp. Ruby trailed behind her walking slowly with stiff legs. "Hear tell tu being romm'd later. Bokht in that." The young girl grinned. "Maybe's Ruby be close behind!" She laughed and cast a teasing glance behind her and despite the trailing girl's glare, Ruby was smiling.

"Mickey don't need be hearing that" Ruby said quietly. She turned her attention to him as he raised his eyebrows quizzically. "Anyways, your daj is dihkin' f' tu. And afore ye be asking, don't jin what she wanting, ain't be asking. She be at yorn an' she ain't seemin' none too happy tu ain't."

The gypsy nodded briefly and watched as Dinah skipped along the path and he looked away as Ruby walked delicately past him in the same direction Stefan had headed. Scratching at the back of his neck, Mickey wondered if Stevo had any idea what future was being planned for him. Part of him envied the sixteen year old. It didn't matter if he knew; Stevo was everything a gypsy was supposed to be and from his perspective, life was heading in the direction it was intended.

Mickey thrust his hands in his pockets and stared at his feet, lightly kicking at the small resistant clumps of grass that survived in the dirt despite the heavy tread of so many gypsy feet. He sighed and accepted he should go and see what his mother wanted of him. Casually he strolled in the direction the youngsters had been heading. There was no great enthusiasm in his step but equally, the gypsy knew he would be reprimanded for arriving late even were he to run straight there. Taking his time, he returned to the family vardo.

Lilly Ray was sat on the caravan's steps as Mickey came into sight and the woman stood up before he had reached her. As he approached he watched as she brought a solid wooden chair from beside the wagon and turned it so the back was facing the small fire that had been lit between the vardo and the bender the girls had been sleeping in.

"Took ye time" his mother said and pointed toward the chair with a pair of scissors she had in her hand.

Familiar with the drill, Mickey threw his leg over the seat of the chair and sat crossing his arms over the back and rested his chin on the very top of the wooden spine of the seat. Staring down into the flames of the fire he waited for his mother to begin.

"Your da has a new shirt for tu" Lilly Ray said in a matter of fact tone as she ran a finely carved bone comb through his hair. "Have to borrow trousers as your best are a few years small."

Mickey's head was yanked every which way as the tangles and knots in his hair caught on the teeth of the intricately decorated comb. There was no sound from him of comment or complaint; though he submitted to the ministrations of his mother infrequently, he knew speaking only prompted her to become more aggressive.

It took ten minutes before the comb was able to run through his shoulder length locks without catching and finally satisfied, Lilly took the scissors out of her pocket and began by halving the length at the back of his head. Mickey sat upright to reduce the likelihood of the pointed blades stabbing into his neck.

"Why can't I just have my hair long?" Mickey queried. He'd never thought it fair his sisters had hair that reached the top of their skirts. The gypsy didn't want hair as long as Virginia or Jemima but he'd willing accept it as a price for not having to endure being shorn whenever it took his mother's fancy.

Lilly Ray swapped back to the comb and the boy winced as he felt the teeth stab into the skin of his scalp. "Men have short hair" his mother stated. "Your sisters have long hair. Tu thinks tu got it bad tu should be thinkin' what it be like for them hasing to comb it all through every day."

"Uncle Mario has long hair." Mickey knew he was tempting things to contradict his mother but he thought it worth a try to mention Mario.

Tugging his hair harder than ever, Mickey's mother paused for a moment before resuming with a little more care and tenderness. The youth couldn't see but the woman had a faint smile on her face. "Mario shee streyino."

There was no arguing that. Uncle Mario was definitely strange. He seemed to be everybody's uncle and yet nobody could explain how anyone was related to him. With his hair tied in a silver ponytail that reached his waist and tattoos on each cheek of falling stars he was instantly recognisable. He would stride out of the woods one day and be welcomed to the Familia as a long lost relative. A few days would pass where he would share news, eat with the kumpania's leaders and then he would be away again to return a few weeks later even when they had moved camp. Everybody knew him but nobody knew where he went.

When Mickey was seven he remembered sitting by a river with a crude fishing line in his hand. He'd caught a fish but it had slipped from his hand as he had unhooked it. Mario had appeared from nowhere, jumped into the river and then stepped back out with the fish in his hand. At the time Mickey had thought it magic and Mario had encouraged the belief.

The man had gutted the fish with a large bladed knife and then given the knife to Mickey. It was the knife Mickey still carried. It was a few years later he watched his Uncle Mario perform the same miracle for a boy of six and this time Mickey figured it out. Mario already had a fish in his hand before he jumped into the water. It didn't lessen Mickey's perception of the man, it only made him smile the more.

Mario was strange but then, by Romany standards, so was Mickey. Why then could Mario be welcomed for who he was and yet Mickey had to live a lie. The gypsy's lie; a gypsy had to be a certain way or he was not a gypsy. Mickey could be a gypsy if he chose to never be who he was. He wondered to himself if maybe Mario lived the same lie. He came and went on his own terms and none knew where he went or what he did. No wife, no children, no family and yet he was always welcome.

Mickey moved his head a fraction and the point of the scissors nicked his neck. A slap and a rebuke from his mother brought the boy back from his wool-gathering.

Leaning forward, his mother spoke quietly into his ear. "Tu realise, this is the last time I be cutting your hair."

Mickey froze as the words sank in. It hadn't crossed his mind but it was easily recognised as the truth. In the future so many things his mother did for him would become the responsibility of his wife. It would be Rosa that would cut his hair just as it would be Rosa that cooked for him. She would be the one who washed his clothes and kept the family purse. When Mickey chose to be somewhere or had need to venture into a town it would be Rosa he would be expected to discuss it with. For all the small things in his life he had turned to his mother for, he would now be turning to his bride.

The gypsy suddenly realised he was going to be the head of the family although he was not so naïve as to think it would give him authority. His own father may be the Big Man in the camp but when it came to family matters, if Lilly ray didn't agree, it didn't happen. The women in gypsy households kept the purse-strings, ran the vardo and had the final say in so much of life.

Staring into the fire the young gypsy understood his life as he had known it was over. Mickey had understood the wedding would sever his relationship with Tom but he hadn't really appreciated all that it meant. He'd hoped to be able to slip away to explain what circumstance had caused. There wasn't simply no future with Tom, there was to be no farewell either.

As the scissors cut hair from over his ears and trimmed his fringe, the gypsy fought back the tears he wanted to shed. To himself he thought of all the words he wanted to tell Tom and knew he wouldn't get to speak them. Once the sun rose in the morning, he was to be Romany through and through.

Blinking away the few tears he was unable to hold back, he took his eyes from the fire and briefly stared ahead. Feeling fingers on his shoulders he saw his mother plucking his trimmed hair from his clothes and throwing it into the fire. Raising his face he held the eyes of his daj and she smiled at his wet face thinking his tears where a gentle sadness they shared where this was to be the last time she treated her son as a boy.

Lilly Ray stepped close and softly allowed the youth a hug before she returned to trimming the last hair to even the cuts she had made. Unnoticed, Mickey plucked a small clump of hair from his leg and thrust it discretely into his pocket.

Satisfied she had finished, Lilly Ray got her son to stand by the fire and brushed the last of the hair into the flames. Once she was certain all the dead hair had been burned, she hugged the boy briefly once more, then sent him on his way. Mickey glanced back at the fire to see his mother standing with her back to him and a hand clamped to her face. He didn't need to see her face to know she was crying.

Chapter Thirty-four

Rosa had to spend her time after the lunchtime meal contained in her da's vardo. The restriction placed on her would ordinarily be something she would rebel at but today she didn't simply permit it, she luxuriated in it. Frequent visitors brought small tokens to her and all her family and friends came by to wish her well.

Even in such a confined space the girl gave no thought to how cramped the single room was with herself and her sisters, Fenella and Daisy fussing around her and the guests dropping by in pairs more often than not.

With her hair washed and combed out, her sister Fenella was tying the long strands into braids that would hold well enough under the crown of coins her da had crafted for her but would fall free easily enough once the girl was wed.

"Been waiting on this day an' tu go and spring it on uz" the seventeen year old girl said. "Wishing tu warned me. Was hoping to weave a flower wreath for tooti had but this'n be have to be doin'."

Unable to take the grin from her face, Rosa tried to appear contrite as she pointed out the wedding was to have taken place in the coming October.

"Tu goin' t' claim 't ain't your plan is tu?"

Rosa blushed and averted her eyes from her sister. It was easy to forget how well her sister knew her. Though a year her junior the two girls had been inseparable until Fenella had wed the man her parents had chosen for her two years previously. It had been Rosa who had done her sister's hair that day just as she now did hers in return.

"You happy Fenny?" Rosa asked. "Is being wed all you wanted?"

The youngest sister stepped away from combing the last of her sister's hair and eyed her sisters as they spoke of married life. Attentive and alert to everything they both said, she was keen to know all she could. Her da had told her he was keeping an eye out for a husband for her after he had announced Rosa and Mickey were to wed.

Though she was only seven years old the girl understood it would be years before her father settled on her future and then again more years would pass before he would permit her to marry. Marcus honoured the customs of the Romany but some of the families thought he waited too long pairing his girls and they pointed at

Rosa's will-full behaviour as an example of what happened when a man let his daughters have too much freedom.

Daisy knew she would have much to learn over the next six or seven years and she took the opportunity to listen as Fenella sat herself on their parent's bed and sighed as she thought the question over.

"Vortimo? All's good" the girl admitted. "Benny were no bad choice. Ain't workshy and 'tween the sheets, he know what goes where." Fenella leant forward and winked. "Ain't believing we got no chavi yet. Hoping time see to that. Maybe seeing puri-daj iffen we got no news soon."

Without sparing her hair a thought, Rosa got up from the chair and sat herself on the bed beside her sister and wrapped both her arms around her, leaning her forehead on the married girl's shoulder she said nothing but comforted her none the less.

Not wanting to be left out as the youngest sibling, Daisy sat on the other side of Fenella and she too put her arms around her. "Tu needs him to poke his karbaro in tu mish" the girl said as helpfully as she could. She pouted and let go of her sister as both Rosa and Fenella laughed at her.

"Dordi Daisy" Fenella called as the young girl turned her back on the two young women. "Hey! Palal!" The girl turned back to the girls and cautiously approached her sister again. Reaching out, both

Rosa and her sister pulled Daisy into a hug to let her know they hadn't meant to laugh at her. The girl snuggled against them both and let their affection turn her frown into a smile again.

"Still not seeing what was so funny." Daisy muttered prompting the older girls to laugh again but this time, gently and including the youngest sister.

Fenella broke free of her siblings and shrugged off her own worries. She reprimanded Rosa for having mussed her hair up and forcefully told her to sit again, pointing at the hard back chair. With a mock curtsey, the bride to be moved from the bed back to the seat and perched back on the front edge and smiled demurely.

For the next hour both sisters worked at Rosa's hair until they were finally satisfied and then they positioned the chain of coins along her fringe so the golden coins hung evenly down on her forehead.

Fenella went to her mother's chest and opened it. She told her sister their daj had left something for her and she lifted out a small package of fine blue silk and slowly unfolded it to reveal a delicate square of lace that when unfolded was roughly two foot square.

"Nana May's veil!" Daisy gasped and Rosa reached out to touch the pristine white material with shaking hands. Wide eyed the girl shed a tear at the sight of the beautiful stitching on the ancient fabric.

Fenella smiled and felt herself growing emotional at her sister's reaction. "Nana May be lending this to I when me were wed, now she said to be lending it to tooti."

"Oh Fenny!" Rosa gasped. "Fenny... I..."

"I know." her sister grinned. "Was the same I thought when she did for me. Says this been worn by our women for last eight generations. Came out of Spain but afore then, none as knows."

In awe of the veil, Daisy tentatively stretched her fingers toward the lace but pulled them back before she made contact. Fenella took the young girls hand in her own and encouraged her to touch the fabric. "Just a touch Daisy, arter today this be put away agin till be your turn."

With the barest of touches, the youngest of the three sisters let her fingertips stroke the material before she again pulled her hand away. She was beaming from ear to ear but she was the only one who kept her tears in control.

Mickey was sat on the step of his vardo. At his feet were Stefan, Paulo, Alex and Johnny. Each of the boys had a bottle in their hands and each had taken it in turns to toast the soon to be wed youth. None of the four understood why Mickey didn't seem to be in a mood to celebrate and even Paulo commented he seemed to be drowning his sorrows rather than celebrating.

"Arvah!" Johnny said. "Were me getting 'tween her thighs tonight I'd be khushto enough I reckons." The fifteen year old grinned lewdly and elbowed Paulo in the ribs knowingly.

Alex laughed with the others "Maybes she ain't all we been reckoning all these years. That it Mickey boy? She kek khushti arter all?"

Mickey laughed with the teenagers but refused to comment. He knew each of them envied him for being Rosa's promised. The girl was everything a gypsy man could want. Her body curved where they wanted it to and she had a walk that stirred enough in the camp her da had been prompted to crack a few heads together.

"Ain't for me to say my chavs, ain't for me to say" the gypsy laughed. In all honesty, there was no way Mickey could make any conversation with the sexually frustrated youths about his betrothed. If he said she was a great lover they would want details, if he told them she was no good they'd tell the world. If he told them the one time they had been together he had been barely conscious they wouldn't have believed him and if he told them he'd rather be lying beside a gadjo boy... Mickey didn't know what they'd do.

Trying to deflect attention from himself, Mickey pointed the neck of his bottle at Stefan. "What about you then Stevo? Hear tell tu and Ruby been making the beast wi' two backs."

Stefan glanced fearfully around their surroundings to check

nobody had heard. "Hush man! Tu wantin' me guts decorating your wedding feast?"

"It be true then?" Alex leant in and the others followed his lead, four heads bent close together. "Tu been doing little Ruby?"

Satisfied nobody was listening to them, Stefan nodded. "None so little. That chavi's one tatto grasni, an' 'er pikkis!" He held his hands in front of his chest to intimate her breast size. Shaking his head as he grinned he added "Thinkin' 'bout having me da pooker wi' 'er da. Thinkin' may be for me to follow Mickey here into wedded life."

"Feck orf!" Paulo said scornfully. "Arter once?"

Stefan almost explained that his one time with Ruby had left him weak at the knees and sore for hours but he quickly stopped himself. He needed to tread softly; the group may be his friends but if he told them too much they'd be slipping into Ruby's tent in the night to test his claims and the boy didn't want that.

"What time tu starting wi' this anyways" Stefan asked. "Tu want us as bait afore tu snatch Rosa?" Mickey looked confused and Stefan raised his eyes skyward in disbelief. "Tu is planning to do this proper ain't tu? Tu gotta grab Rosa from her vardo while we lead away her guards!"

Mickey rubbed his face and nodded. Grumbling that he knew what he had to do and effecting annoyance that Stefan inferred he didn't. The reality was the gypsy hadn't given the traditions much in the way of thought. None of the planning of the wedding had been discussed with Mickey and until the moment Stefan had mentioned it, he'd been expecting to be fetched and brought before the vicar with no further action on his part.

It was as the boys began to discuss the practical aspects of what was expected that Jacky Ray strode up to them. With their heads bowed together as they plotted, they didn't notice him arrive until he grunted his approval of their plan. "Khushti. Sees tu pookerin' this'n."

Satisfied his son was taking his role seriously he pushed past his son to enter the caravan. Pausing on the top step he looked down at his son. With a comment that the boys should get something to eat he told them once the shadow of the vardo touched the fire they could make a start.

Reverend Stewart had returned to the gypsy camp and had been directed back to Jacky Ray's vardo when it proved impossible for him to find it on his own and Mickey's father made the vicar stand on the top step of the caravan facing out into the camp.

Daniel Stewart was still uncomfortable with his role and had spent half an hour on the vicarage telephone with his Bishop trying to both explain the situation and to seek advice. As events had transpired Bishop Carmichael had some understanding of Romany weddings and had advised the vicar to simply go along with whatever was asked of him. "They will marry with or without your efforts and there is no harm in your officiating. I do appreciate the wedding will have no legal standing but I assure you, for them, it won't matter in the slightest."

Jacky Ray walked to the side of the caravan and picked up a large metal stick that was suspended from a circular disc of copper that hung for no obvious purpose from an arm extending out from the vardo. As he swung the stick against the gong, Reverend Stewart jumped noticeably.

The gong was struck a further two times before the stick was returned to hang motionless beside it. Slowly, over the course of five minutes, a crowd began to gather. Men, women and children of the Romany gathered at the summoning by the Rom Baro. Most of the people arriving held part drunk bottles in their hands and additional supplies could be seen poking from pockets. There was a buzz of muted conversation as everybody knew why the gathering had been called, even the children seemed excited.

From the other side of the camp a loud clamour went up. The sounds of shouting and bottles and cans being banged together echoed through the early evening air. A second roar of voices screamed out in response to the first and the vicar looked to Jacky

Ray in terror as to what may be occurring. Mickey's father placed his hand on the wrist of the vicar and winked reassuringly.

The sound of the chaos grew closer to the gathered gypsies and at one end of the naturally formed circle, people stepped out of the way as Mickey Ray strode bare-chested into the circle towing a young woman behind him. Even with her face covered by her veil there was no mistaking Rosa even though everybody knew who they were there to see.

Nobody had expected Mickey to be shirtless but the nods and whispers among the crowd suggested they approved. The boy was their champion in all the recent fights that had been arranged and there was something right about him showing his muscles off.

Behind Mickey came his entourage of friends who had played the part of distraction that their friend could abduct Rosa from her father. Finally Marcus stepped into the circle flanked by his daughters and with his wife trailing behind. Mickey stepped forward to the vicar and spoke loudly. More for the gathered kumpania than for the vicar.

"I've fought and brought this ghel here that we may be wed. Behind me be her da an' he has shown he can't keep what be 'is. Asking you now, will you be wedding us?" Mickey turned then to Rosa and to show he had brought the right girl to the ceremony, he lifted her veil and smiled genuinely at her.

The vicar licked his lips nervously and glanced from Mickey's father to Rosa's. Receiving nothing back but grins he assumed he was meant to continue. The words he spoke were those told to him by Jacky Ray but the man had made a few adjustments that Mickey's father had accepted.

"I will marry you before God if none here have objection" he said and paused for a moment.

"Get on wi' it, none be objectin'" Jacky Ray muttered to laughter from those close enough to hear.

"Yes, well... right" Reverend Stewart muttered to himself. "What do you bring that may bind you together?"

Mickey Ray reached across to Stefan who passed him a loaf of bread and Mickey's own knife. Mickey handed both to the vicar and watched the man close his eyes as though he felt everything he understood of marriage was being mocked somehow.

Daniel Stewart tried to tear the loaf in half as he had been told but with the knife in his hand he couldn't manage and he paused while he passed the blade to Mickey's father who took it but shook his head silently, grinning the entire time. Unencumbered, the vicar managed to rip the bread into two almost even pieces and passed one piece to Rosa and one to Mickey. He took the knife back from Jacky Ray and swallowed hard.

Mickey and Rosa both held their hands out to the vicar who

pushed the steel blade forward with shaking hands and attempted to slice the palm of the boy in front of him as he had been told to do. Mickey locked eyes on the man before him and he wrapped his fingers around the metal, squeezing it tight until he felt it cut him. He took his hand away and opened his palm to show the blood.

The vicar turned his pale face to the girl and as he reached toward her, Rosa didn't hesitate, she grabbed the knife in the same fashion Mickey had and forced it to slice into her flesh as well.

With his part almost complete, the vicar retreated to the steps of the vardo and leant heavily against the wood of the door. He watched the rest of the ceremony unfold in front of him.

Rosa spoke first. "I be yours Mickey Ray. Me binds meself to tooti." She held her cut palm over the bread in her other hand and let the blood drip from the wound onto the loaf.

"An' I be for tu Rosa, my Rosa Ray. I binds mesel' to tu also." Mickey mimicked her action until they both held bread upon which they each had bled. They exchanged loaves and in unison, they each bit a chunk from the bread the other had blooded.

The crowd erupted in wild cheering and Mickey's father nudged the vicar.

Reverend Daniel Stewart perked up and raised his hands in the air, the gypsies quieted for a moment. "I now pronounce you husband and wife." The earlier roar was a shadow of the yell that ripped through the camp as every voice celebrated the joining of the two gypsies.

With the bread having served the purpose it was brought for, Mickey dropped his to the ground and Rosa did likewise. The youth reached his hands to Rosa's veil and as he lifted it free, he passed it back to Fenella who carefully folded it and rewrapped it in silk.

With trembling hands, Mickey lightly teased the braids of his wife's hair until it all fell free. From behind him, his mother passed him a headscarf that he placed over her. He couldn't reach to tie it in a knot at the back of her head but the deed was more symbolic than practical. From now onwards, Rosa would not be seen outside of her home without her head covered. The bride beamed at having become a true Romany wife and now she just sought the last obstacle.

Rosa stepped forward to the vicar with her hand clasping Mickey's like the prize she knew it was. "D'ya mind?"

The vicar looked at the girl in puzzlement until Jacky Ray's voice laughed out at him. "You're in t' way vicar!"

Embarrassed, the vicar stepped down from the caravan's steps as Mickey and Rosa squeezed past him to spend their first night together as a married couple. Until Mickey acquired his own vardo, it would be the only time they would have privacy but for tonight, it was their home alone.

"Tu did well vicar" Jacky said as Marcus joined them. He

pushed a bottle of Nana May's ale into the man's hand. "Tu did very well."

Chapter Thirty-five

Tom hadn't bothered with work on the Monday and with the sun already up on the Tuesday, they would have realised he wasn't going to appear at the common to help with the logging today either.

Most of Monday had been spent in the town, he'd returned the books he'd borrowed on Saturday to the library even though he'd only completed the book about the Dawn Treader. Miss Corbett had been surprised to see him back so soon but hadn't engaged him in a lot of conversation.

It seemed everybody knew about his mother but nobody was willing to talk about her more than to offer brief condolences. Tom was more than a little relieved as he found it difficult to say anything other than accept their sympathy. Fortunately his mother's death did mean a lot of people seemed to be going out of their way to avoid him.

Scouring the shelves of the library for any information he could find about living off the land, Tom struggled to find anything of use until he gave in and asked Miss Corbett. The spinster assumed the boy was trying to find a way to reduce his living costs and pointed him toward a section at the back of the library that appeared to deal with horticulture and gardening and though he found a book that identified what mushrooms were edible, he found little else there.

Under his own steam he managed to locate a book on scouting that didn't seem to tell him everything he needed to know but gave a little practical insight into making a camp. He added it to the book on mushrooms and continued looking.

Now it was Tuesday and Tom was packing a knapsack he'd found in his mother's closet that he assumed must have belonged to his father. The library books were packed at the bottom and the boy had added a long bladed kitchen knife and the carving knife from the drawer. As an afterthought he added the vegetable knife thinking he was going to need something with a smaller blade for sharpening sticks to points.

In the shed that had been pretty much ignored for most of his life Tom found a fishing rod. He left the rod but took the reel of fishing line thinking he could improvise a rod of his own. He'd already accepted space was going to be an issue and if he could make something on his travels he wouldn't need to take some items.

The shed also provided a sharpening stone and he came across a tin of air pellets but try as he might, he couldn't find the gun they had to belong to. Packing the knapsack with everything he had found he squeezed a bottle of lemonade in beside a change of clothes thinking the glass bottle should prove useful when empty. The one thing he was missing that he'd hoped to find was a large square of material that if not waterproof would at least be water resistant. His memory told him they had a groundsheet from a tent but he'd looked everywhere and been unable to find it.

Tom had everything he could think of he could find that might prove useful but he was annoyed with himself for not being able to anticipate some things he would want. There had to be things he was overlooking but he hoped Mickey would provide what he hadn't found.

Setting the bag on the kitchen table Tom went to the larder and pulled out as much as he thought would still be able to be squeezed in the bag. Ignoring anything fresh except what remained of the beef and the last of the sausages, he stacked a half dozen tins on the table and ran his eyes over the food that remained.

A lot of the larder contained ingredients that would be no use on their own. If it was in a paper bag he ignored it, if it was in a tin he considered it. His frustration was the box of half a dozen eggs that only had two missing. Carrying something so impractical simply wasn't going to work but he suddenly had an epiphany. Carefully Tom withdrew the four eggs and settled them in the bottom of the kettle and put it over the heat of the rayburn. It wouldn't matter if the shells broke if the egg was already cooked.

While the kettle bubbled away Tom began to say goodbye to the house that had been his home for as much of his life as he could remember. Starting in his bedroom he glanced around the room and felt a sad weight press down on him. There was nothing he was leaving behind he would need but the room had been his sanctuary for so long.

It was an effort but he could just recollect his father leaning over him to kiss him goodnight; he had been almost been five. He remembered his mother coming into his bedroom and waking him one morning to tell him his father had been killed in the war; he had been eight. So many of his memories in the house were filled with pain, even the good memories. Tom shook his head and walked out of the room. He ignored the door to his mother's bedroom and stomped heavily back down the stairs.

In the kitchen he retrieved the boiled eggs and picked up the knapsack, thrusting one arm through a loop to carry it on one shoulder. He paused and gazed at the door to the living room. The door was closed. Tom hadn't been in the room since Mickey had been to the house, he couldn't face it. Part of him needed to say goodbye to the keepsakes of his father on the mantelpiece but swallowing hard, he turned his back on the past and stepped toward the front door.

Once he was in the garden Tom pulled the front door closed behind him and hesitated with hand still on the latch. Had he forgotten anything? The neighbour was looking after his cat as Tom had asked if he would. Tom had implied he was going to visit a relative for a few days and Mr Johnson hadn't queried the lie for a moment.

The fire in the rayburn would burn out by evening, he had as much as he could carry that may be of use and Blackie was going to be looked after. Tom still felt as though he'd forgotten something but short of scouring the house again, he had to accept he was as ready as he could be. Leaving the door unlocked, the youth walked down the path and through the garden gate to head toward the gypsy camp.

The sound of engine came to Tom as he neared the main road, he didn't give it much thought even though vehicles were still rare enough to provoke interest, his mind was elsewhere. The youth was considering the best approach to meeting with Mickey but as loath as he was to pass through the mass of tents and caravans, he didn't want to repeat his risky crossing of the river.

Crossing the road and passing the five bar gate to the field, he couldn't help but notice the dozen cows were lying down and he knew enough country law to know it portended rain. Even the prospect of a dowsing didn't dull his mood; Tom was euphoric at what his future held. As much as his emotions had been ripped and mended the last few days, he was looking to travelling the road with the gypsy.

Further down the lane his steps took him and as he moved under the dense overhang of interlocked branches, the rain began to fall. It wasn't so hard as to flatten the leaves but the darkening of the sky combined with the shadow of the trees that lined both sides of the lane was sufficient to dull his mood as much as the road.

At the end of the parallel rows of trees Tom could see the green of the grass at the bend in the road and slowing his steps in the hope of the rain easing before he reached the open again, he glanced behind him. At either end of the natural tunnel it was as though the sun still shone and it was only where Tom was kicking his heels it rained.

Even with his slow pace he reached the last of the shelter before the shower lifted. There was no doubt it had eased and determined not to have his cheer diminished, Tom continued on down the lane toward the stone bridge. Turning his collar up against the drops that dripped down his neck he pulled a face that he hadn't chosen to take the hat of his father's that had been on the worktop in the shed.

Clearing the bend in the road as he stepped on the bridge Tom swallowed hard and gazed toward the left. The boy had not noticed the absence of noises from the camp due to the rain striking the leaves above him but if his hearing had failed him, his eyes did not.

The meadow was empty; void of all caravans, benders and tents. No gypsies strolled the flattened grass, no smoke rose from fires, no children screamed with glee as they were chased around their wheeled homes. The gypsies were gone.

Standing open-mouthed, Tom's eyes scanned the terrain from road to river. Some few wooden splints that had been supports for tents were discarded on the ground, a few fragments of cloth fluttered feebly in the wind and a fox was gnawing on something a short distance away.

Tom put his lips together in a tight line and looked again, hoping for something to have changed in the second it had taken to scan from one side of the meadow to the other. The clouds parted and the sun shone down on the damp grass. As though waking, the fox, the mangy red creature realised he wasn't alone, he made one more attempt to chew at the remnants of a discarded meal before turning and heading away from Tom at a gentle lope.

All the youth's good feeling evaporated at the sight of the denuded, bare ground. Where there should have been a gypsy camp was a desolate expanse of brown dirt made damp by the recent shower. Indiscriminate squares of flattened, yellow grass showed where the camp of seventy plus people had spent the weekend.

With a hollow sensation in the pit of his stomach, Tom walked out into the empty ground with his eyes scouring the meadow for some sign or indication the absence was temporary; he knew it was not.

Raising his eyes toward the forest that bordered the camp the youth felt his body flood with nausea as a last desperate hope took hold of him. The clearing; Mickey said he would meet him at the clearing. Permitting himself a nervous smile, the youth's pace increased as he strode purposefully across the centre of the meadow toward the ancient oak on the far side; the big tree, the baro rukh.

Mickey had to be there, he'd promised.

Tom's steps hurried him toward the tree that denoted the beginning of the path. Clenching and unclenching his hands he could feel the dampness on his palms that had nothing to do with the recent rain. Unblinking he strode forward.

Skirting the trunk of the tree, his steps put him on the path and his heart beat loudly. Blood coursed through his body and he could feel and hear it pounding as he drew closer to the arranged meeting with each step. He'd be there, Mickey would be sat on the stump in the clearing and he'd grin when Tom came into view; he'd be there, he'd promised.

Ten yards in to the wood Tom's steps faltered. What if he wasn't there? Tom ignored the thought and deliberately placed one foot in front of the other. He'd be there, he promised.

The clearing came into sight and the youth wiped his mouth with the back of his hand. He couldn't see Mickey, he was hiding. The gypsy would think it funny, Tom would arrive and think he was alone, then Mickey would step out from behind a tree and laugh, they'd both laugh. Mickey would cross to him and they'd embrace.

Mickey had to be there, he'd promised.

Alone in the clearing Tom cast his eyes around the empty space and waited. Unshouldering his bag he lowered it to the ground and turned a full, slow circle, seeking a sign of where the gypsy could be hiding.

There was something on the stump. Tom wondered that he hadn't noticed it sooner. Walking to the stump he realised it was an empty beer bottle. It had no label and the cap was missing. Beneath the glass bottle was a square of paper. Moving the bottle to the side, Tom picked up the piece of paper. The rain had touched the edges but the rest of the note felt crisp and thick in his hands. It had been folded in half and the youth raised it to his face and unfolded it, a second, smaller piece of paper fell heavily to the floor.

Ignoring what had dropped to the ground, Tom stared at the letter in his hand. The note wasn't written on expensive notepaper like his mother had used. The paper was coarse and the pulp of the wood used hadn't been powdered but made crudely from wafer thin flakes and shavings. Where it had been folded a few splinters stood proud at the edge of the virgin parchment. The writing was in a black ink, clearly not from a fountain pen judging from the flow of spattered and ragged letters that were scrawled across the page.

Tom read the note through once to try to determine the words; the script was scruffy and hard to decipher and even when he managed to identify the words, he then had to translate or guess some of the Romany words.

Reading the letter through a second time, Tom knew tears were running down his face. The tears didn't matter. He read the words a third time and a sob caught in his throat. Raising his hand to his mouth the nausea returned. Weak legged, the youth turned and lowered himself to the stump, sitting with the letter still in one hand, he rubbed at his eyes with his other.

He stared at the thick paper and tried to read it one more time but he couldn't focus through tears and he bowed his head.

Tom,

sorry. had to go avree. not my want. i'nt wat i wish. no choosing of my making.

i wedded now. have no choosing in this. pleese not be thinking ill of me. life I want is gone from me. want being wit tu but not to be. want tu in me life, not to be.

leave tu me heart. leave tu what is me, never be losing this an I always be wit tu.

your mickey.

Tom dropped the piece of paper to the dirt at his feet and pressed the heels of both hands to his eyes. Sniffing, trying still to contain his grief, sobs began to shake him. He coughed and his chest heaved. Tom's lungs contracted, the sobs grew louder, more pained. Taking his hands from his eyes, he held his head in both hands.

Tear-drops fell onto the letter at his feet, a breeze stirred and the paper fluttered. His mother's notepaper would have blown away. Crying hard and making no pretence anymore, Tom reached down and retrieved the note. As hurtful as it was, it was all he had of Mickey. Mickey had broken his promise.

Mickey was gone. Tom was alone, he had to accept it. Mickey wasn't going to surprise him, Mickey wasn't hiding, Mickey wasn't waiting for him. Tom wept, the accumulated grief of a decade crept up on him. Why did everybody leave him? His father had left, his mother and now... Mickey was gone too.

Tom had always been alone but today, now, his heart broke as he tried to find something in his life that was worthwhile, something that meant something. He sought through the memories of his life for something to cling to and found nothing. Tom was utterly alone, alone and unloved. Slipping forward, Tom slid to the dirt from the tree stump. He folded the letter, then unfolded it again, he read it once more then crumpled it into a ball in his hand. He unfolded it and flattened it against his leg, smoothing the creases he had just scored into it.

Little by little Tom managed to pull back his weeping. Still empty, still hollow, the youth was physically shaking.

At his feet, Tom noticed the second piece of parchment that had fallen when he had opened the letter, it had slipped his mind. Frightened of what the second note may contain, Tom held it in his hand and stared at the blank folded square.

Turning the coarse paper over in his hand, it was apparent it had been folded a number of times. The creases along each edge were sharp, much neater than the crease through the centre of the letter had been. One side had a fold like an envelope and slowly, the boy raised the edge to discover a second fold.

Taking his time Tom repeatedly unfolded tidy creases as the paper began to expand with each unfolding. All that was left were two central creases. Unfolding the penultimate one, something fell from the sheet and dropped into his lap. Looking at the paper Tom was puzzled to see it was blank. He flipped the parchment over, the reverse side held no text either. Tom looked to his lap to see what had fallen.

In his lap, caught on the bunched fabric of his trousers was a black circle, an inch and a half in diameter. Tom picked the circlet up between his thumb and forefinger.

Neatly wound and fastened together by a strand of cotton, Tom held the loop in the flat of his hand and trembled. The words Mickey had signed off with echoed in the youth's mind as he stared at his palm. 'I leave you what is me'.

The lock of hair was Tom's breaking point. He understood all it meant and his face screwed up as he clutched it to his chest. His lungs locked and his breathing halted as he tried desperately to not lose himself and he failed. A plaintive wail broke from the boys lips and he fell to the earth. The letter fell beneath him and he curled into a foetal ball with the lock held tightly in his hand close to his heart. Even on the ground he keened and cried without restraint.

Epilogue

Saturday 1st June 1963.

The horse towing the gypsy caravan was inured to the traffic that passed by as it steadily plodded along the road toward Appleby. Sat on the bench holding the reins, a boy of nine glanced at his father and received a reassuring smile that told him he was doing fine.

Jack wanted to call his mother so she could see he was managing the massive horse despite her initial concerns but she was inside the wagon with his sister and younger brother.

Jack Ray usually travelled between camps in the Land Rover but his da had insisted that Stevo and Aunt Ruby take the battered vehicle ahead. At first Jack had worried he was missing out but then his father had told him he wanted the ten year old to take the reins for the day. The responsibility was immense, it wasn't as if the road was going to be quiet. In truth, the boy was less intimidated by managing the caravan as he was at being the one to lead the kumpania into Appleby.

The horse fair was still the biggest in the country and he knew the respect he would gain to be steering the lead vardo to the gypsy lands could never be taken away.

Ahead of the piebald horse Jack noticed a man with his thumb out seeking to hitch a ride and the boy studied him closely. They didn't pick up hitch-hikers but the youngster was always fascinated by them. They seemed to cross the barrier between traveller and gadjo and as such, they were a curiosity the boy would welcome knowing more of.

The man turned at the sound of hooves behind him and stopped walking as the caravan drew close. He was scruffily dressed and in need of a shave; Jack realised the man wasn't one of the adventurous wanderers he had grown used to seeing but was actually a vagrant.

Thomas Quatrell watched the gypsy vardo bearing down on him and he stepped on to the verge in order to let it pass. Staring at the boy and the man sat at the front of the caravan he locked eyes on the man sitting beside his son.

Mickey Ray stared at the man at the roadside. He wanted to leap from the caravan's seat to speak with the man but he knew he couldn't. As they drew level the gypsy continued to stare at the man. His clothing was old, worn and stained from many nights sleeping rough. The collar of his coat was open to the summer heat and Mickey could see the necklace that hung low on the man's chest beneath the open shirt.

Unconsciously, Tom's hand strayed to the locket on the chain around his neck and he clasped his hand over it as his past drew level with him. The horse stopped at a command from the reins and Jack looked to his father.

Mickey Ray took his hand from the leather reins and stared at Tom. "Does you go to the fair?"

"Arvah, jilling f' a dihk" Tom replied, even his accent a fair mimicry of the Romany tongue.

Gesturing for the man to climb up, Mickey got his son to shift along to make room for the stranger. Tom climbed up and sat beside the boy and thanked Mickey for stopping. Briefly touching his hand to the necklace that held the lock of hair he'd been left a decade before, Tom smiled as he stared at the road ahead. On the other side of his son, Mickey Ray told Jack to get the horse walking again and he too smiled as he let the black and white horse lead them on.

The end.

About the Author

Living in England on the Hampshire / Surrey border, CJ is a married father of three grown sons and has written for pleasure for more decades than he cares to admit. Growing up on an old fashioned country estate, he would often be found among the trees of a nearby wood with a book for company

CJ has been writing for decades but only chose to begin writing to publish in 2014. Reading fantasy for pleasure, he was as surprised as anybody to find he is more comfortable writing emotional stories than chasing down action and adventure.

The Gypsy's Lie is his fifth published book and he feels a strong resonance toward readers from the lgbt community having made contacts through a number of sites while researching Her Name is James. CJ has reservations about promising more stories with gay or trans characters but as he freely admits, he hadn't expected writing the two he already has. When asked what is next, he smiles and replies "If I have to wait and see, so do you!"

Other books by this author

LGBT / Coming of age.

Her Name is James

Dark fantasy

Dark Angel Trilogy
Dark Angel
Hell on Earth
Lucifer

- **Connect with CJ Heath**

Follow me on Facebook:
https://www.facebook.com/HerNameIsJames

Follow me on Twitter:
http://twitter.com/writecjheath

Visit my website:
http://www.cjheath.com/

Printed in Great Britain
by Amazon